Broken Together

Sarah Norkus

Broken Together
Copyright © 2019 by Sarah Norkus
Published by West Alden Publishing, LLC

This novel is an act of fiction. Names, characters, places, and incidents are products of the author's imagination or used fictitiously. Any resemblance to actual events, locales or persons, living or dead is coincidental.

Print Edition ISBN 13: 978-0-99760-025-4

Cover designed by Bonnie Watson (http://wisdomnovels.com/art/)
Editing and interior design by Rick Steele Editorial Services
  (https://steeleeditorialservices.myportfolio.com)

Printed in the United States of America

I dedicate this novel to all those who have gone through a painful divorce. May God grant you the peace that passes all understanding.

Broken

The white charter boats bobbed gently in their berths at Rudee's Inlet. Arabella Stanford took a bite of her crabmeat omelet and chewed contentedly as she gazed out the window of Rudee's Restaurant. She was thinking about a portion of the verse from Philippians 4:7–the peace of God that passes all understanding. She felt that peace washing over and through her.

"Bella."

Bella continued to chew contentedly.

"Bella."

She sighed blissfully.

Bella!"

"Um...what?" Bella slowly swiveled her head back towards her brunch companions seated across the table from her.

Alicia sighed in exasperation. "I said your name three times. What is so fascinating out the window?"

"Oh, sorry." She looked at Alicia and then at Charley. "You know that rare moment when you feel perfectly at peace. Just so...calm inside...so good. I'm having that now."

Charley and Alicia looked at each other and then at the nearly empty flute of mimosa next to Bella's plate.

"No more bubbly orange juice for you," Charley said.

"Jeez, we can't take you anywhere." Alicia raised her flute to take a sip.

Bella's grin was wide as she lifted her glass. "To my very best friends...I love you both."

The three tapped their flutes together and took a drink.

Alicia raised her glass. "To the fifteenth celebration of our April birthdays."

Charley started to raise her glass again and then lowered it. "Really! Has it been fifteen years?"

Bella beamed at Charley. "Yes, it has. Fifteen, fun, wonderfully blessed years...from the moment we met our freshman year at William and Mary College."

She laughed with abandon as she toasted her friends, drained her glass and glanced out the window at the idyllic scene of white boats swaying on the green waters and seagulls calling and floating on the air currents. A movement to her right caught her eye. A car was pulling into a slot in the parking lot. She started to turn away when the personalized license plate caught her eye–JUSTICE. *That's odd*...she mused, since her husband, Daniel, had the same license plate. Even the car was the same. But what would he be doing in Virginia Beach? He said he would be in Washington D.C for the weekend, playing in a golf tournament with his best friend, Mike.

The driver's door opened, and her husband stepped out, shutting the door behind him. Bella started to rise out of her chair to go meet him in the parking lot.

"Bella? Where are you going?" Charley said.

As Bella watched, her husband walked around to the passenger side and opened the door. A stunning woman with long dark hair stepped out. *A colleague?* Bella slowly retook her seat, confusion stamped on her face.

"Bella, what's wrong?" Alicia turned to see why her friend was staring out the window with such a weird look on her face.

Bella's eyes widened in shock, as the woman reached up and curled her hand around Daniel's neck. She rose on the toes of her fashionable high heels and kissed him lightly on the lips before lowering back onto her heels. Her husband then kissed the dark-haired woman lightly on the forehead before reaching for her hand. They both turned and headed for the entrance to the restaurant.

"What...no!" Alicia gasped.

"What?" Charley swiveled around in her seat to look out the window and let out her own gasp.

Her friends' comments were drowned beneath the roaring in her ears. Stunned beyond belief would be the term she would associate with what she felt...later... when she had time to think about this terrible life altering moment. But now–she could not think. Her brain could not or would not process what her eyes could not turn away from.

"Oww!" Bella tore her eyes from the window and looked down. Alicia was squeezing her hand so hard it was turning white.

"Look at me, Bella."

She drew her violet eyes up to Alicia's furious green eyes. Comprehension of what just happened slammed into her chest like a sledge hammer. *Daniel with...another woman.* She couldn't breathe.

"We're leaving now." Alicia rose from her chair tugging on Bella's hand until she stood upright. "Can you pay the bill, Charley? We'll meet you in the car."

Bella placed a trembling hand on her chest, struggling to draw breath as Alicia grabbed their purses.

Alicia could not remember being this mad in her entire life. Her whole body shook with outrageous indignation. "Don't you say one word to that...bastard." *Forgive me, Lord.*

Alicia's grip on Bella's hand tightened as she steered her to the exit. Before she reached it, Daniel entered his hand on the small of the woman's back.

If her heart hadn't been breaking for Bella, she would have felt immense satisfaction as the blood drained from Dan's face.

Bella was staring at her husband, tears streaming down her cheeks.

"If you know what's good for you, Dan, you'll move out of the way." Alicia's eyes stared daggers into Bella's husband's eyes.

Daniel took a couple of steps closer to the wall.

Alicia hurried her friend to her Chevy Equinox opening the passenger door for her. Bella shook her head and reached for the back door. She slid onto the seat, covered her face with her hands, and began to sob.

Tears welled in Alicia's eyes. "Oh, Bella, I'm so sorry."

She shut the door and hurried around to the driver's side. She kept her eyes on the restaurant door, half expecting Dan to come charging out demanding that she turn over his wife. The minutes it took for Charley to pay the bill and get in the car felt like an eternity. She slammed the gearshift into reverse and left the parking lot. She took deep breaths trying to quiet her suddenly quivering insides as she shot down the road towards Charley's house.

Alicia looked over her shoulder and backed down the concrete driveway, missing the mask of worry plastered on Charley's face as she stood frozen next to the walkway beside her house. She would call her friend later to discuss the best way to support and comfort Bella. Right now, her mind urged her to *hurry, hurry, hurry.* She needed to get Bella home before Dan got there. She maneuvered through the upscale neighborhood on the waterway and headed for the interstate. They should reach Bella's house in Williamsburg in about an hour and a half if the traffic wasn't too bad.

Bella's crying abruptly ceased.

"Bella?" Alicia glanced into the rear-view mirror and then switched her gaze back to the road.

"How… could he…do this to me?" Bella's words came out rough, jagged.

"Oh, honey, I don't…I wish I knew."

Bella hiccoughed. "I don't understand. There were no signs…nothing to show that he was…he was…" She started weeping again.

Alicia started to open her mouth then shut it. *What could she say?* Nothing was going to make Bella feel better. *Nothing...for a very long time.* She flipped the turn signal, her heart a heavy stone in her chest.

With dull eyes, Bella stared out the window, as Alicia's tires ambled onto the pebble and concrete driveway in front of her beautiful two-story brick home. Daniel had been so proud when they moved into their house on the golf course three years ago. His raise had been substantial, and they had finally been able to afford the mortgage and the monthly fees for a house in Governor's Land.

Alicia opened her rear door and reached in, pulling Bella to her feet and embracing her with a hug that enveloped her with warmth. Bella closed her eyes tight, wanting to stay there forever—secure in her friend's arms—until the nightmare was over. Alicia then pulled away, and Bella took a deep shuddering breath.

"Don't worry about Noah. He can stay with us for as long as it takes...", Alicia said as she cleared her throat. "The boys would love for him to spend the night."

Bella's lips trembled. "Thank you."

"Do you need me to stay until..."

Bella cut her off. "No, go before he gets home."

Alicia handed Bella her black leather purse and squeezed her arm.

Bella's heart seized in her chest, as she watched her friend back down the driveway. *Lord, I'm afraid.* She turned and walked to the red brick steps grabbing the railing for support as she climbed the two steps. Her hand shook as she dug in her purse for the keys. The brass lock rattled, and it took three tries before the key slipped in.

Bella paused in the foyer, gazing at the golf course through the slats in the white blinds hanging from the four large windows in the living room. *He said he was going to a golf tournament.* A golf cart, with two men seated inside, drove by, and she blinked, drawing in a ragged breath. Her eyes refocused on the living room as if viewing it for the first time.

The room was designed to welcome guests with cheery comfort. The walls were a pale gray. A pewter gray couch strewn with accent pillows faced the slate fireplace to the left of the windows. A matching loveseat sat to the right of the couch facing the front door. A black leather recliner sat across from the loveseat. Three chrome and glass end tables and a sand colored area rug complimented the grouping. Candles, artificial flowers, and other decorative items were place tastefully throughout the living area.

The scene before her–that had always brought such contentment when she opened the front door–mocked her. *A happy family lives here…you don't belong… leave.* Bella, ready to obey the inner voice, started to turn when a photo on the gray colored mantle caught her eye. She set her keys and purse down on an onyx entryway table and walked across the white tile floor of the foyer–past Daniel's study, the guest bath and master suite on the left and the dining room and staircase on the right. Her fingers still shook as she stepped over to the mantle and lifted down a photo of Daniel building a sandcastle with a three-year-old Noah at the beach. The grandfather clock in the entryway bonged, but she didn't raise her head to look. Time had no meaning . She replaced the photo and ran a finger across the glass of the photo next to it–her and Daniel in each other's arms smiling at the camera. Her finger paused on her radiant face as a sob caught in her throat. The image wavered as her eyes flooded.

The click of the door latch announced her husband's arrival. Bella gripped the mantle edge, her knuckles turning white. She closed her eyes, forcing tiny rivulets of water down her cheeks. *Oh, God, I can't have this conversation. I can't.*

"Bella?"

Bella raised her head and turned her eyes toward her handsome husband. Conflicting emotions squeezed her heart…grief, sorrow, anger, and fear. But buried beneath the other emotions she could still feel her love for Daniel with every beat of her heart. She closed her eyes as a sob escaped.

Rapid footsteps crossed the floor and strong arms enveloped her. She fought the arms, and they released her. Needing a barrier between them, she moved to the back of the loveseat. Her chest heaved as more sobs escaped. Her husband stood by the mantle, his face a mask of guilt and sorrow.

"Bella, I'm sorry. I never intended…"

Bella's sobs came to an abrupt halt. Shallow breaths emphasized her words. *"You never intended."*

His blue-gray eyes pleaded with her. "God, Bella...I really am sorry."

Bella took deep breaths in a desperate attempt to get her emotions under control. "You're sorry? After what I saw at Rudee's....*you're sorry.*

"Bella, I wish you had never seen..."

"Then you don't deny what I saw. You don't want to give some excuse..."

His shoulders sagged. "No. I met Melissa..."

Bella screamed. "I don't want to know her name!"

Daniel jerked back. "Of course."

Bella gripped the back of the loveseat, her insides quivering, the betrayal beyond unbearable. "I love you so much. How could you betray me like this? I would never cheat on you. I'm a Christian, and so are you! Turning our lives over to Jesus meant..." Bella took a breath and then shouted. "I would never give into—lust!"

"For the record I haven't given into lust."

Bella's chest heaved with her agitated breathing.

"I haven't."

She hadn't felt this grief-stricken since the passing of her beloved grandmother. She bowed her head, putting her hands over her face as her shoulders shook.

"Bella." Daniel came around the loveseat and wrapped his arms around her again.

Bella didn't fight him as she continued her silent weeping.

Daniel's voice vibrated with emotion. "Oh, God, Bella, you have no idea how sorry I am. The pain you're in is tearing at my gut. Can we sit down and talk about this?"

Bella turned in his arms. "Do you love me?"

"What?"

"You heard me," Bella whispered.

"I…" Daniel paused.

An unimaginable fear rose up and pulsated through every nerve ending in her body. What if he said he didn't love her? *No! I couldn't bear it.*

She jerked out of her husband's arms, her body trembling. "Leave, Daniel…now."

Daniel dropped his arms. "What?"

She stepped back to the mantle voice quivering. "I said, leave."

"Bella, you're pushing this way out of control. If you would just listen to what I need to tell…"

"No!"

Daniel lost his temper. "This is my house, too!"

"Then I'll pick up Noah and go to my parents."

Bella watched the war of emotions skitter across Daniel's chiseled features. She jumped when he slammed a fist onto the back of the loveseat. He pivoted on the soles of his shoes and stormed into the master suite. With her whole body shaking like a traumatized puppy, Bella collapsed on the couch. She grasped her hands together. *Oh, Jesus, help me.* Wire hangers jangled as clothes were ripped from them and drawers screeched as they were yanked open. She gripped her hands tighter.

The banging stopped, and silence ensued. Bella's eyes were drawn to the bedroom doorway. The quiet stretched for an eternity before Daniel emerged–with a garment bag in one hand and the other hand pulling a suitcase on wheels.

"I'm sorry I yelled at you. I understand if you need space." He cleared his throat. "You can reach me on my cell. I'll be at the Williamsburg Inn." He took in a breath. "You may not believe me, but the love I feel for you hasn't changed."

His tall figure strode across the foyer. He opened the front door and closed it quietly behind him.

Bella stared after him, as her perfect life shattered like an exquisite crystal vase into tiny glass shards…falling to the floor and glittering dully at her feet.

Bella blinked, her sticky eyelids opened to narrow slits. Groggy to the point of absentmindedness, she lifted a leaden arm to wave off the noise, but it was insistent. Pain pierced her head, as she rolled to a seated position on the couch. Shadows had deepened in the room. Daylight was fading to twilight. The music stopped, and her iPhone beeped.

Bella groaned. The pain in her head made it hard to think. She remembered brunch with her friends to celebrate their birthdays. Had she gotten drunk? No, she never had more than one dr…

Her eyes tried to widen and failed. *Daniel,…that woman.* Her headache increased as she remembered. Daniel was gone. She had been sobbing her heart out on the couch—and must have fallen asleep from sheer exhaustion.

The cell phone in her purse chimed abruptly with its musical ringtone again. With her vision limited and her feet unsteady, she wobbled like an old woman to her purse, grabbing hold of the leather chair to steady herself before pushing off to the entry table. She jerked the phone out of her purse and pushed the green icon.

"Alicia?" She tried to swallow. It hurt to talk.

"Bella! I've called you at least five times and left four messages."

Bella cleared her throat. "I fell asleep and didn't hear the phone."

"You sound really hoarse."

Bella rubbed her throat and remained silent.

"I've been so worried. I just wanted to make sure you were alright after you and Dan talked."

"I...made him...leave."

"Good." Alicia's fierce tone came through loud and clear.

Bella gripped the phone harder and closed her eyes.

"Bella, I'm sorry I shouldn't have said that. I'm just so mad at Dan."

"I know." Bella murmured.

"Do you want me to come over?"

Bella shook her head.

"Bella?"

"No...thank you, but, no. I need...I don't know what I need."

"Noah's fine. He's having a great time with Cameron and Kelen.

"Oh, God, I forgot about Noah. How could I forget about Noah?"

"Bella…stop. You're in shock. You need time to process what happened. Noah can spend the night here, and we'll take him with us to church. After church we can drop him off. But I think you should call your mom and ask if she could take him for a couple of days–just until you can get a grip on the situation and decide how to break the news to Noah that his dad is…uh…away."

Bella's fingers rubbed her pounding head. "You're right, I will. I'm sorry, I have to go."

She disconnected the call and shoved the phone back in her purse. She made her way slowly into the master bedroom turning left into the bathroom. She opened a drawer in her vanity and pulled out a pill bottle. She shook out two ibuprofen and tossed them down her throat, chasing the pills with a cup of water. She put the pills back and shut the drawer.

Lifting her head, Bella staggered back in shock. *Her face!* A demented clown face stared at her from the mirror. Skin ghostly white and blotchy, a nose to rival Rudolf the Reindeer, black streaks trailed down from her lower eyelids to her chin–but her eyes were the worst. Red-rimmed, bloodshot…the upper lids were swollen to almost the size of grapes. She looked like she had been on a weeklong bender.

Daniel saw her like this. An image of a woman with long silky black hair, high cheekbones, and large almond-shaped brown eyes with long lashes wavered next to her image in the mirror.

"No!" Breathing hard, Bella snatched the washrag off the rim of the sink and scrubbed at the image of the dark-haired woman in the mirror until it disappeared.

With a hand that trembled, she yanked the left handle on the bronze faucet. Water poured into the ceramic sink. As soon as the water warmed, she wet the cloth, ran it over a bar of soap and scrubbed her face hard enough to take off skin. Tossing the cloth in the sink, Bella averted her eyes from the mirror, as she frantically stripped her clothes off. She started to shiver. She needed hot water... lots of hot water. She stepped into the oversized shower with multiple heads and turned them on as hot as she could stand it.

Steam billowed around her as her skin turned an alarming bright pink. *Too hot...too hot.* She turned off the hot tap and screamed when the cold water doused her. She shut it off with trembling fingers. Soaking wet and shivering in the tile and glass box, one thought repeated over and over in her mind. *I can't lose him, I can't lose him...please Jesus...I can't lose him.*

Bella opened the glass door and stepped onto the teal colored bathmat. She lifted the white towel off of the hook by the door, dried herself off, and then wrapped the towel around her body. Water dripped from her short strawberry-blonde hair, down her chest and back while she walked back to the white vanity. Without the benefit of a brown brow pencil and mascara, her eyebrows and eyelashes were also a reddish-blonde color. She looked marginally better, but she needed ice for her swollen lids. The pills kicked in, and the pain in her head receded to a slight throbbing.

The large bedroom was dark as she slipped into her black pajama bottoms and gray top. Towel secured to her head, Bella flipped on an overhead light in the foyer and walked across the right corner of the living room into the kitchen. She grabbed a glass by the sink and walked over to the stainless-steel refrigerator. She pressed her glass to the automatic ice dispenser and held it there until ice started to drop. She opened a drawer beneath the black granite topped counter and lifted out a clean dishrag. Bella walked over to the farmer's sink and dampened the dishrag.

With fingers that had finally stopped shaking, she reached into the glass and removed two cubes, wrapping the rag around them. She peered across the sink at her reflection in the dark panes of glass. As she raised the dish rag to her swollen right eye, a thought too horrifying to contemplate crossed her mind, and her hand froze in midair. *No, God, please, no.* What have I done? Bella dropped the rag into the sink and rushed to her purse to retrieve her phone.

The Star Wars battle was reaching a fevered pitch as Alicia took one more sip of coffee before pushing her chair back from the large round table and picked up her ringing cell phone from the kitchen counter.

"Hey, Charley."

"I couldn't sleep last night. I'm worried about Bella. Have you talked to her?"

Alicia glanced into the living room to make sure Noah wasn't within hearing distance.

"Late yesterday. I don't have any details, but she kicked Dan out."

"It's nothing less than what he deserved, but poor Bella."

Alicia's husband, Jarod, walked into the living room. He raised an eyebrow.

"Sorry, Charley, but I need to go get ready for church. I'll call you back after I drop Noah off and talk to Bella."

Alicia set the phone back on the mocha- and ebony-speckled granite counter.

Jarod raised an eyebrow again.

"Charley, asking about Bella."

Before Jarod could comment, Luke Skywalker and Darth Vader rounded the corner from the hallway into the living room, brandishing light sabers.

Jarod raised his voice above the battle cries. "Kelen, Noah, back in the bedroom. No light sabers in the living room."

Without missing a beat, the boys backed around the corner, sabers clashing.

Jarod strode to the counter. "I know we talked about it yesterday, and you vetoed the suggestion, but I can talk to Dan. I'm his deacon and his…"

"I know you weren't about to say friend. You tolerate his arrogant persona because Bella and I are best friends." Alicia shook blonde highlighted brown tresses. "There is no point trying to talk to that man. He'll tell you to mind your own business."

Jarod winked at his wife. "I can be very persuasive."

Alicia laughed and then sobered. "No, we have to give them time to work it out on their own…and be there for Bella no matter what happens."

Alicia leaned over and kissed her husband. "Please go and get Luke and Darth dressed for church."

Sunlight glinted off the panes of glass in the window to the left of the dark green door of Bella's house. Alicia was blinded for a second as she pulled into the driveway and put the car into park. Noah unhooked his seatbelt and jumped out, running for the front door. Alicia was emerging from the driver's side when the door opened to Noah's frantic knocking. Her jaw dropped.

"Thanks for dropping Noah off, Alicia." Daniel backed up a step and shut the door.

Frozen in place, Alicia stared at the door. *What...why is...Dan here?* Limbs functioning once again, she collapsed onto the driver's seat of her vehicle. Her eyes narrowed. Had that been a smirk on Dan's face? Her face heated as the anger built. She switched the ignition back on and backed down the pebbled driveway.

On any other day, Alicia would be admiring the manicured golf course on the drive through Governors Land, but her green eyes didn't budge from the road in front of her as she tried to figure out what happened between late yesterday afternoon and now while her stomach churned. Had Dan come back and gone on a full-fledged charm offense, or had Bella called him to come home?

She turned right onto Route 5. The acid in her gut increased. During the ten-minute trip back to Ford's Colony, Alicia dissected the two possible scenarios. Conclusion—neither boded well for her friend. She had seen with her own eyes the intimacy that had passed between Dan and the woman at Rudee's Inlet. That emotional bond was strong. Dan needed an extended separation from his wife and son to feel their loss and weigh that against whatever he felt for *that* woman. But that hadn't happened...and if Bella had already forgiven him...Alicia's stomach flipped. This wasn't over.

✦ ✦ ✦

The white slat in the mini-blinds snapped back in place, as Bella pulled back from the window on the second floor. She had retreated up the stairs at the sound of a car engine. She couldn't face Alicia. Alicia wouldn't understand that she didn't have a choice. She had to call Daniel and ask him to come home.

She pivoted and faced her son's Star Wars-themed bedroom. She sat down on one of the twin beds, twisting her gold wedding ring around her finger as she remembered her terror the evening before.

Staring at her reflection in the kitchen window, a vision had formed in her mind... Daniel, in his room at the Williamsburg Inn, placing a call to Melissa...*how she hated that she knew the woman's name*...telling her that his wife had kicked him out and Melissa commiserating, then asking or suggesting she come to the Inn for support.

Bella sighed deeply. She and Daniel had had a long talk, and he had confessed everything. He told her that he had an addiction. He surfed the web—not for porn—but for pictures of beautiful Asian women. It had started when he was a teen. Within a few months, he was spending hours every day clicking on site after site of these women. He began to suspect it was becoming an addiction and tried to stop...but he couldn't.

Daniel told her he justified it in his mind, because it wasn't porn, and he wasn't hurting anyone...until now. He had looked at her with anguished ridden eyes as he continued. Melissa was a client. The first time she walked into the office, it felt like all the air and been sucked out the room. As she talked, all he could do was stare at her beautiful Asian face. And then he proceeded to ask her to lunch.

Daniel's words had ground to a halt. He looked down at his clasped hands and took in a shaky breath. Then he told Bella that he wouldn't hurt her with the details, but they had been seeing each other for three weeks.

Silent while Daniel had been talking, Bella had summoned the courage to ask the one question she was dreading the answer to. Her relief had been palpable when Daniel swore on Noah's head that there had been no sex.

He had lifted one of Bella's trembling hands out of her lap and told her that she would have to be patient with him while he worked through his addiction. He had emphasized that she was the best wife and mother he could ever have wished for and that he loved her.

Voices murmured from the room down the hall. Bella looked down at the band she had been twisting. She closed her eyes. *Lord, help me to be able to forgive Daniel of this sin of addiction. I'm hurting, Lord. I'm hurting badly. Help me to be understanding. And please help us to come back together as one.*

Bella opened her eyes and took in a breath before rising from the twin bed and walking down the hall on bare feet to the entertainment room. While standing in the doorway, she spotted Daniel and Noah concentrating on building something out of their Star Wars Legos.

Two heads of identical wavy brown hair were so close together, they were almost touching, as they bent together over their construction project. She didn't need them to glance up to see the matching noses and lips or same shade of hazel eyes. Noah was Daniel's Mini-Me. The corners of her lips slowly rose up at the tranquil scene, and a calming wave washed over her anxiety. Daniel looked up, lifting a hand in her direction. Hesitating for a brief second, Bella took a step over the threshold and grasped her husband's fingers. He pulled her down beside him kissing her cheek. She picked up a Lego handing it to her son.

+ + +

"I can't believe it either, Charley." The shock was dissipating but wasn't completely gone.

"And Dan shut the door in your face." Anger laced Charley's words.

"I could be wrong, but it felt like he was sticking it to me for what I said to him at Rudee's."

"I am so mad right now I could...I could...oh, I can't think what I could do... I'm too mad."

Alicia barked out a laugh. "You and me both."

"What do we do now?"

Alicia sighed. "I don't have a clue—the ball's in Dan's court."

"I say we give it a couple of days, and if we haven't heard from Bella then we call her."

"Sounds like a plan to me."

Alicia jerked the phone away as a screech exploded in her ear. Charley admonished one of her girls.

"Sorry, Madison jerked Elsie out of Hannah's hand."

"The continuing saga of the princess wars."

Charley sighed. "What I wouldn't give for a couple of boys right now."

"That could be arranged," Alicia said.

"Great, let's swap for a week."

Alicia gasped. "Hold on…not a fair trade…three girls between one and six for two boys nine and eleven?"

"Who said it had to be fair?"

Alicia smiled into the phone. "Let me think on it."

"I won't hold my breath."

Alicia swapped her cell to the other hand as she reached into the polished steel fridge for a pack of pork chops. "I will, promise. Keep Bella in your prayers. I've got to go and start dinner."

"Me, too…been praying all day. Bye."

Alicia set the pork chops on the counter and shut off her cell. As she set the iPhone beside her purse, Jarod walked through the front door with her sons.

Kelen ran up and hugged her. "Mom, the new Star Wars movie was awesome. But Hans Solo died."

"Well then I'm glad I didn't go. I hate it when the heroes die."

Kelen raced off for his room.

"Still a great movie," Cameron said.

Alicia blinked her surprise. She would have sworn her son had shot up an inch since he left for the movie. Cameron was now only a head shorter than she was. *Stop growing. I want my little boy back.*

"Mom, something wrong?" Cameron looked at her, a frown on his face.

Alicia shook her head and smiled. "Just waxing nostalgic."

Cameron's brows drew together. "What?"

"Nothing, shoo. I'm making dinner."

Jarod waited until the coast was clear. "Well?"

Alicia smiled grimly. "Dan was there when I dropped off Noah."

Jarod's brows pulled together, but he stayed silent.

"Let's talk about it later; I'm still upset."

"Okay. Need any help?"

Alicia slit the cellophane covering the pork chops with a knife. "No, go relax."

As Jarod left, Alicia's mind started to drift back to Bella, but she firmly pushed it away. It was time to stop stressing about Bella's marriage and give it totally to God. She opened a lower cabinet and pulled out a baking pan.

CHAPTER

4

Springtime tourists bustled by outside of The Trellis restaurant in Colonial Williamsburg, where Alicia sat at a table for four, shoulders tense, and one finger rolling the white linen-wrapped silverware back and forth. She was the first to arrive.

Bella had called two days after Alicia had dropped Noah off at her house and had asked for a week with no contact and then she would meet them for lunch at The Trellis. After Bella hung up, Alicia had stared at her cell, contemplating her motive. Bella obviously wanted to meet at a bustling eatery where a certain subject could be avoided. Not happening.

Alicia chewed her bottom lip. But now she wasn't sure. The tables *were* set close together in the small café-styled bistro. She picked up her glass of water and took a sip, as Charley strode in the door. Charley still carried forty pounds of baby weight a year after the birth of Addie and not concerned in the least about shedding the extra pounds. A personal trainer, Alicia would like Charley to be physically fit and eating healthy foods. But it was Charley's body and her choices.

"Not here yet?" Charley glanced towards the restrooms.

Alicia shook her head as Charley pulled out a chair.

"Windy out today," Charley said as she combed a few strands of her premature grey hair behind her ears.

Alicia couldn't help but stare at Charley's gorgeous hair. Locks of her thick mane were held back from her face by a large barrette allowing the pewter-colored tresses to cascade down her back like a waterfall. A bestselling water color artist—Charley embodied the word *eclectic*. Alicia grinned at her choice of clothing and accessories for the day—black pants, white bohemian blouse, large turquoise earrings, matching necklace and watch.

"Did I smear my lipstick?"

Alicia's eyebrows pulled together. "What?"

"You were staring at me."

Alicia's green eyes flashed with amusement. "Too pretty to be looked at?"

"Ha…ha."

"Hey."

Alicia and Charley jerked as if hit with a cattle prod. Bella stood next to the table. Alicia's shoulders tensed again, as her friend pulled out a chair. She didn't look good. The make-up had been artfully applied, but she could still see the frown lines around her mouth and dark circles under her lower eyelids. But it was the eyes themselves that told her story—normally a beautiful sparkling violet, they were listless and dull.

A waitress, sporting a bright smile, approached before Alicia could voice her own hello. As the server walked away with their drink order, Charley spoke words that both amazed and shamed Alicia. "We love you and support any decision that you've made regarding your marriage."

Anger blossoming in her chest, Alicia had been ready to blast Dan up one wall and down the other in defense of her friend, but Charley had intuitively sensed Bella's deep pain and addressed it with compassion. Bella visibly relaxed. She had obviously been prepared to go to battle over her decision.

Her rage faded as Alicia gripped Bella's fingers across the table. "Absolutely...we will, Bella."

Bella swiped a hand across her misting eyes. "Thank you. I was afraid you would be mad at me." She grabbed Charley's hand in her free hand. "I need you both to be strong prayer warriors for Daniel. What we saw at Rudee's isn't what we thought it was..." Bella took a breath. "Daniel has an addiction."

The women released hands as the waitress returned with drinks. Having no interest in the menus, they asked for the young woman's recommendation and all ordered the chicken salad.

As she picked up the menus and left, Alicia's brows puckered. "An addiction?"

"It started in high school."

Bella dismissed what they had seen at the restaurant as an end result of years of trolling online for pictures of Asian women. There wasn't an affair, just an abnormal infatuation...obsession with...Bella's words trailed off. Her eyes pleaded that they understand.

Charley, ever the diplomat, declared, "Of course we will pray for Dan."

Alicia waited until their meal was served and then cautiously asked, "Will Dan be getting help for this addiction?"

The doubt was stark in Bella's eyes. "Well, no, he says he doesn't need to see a therapist. Almost losing his family cured him."

Charley flicked a quick glance at Alicia. "I'm sure you're right, Bella."

Bella picked up her fork and took a bite of chicken salad. Alicia took the hint and tried to eat, but it was difficult to do in this awkward situation. Darting a glance at her friend, the word that came to mind was *desperate*. Bella was desperate to move on...yet at the same time, desperate that her life go back to the way it had been. *Opposite sides of the same coin.* Alicia's grip on her fork tightened. How would it affect Bella...if what she wanted...didn't happen? Dan had crossed the line from fantasy to reality. If the addiction was strong...could he really will it away?

"...a client."

Alicia pushed her ominous thoughts away. "I'm sorry, what were you saying?"

Bella took a breath. "I was saying that the woman was a client. That's how they met."

Charley shifted in her wrought-iron padded chair. "Really, Bella, you don't have to talk about it."

"I just need you to understand. He didn't go looking for one of these women. She walked through the door, and the addiction took over."

Alicia knew she shouldn't go there…shouldn't ask the question…bit down on her lip so she wouldn't…

"Is she still his client?"

Her mouth opened in shock, as her eyes focused on Charley. Charley took the hint. "I'm sorry, Bella, I shouldn't have…"

"No, it's okay. She is no longer his client."

Charley gave a relieved sigh. Bella laid down her fork and pulled her shoulders back. "I want…no I need for our lives to go back to normal. Pray for Daniel, and pray for me, but I won't talk about this topic again." She forced a smile. "Now, Charley, tell me the latest in the saga of the princess wars."

Alicia forced her own smile, as she ate another bite of her chicken salad. As Charley and Bella talked, she closed her eyes and said a quick prayer in her mind. *Lord, please help Bella. She's in a lot of pain, and although I pray Dan will keep his promise, I'm worried he won't. Let your presence calm her and give her strength. Amen.* She opened her eyes, took in a deep breath, and joined the conversation.

Noah trotted around the paddock on his gray gelding, Skywalker. Bella leaned up against the black wooden fence and breathed a sigh through her smile. She had been a bit apprehensive when her father had surprised Noah with the two-year-old horse for his tenth birthday in March. Last summer, Noah had complained that he was too old for his pony, Skittles—the name Noah had bestowed on his new pony when he was five.

Noah waved as he trotted past. She had to admit her fears were groundless. He had apparently inherited his grandfather's genes, with one of the most natural seats she had ever seen on a ten-year-old.

Her father moved closer, laying an arm around her shoulders. "Doesn't he have the most natural seat you have ever seen?"

Bella laughed as she laid her head on her father's shoulder. "That was exactly what I was thinking."

Her father gave her a squeeze. "It's good to hear you laugh."

"What do you mean, Dad?"

Her father pulled away—he looked her in the eye as the sun glinted on her father's head, turning his longish hair a burnished copper. "Your mom and I have been worried about you. For the last few weeks your voice on the phone seemed…stressed." His blue eyes expressed relief. "We didn't want to pry."

Bella squeezed her father's rough hand. "Thank you." Her lips turned up in the corners. "You know me…if I'm not worrying, I'm sleeping."

Both laughed at the inside joke first voiced by Bella's mom, Ginny, when Bella was a child. Ginny told her friends at church that when Bella was five, she would wake her up out of a deep sleep at least twice a week to make sure she hadn't died and gone to Heaven.

"What's so funny?" Ginny appeared beside them, handing both Bella and her husband, John, a bottle of water.

"I told our worry wart how glad I was to see her smiling again."

Ginny laid a hand on her daughter's cheek. "You had us worried there for a while."

"Sorry, mom." She leaned down to hug her petite mother. "Everything's fine."

When she rose back up, her eyes took in the lush acres of land that comprised the horse farm. Peace washed over her as she gazed at the scenery. Her father had been a corporate lawyer with a billion-dollar company for the last thirty years. He had retired at sixty to pursue his dream of raising Standardbred horses.

Her grandfather had been the editor of a harness-racing magazine in Lexington, Kentucky, and her father had spent a lot of his youth at the race track, developing a love for the trotters and pacers of the sport. Many of the foals they raised on the farm went on to race at the nearby Colonial Downs racetrack.

"Papa, can I canter."

Skywalker approached them from the left side of the paddock at a trot. Bella's pride swelled in her chest, as she gazed at her son sitting atop the handsome horse.

John denied the request. "Skywalker's not quite ready to…"

"You rode her at a canter last week, and she did fine. I'll show you."

Before his grandfather could respond, Noah gave a light flip of his whip to Skywalker's withers. But instead of increasing his gait, Skywalker stopped dead in his tracks. Noah flew forward out of his stirrups onto the colt's neck. The redistribution of weight confused the horse and he bolted in alarm. Noah fell to the packed earth with a thud and cried out.

John jumped the fence and ran to his grandson. Bella and Ginny climbed up and over as fast as they could. Bella's heart pounded in her ears. When she reached the crumpled form of her son, he moaned—his face the color of wallpaper paste.

"Oh, Noah." She started to pull him into his arms.

"No, don't move him. I think his arm is broken." Her father pulled his smartphone off the clip on his belt and punched in 9-1-1.

Bella brushed her son's dark hair off his forehead as John talked to the dispatcher. "It's okay, honey. You're going to be okay."

"My arm hurts bad, mom." Perspiration had popped out on her son's forehead.

"I'm sorry, Noah." Bella took a breath to calm the quiver in her voice. Noah didn't need to know how scared she was. "We have an ambulance on the way, and the doctor will fix you right up."

"Don't let him move, Bella."

John slipped the phone back on his clip and jogged to the other end of the paddock to help his wife calm the gelding. Bella turned her attention back to her son.

"Don't let papa be mad at Skywalker. It was my fault." Noah hissed out through clenched teeth.

"He won't." She sat next to Noah, lightly rubbing his good arm, exhaling a breath of relief as the sound of sirens reached her.

The doctor had finished splinting Noah's arm, when Daniel jerked aside the curtain and stepped into the exam room. By the thunderous look on his face, Bella knew to keep her mouth shut. Daniel took in a breath, harnessing his strong emotions and addressed the doctor. "How is my son?"

The young resident laid a gentle hand on Noah's good arm. "He has a greenstick fracture. I've splinted the arm to stabilize the break and, in a day or two when the swelling goes down, I'll put on a plaster cast. The bone should heal in about three weeks. As breaks go, this is fairly minor."

Daniel visibly relaxed. "Thank you, doctor."

The resident turned to Bella. "You can take him home now. Give him ibuprofen or aspirin if he complains of pain."

He gave Noah's arm a squeeze. "I'll see you back on Monday, young man."

Daniel helped Noah down from the exam table.

Bella took her son's hand. "Ready to go?"

"He's going with me." The thunderous look was back.

Bella forced a smile as she let go of her son's hand. "I'll see you at home."

"Noah is not riding that horse again." Daniel trembled with rage.

"Ssshhh, he'll hear you yelling." Bella's eyes darted towards the staircase.

"I could care less. My son could have broken his neck today."

Bella started to retort then clamped her lips tight. She had had the same thought when she watched him fall.

Daniel's eyes narrowed. "You dismissed my concerns when he started riding his pony and again when I said he wasn't ready for a horse. You told me that you had been riding since you were three and never had a fall. I gave in over my better judgment because Noah begged me to let him ride, but I won't this time. His riding days are over."

"Oh, no, Daniel, please. He loves riding. He loves Skywalker. You will break his heart."

"No, you will break his heart because you're going to tell him."

Bella's eyes widened. "What?…No."

"Yes. This was you and your father's idiocy, and you will end it. I will not take the chance of Noah breaking his neck and being paralyzed for the rest of his life." His voice hardened. "And you will not make me the bad guy. You will tell him that we both agree that riding is too dangerous."

Bella's tone was desperate. "But he'll be starting up tennis in a month, he could just as…"

Daniel turned his back on his wife and left their bedroom. Bella dropped to their king-size bed her eyes filling with tears. "How am I going to tell Noah?" She whispered. She swallowed hard, took in a deep breath and rose off the bed. She made her way slowly up the staircase.

She paused in the doorway of the entertainment room. Noah's fingers were moving at lightning speed across the controller, his splinted arm forgotten. His favorite Xbox game loomed larger than life on the flat screen television.

"Noah, pause the game for a minute."

"Aw, Mom, I can't stop now. Please let me finish."

"Okay." Bella set beside her son on the leather sofa as he battled the Empire's forces.

Ten minutes later, Noah yelped with glee, as his rebel forces won. He turned to her with a huge grin as he laid the controller aside. Bella's stomach churned at the thought of destroying her son's happy moment.

"Honey, I have something I have to tell you that you aren't going to like."

Noah's grin started to fade. "What, Mom?"

"Your father has…" Bella stopped and cleared her throat.

"Your father and I have decided it's too dangerous for you to ride Skywalker."

Noah's eyes started to glisten. "No, Mom."

Bella used her fingers to wipe at the moisture forming in her own eyes. "I'm sorry, Noah, but you could have broken your neck and been paralyzed today. It's for your own safety."

Tears ran down Noah's cheeks. "Dad made you agree with him…didn't he? He hated me riding Skittles, and now Skywalker."

Bella shook her head and closed her eyes against the pain in Noah's eyes. "No, we both agreed that riding is too dangerous. Maybe…maybe when you're older."

Noah's feet pounded out of the entertainment room and down the hall. Bella jerked as a door slammed. She put her hands over her face and wept silently but abruptly stopped as footsteps sounded on the steps, prompting her to wipe her face and stand up. Daniel didn't even glance in her direction as he passed her on the way to their son's room. For no reason at all, her heart pounded in her chest, and she shivered as a chill blanketed her body.

Alicia hurried into the dining area of the Two Rivers Country Club. She pulled out the cream upholstered chair and sat down. "I'm sorry I'm late. My last client had questions I needed to answer."

"Not a problem." Charley and Bella chorused together.

Alicia laughed and then turned to Bella. "Why are we meeting here? It's our turn to drive to Virginia Beach for lunch. Charley's driven down here twice in a row."

Charley grinned at Alicia. "Bella insisted on treating us to lunch at her club."

Alicia breathed an inward sigh of relief. She had been wondering if there would be anything she could afford off the expensive menu. Both she and Jarod had jobs they loved, but added together, their earnings were modest.

Two children ran across the lawn outside, yelling in delight. "How can they stand the heat?" Alicia shook her head. June was turning out to be a scorcher.

A waiter in formal attire discreetly placed glasses of water on the table and retreated a step—waiting.

"What do you recommend, Bella?" Charley's eyes swept over the menu.

"The swordfish."

"Sold."

Alicia's eyes widened at the price.

She started when Bella placed a hand on her arm. "Stop looking at the price and order want you want."

Warmth infused her cheeks. "The chicken salad."

Bella huffed out a breath and turned to the waiter. "Three swordfish."

He nodded. "Excellent choice." After gathering the menus, he quickly exited toward the kitchen.

Bella turned back to Alicia. "You love swordfish."

Warmth spread to Alicia's heart, as she thanked her generous friend.

"You're welcome." Bella frowned while glancing out the tall window in front of her. "It is in the nineties. I probably shouldn't have let Noah go to his tennis lesson."

Charley took a gulp of water. "Tennis? Didn't he break his arm a few weeks ago?"

"It's healed. Back to one hundred percent."

"Is this the first lesson?" Alicia reached for the bowl of lemons and limes.

"Yes."

Alicia squeezed a lime from the bowl into her water. "Is he still mad about not being able to ride?"

"He seems to be getting back to his old self." Bella sighed. "My dad is heartbroken."

Alicia bit back the retort she wanted to utter about Dan's decision on the riding. "Whose idea was the tennis lessons?"

"Daniel's, of course. I never liked my tennis lessons. I only learned because Daniel wanted me to partner with him in doubles matches."

After a few more minutes of idle chatter, the waiter returned with their entrees, and the friends sighed with delight from their first bites to their last. Charley burped discreetly, "Absolutely... marvelous."

Bella cleared her throat to get everyone's attention. "I was wondering if ..."

"Mrs. Stanford?" A young woman stopped beside the table.

"Yes."

"I'm sorry to interrupt your lunch, but you're needed at the tennis courts." Seeing the stark fear on Bella's face, the messenger hastened to add. "Your son is fine, just a bit overheated."

Bella pushed her chair back and rushed from the room. Alicia followed while saying a quick prayer in her mind.

Charley shook her head and laughed good-naturally as her eyes followed her friends out of the room. "Well, at least I didn't get stuck with the check again."

Noah sat on a folding chair next to the green tennis court fencing with an ice pack on his forehead and another on the back of his neck. Bella rushed over to her son, as Alicia stood next to the entrance to the courts.

Bella squatted down beside him. "Are you okay, honey?"

Noah turned pink cheeks toward his mom. "Yes, mom. I want to go back and play but the coach says no."

A young man with an athletic physique walked over from mid-court. "Mrs. Stanford, Noah's fine. His cheeks turned a little red …I had him sit down with ice packs."

Bella rose from her squat. She handed the packs to the coach. "Thank you." She placed a hand on Noah's shoulder. "Come on, honey, no more tennis today."

Alicia's eyebrows rose as Bella approached. "He's fine."

"So weird that we were just talking about this same scenario…I guess I'll go and wait on the boys. They'll be done with basketball camp in about an hour…oh wait, you were about to ask Charley and me something before that woman showed up at the table."

Bella shook her head and plastered on a smile. "It can wait. Come on Noah, I have to go back and pay the bill before we go home."

Alicia laid a hand on Noah's head and tousled his hair. "See you later, buddy." She turned to Bella. "Thanks for lunch."

"You're welcome."

Alicia gave her a quick hug, her smile faltering a bit when she pulled back. Though Bella's lips were smiling, her eyes weren't. Was it uncertainty?…uneasiness?…anxiety…? She had no time to define it, as Bella turned away with Noah's hand clutched tightly in hers.

Two teenage girls clad in one-piece bathing suits rushed by, goggles and swim caps gripped in their fingers, as Bella stepped on the sidewalk from the parking lot. She wore a wide-brimmed straw hat and sunglasses. The July sun was still fierce in the early evening hour. She walked under the covered portion of the walkway and through the wrought-iron gate to the Governor's Land pool. She paused and looked around. 'Two Rivers Typhoon' swimmers intermingle with the …? Something 'Sharks.'

She spotted Noah, in his royal blue Speedos in the small, but crowded pool area, along with Daniel, standing next to Neil and his son Marcus, Noah's best friend. To her right she was relieved to spot Alicia under a Crepe Myrtle's shade. Alicia always came early, saving her a spot in the shade. Bella had never done well in the heat. She had developed heat exhaustion on a number of occasions and learned to bring ice packs on days when the heat reached the nineties and when she knew she would be out for more than an hour. Except for the one tennis practice, Noah had not shown the same tendency.

She wove her way through the crowd carrying her collapsible chair, snack bag, and drinks for the swim meet. After pulling her forest green chair out of its bag and setting it up, she leaned down and gave Alicia a hug. "Thanks for saving a spot. Where are Cameron and Kelen?"

"Running around with the other boys that aren't swimming."

Alicia's boys weren't on a swim team, but she always came to support Noah at home meets.

Bella lifted her water bottle out of the side pocket of her pink striped bag and lifted the built-in straw on the top of the bottle. As refreshing ice-cold water trickled down her throat, she gazed at the pool and its racing lanes. "I don't think I can stay for long. The temperature was ninety-five when I left home."

Alicia glanced in Dan's direction before focusing back on Bella. "What did you want to talk to me about here that you couldn't on the phone?"

Bella shrugged. "I didn't want Noah overhearing. It's probably nothing, but..." She chewed her lower lip.

"Is Dan...?"

"No...Daniel's just busy. There have been a lot of late nights, and he's had to work some Sundays...a five-star client...millions in revenue for the firm. He said a couple of months more and things will be back to normal."

Bella wouldn't share with her friend that Daniel was aloof, distracted around her, less affectionate, and had very little interest in being intimate. When she had finally summoned the nerve to ask him about it, he said it was the guilt still eating at him. She was trying to be understanding, but it was hard.

Alicia's brows pulled together. "Okay, what's the issue?"

"We have always done everything…as a family. I mean we don't even go out with friends without Noah. He's never had a babysitter. And my folks have only watched him a couple of times in ten years."

"Yeah…so?"

Bella took her sunglasses off and sighed. "Daniel's been excluding me from outings with Noah."

Alicia's brows shot up. "What?"

"Every Saturday he plans special outings for him and Noah…movies, miniature golf, bike trips, hiking, even a whole weekend at the Great Wolf Lodge without me."

"Does he say why?"

"He's says it has to do with the guilt he feels over what he did to us as a family and the fear that he almost lost his son."

Alicia's eyes narrowed. "His son…not his wife?"

Bella chewed on her lip again. "He said it has nothing to do with me. He just needs to bond with his son. But it's every weekend. Last weekend, Daniel said they were going to play miniature golf, and I said I'd like to come along." She took in a deep breath. "That's the first time I have ever had to ask to go somewhere with my husband and son, and he said 'no.'"

Alicia started to speak, then pressed her lips together. Bella waited, wondering what was going through her friend's mind.

Alicia tapped her forefinger on the arm of her chair. "When did this start?"

"The first weekend after ...Daniel's mistake. And at first, I have to admit, I was relieved. I was sure it meant that Daniel knew he had almost done something he would have regretted the rest of his life, and he wanted to make up for it by making Noah's his number one priority."

"Noah...not you and Noah?"

Bella acted as if she hadn't heard Alicia's remark. "I don't think he means it the way it sounds." She took a breath. "I need your help. I'm not sure how to approach him about it. I want our lives to go back to the way they were before...when we did everything together. I don't want us going our separate ways every Saturday."

A bell clanged, and the six-year-old boys dove from the starting blocks into the water in the freestyle event.

Alicia watched for a minute, then turned to Bella, her face inscrutable. "Bella, you told me the explanation Dan gave you as to why he wants alone time with Noah. Now tell me what you believe."

Bella frowned. *What I believe?*

Her spine stiffened. "I believe he's telling me the truth. What other explanation could there be?"

Alicia chewed her bottom lip.

"What? Tell me. I want your opinion."

Alicia gave a slight nod. "Okay, but it's only an opinion. What if he resents you for catching him?..." she sighed. "...making him look bad. Maybe he's punishing you through Noah."

Bella shook her head. "No, I'm sure you're wrong. He would never do that."

Alicia took her hand. "Then don't be afraid to be honest with him. Tell him how you feel."

"But what do I say?" Bella tried to clamp down on the quiver in her voice.

"Exactly what you said to me."

Bella nodded as she looked over at her husband. He was staring at her intently. When she caught his eyes, he gave a brief smile and turned back to his conversation with their son. Bella shivered, the stare unnerving her... but she didn't know why.

"Bella!"

Bella jerked in her chair. Kelen ran up, face flushed, grinning from ear to ear, and shining with sweat.

Her thoughts dissolved, and her heart lightened as she pulled Kelen down for a hug.

Bella sat on her living room sofa, using the fingers of her left hand to pull at the fingers on her right hand. She stilled her hands when heavy footsteps sounded on the staircase. Her tongue flicked out and licked her lips. Daniel strode purposely to their bedroom.

"Daniel."

His chiseled jaw swung in her direction.

"Do you have a minute?"

"I need to get in the shower. I'm hot and sweaty from the swim meet."

"Okay, I'll wait until you're done."

The jaw tightened. "It's late. We can talk tomorrow."

Bella stood. "Please, it will only take about ten minutes."

"Ten minutes, after I get out of the shower." He entered their bedroom.

Bella turned off lights and followed her husband. She ignored the butterflies fluttering in her stomach, as she removed the gray and white scatter pillows from the bed and turned down the lightweight comforter. She sat on the edge of the bed pulling at her fingers again.

"Well?"

Daniel stood in front of her in black pajama bottoms, his muscular chest covered with a light dusting of curly dark hairs. At the sight of him, Bella impulsively jumped up and wrapped her arms around her husband's waist laying her head on his shoulder. He tensed and pulled back. She looked up. He cleared his throat. "I think what you have in mind will take more than ten minutes, and I'm tired."

Eyes wide, Bella removed her arms from around her husband's waist. Sex was the last thing on her mind, but... Her brows drew together. How long had it been since the last time *he* had initiated their lovemaking?

Noticing the look on her face, he hastily added, "It's been a brutal day at work, and then it was straight to the swim meet. I'll make it up to you tomorrow." He kissed her forehead. "Now what do you want to talk to me about?"

Bella sat back down on the bed. "Noah."

"What about him?"

"I want to be included on the Saturday outings. It's been three months. And your bond with Noah is tighter than ever. We need to bond together as a family. The only thing we do as a family is go to church, and once there Noah goes off to his class. After church you always play golf until dinner."

Bella stared down at her lap. "I want the life we had before…" She couldn't finish.

Daniel stayed silent.

Bella looked up. "I want…"

Daniel interrupted. "You have him to yourself all week and you want to begrudge my one day with him."

Bella voice quivered. "This isn't about time with Noah. This is about time together as a family."

Daniel's right hand scrubbed at his cheeks and chin. He sighed. "Fine. Plan an outing for the second Saturday in August. Now, I'm going to bed."

Bella jumped up and hugged her husband. "Thank you." She headed to the shower with a spring to her step.

8

The gray light of dawn lightened the window panes next to the round wooden table where Alicia sat sipping her coffee. She wasn't sure how she was going to make it through her seven o'clock training session...or the eight o'clock...or the rest of the day. She was exhausted. She had dropped to her knees beside her bed the night before, praying for Bella's marriage, and, once in bed, had tossed and turned all night from worry. *I have got to stop taking Bella's situation personally.*

Her iPhone rang, pulling her away from her thoughts. Alicia looked at the name and slid her finger across the face of her phone. "Charley, the only thing that would get you up at this hour is an earthquake."

"Or—two girls with diarrhea and throwing up—all night. They just fell asleep. I knew you would be up and thought I'd give you a quick call while my coffee is brewing."

"Why aren't you going back to bed?"

"Can't. My irreplaceable husband, who takes care of the girls in the morning so I can sleep in, is on a business trip, and Addie will be up soon. She's learned to climb out of her crib. I'll probably consume ten cups of coffee before the day is done to stay awake."

Alicia yawned. "Me, too."

"Seriously? Alicia, you're the energizer bunny. You're never tired."

"I didn't get any sleep, either."

"Boys sick, too? Something's going around. Half of Hannah's Sunday school class is sick with stomach flu."

Alicia took a sip of coffee. "Boys are fine. I'm worried about Bella."

Concern laced Charley's words. "Why?"

Alicia repeated the conversation from the day before at the swim meet. After she finished, a few seconds of silence ensued.

Charley cleared her throat. "I just felt a chill, Alicia. Something's not right."

"I know." Alicia sighed. "But I've decided I can't keep worrying about Bella's marriage. I have to put it in God's hands. Otherwise, I'll have to inject the coffee intravenously."

She looked up, as Cameron stumbled into the kitchen yawning. "Who are you talking to this early, Mom?"

"Let me let you go, Charley. Cameron's up. Can't wait for our day at the beach." She disconnected the call.

"Hey, sleepyhead, why are you up early?"

Cameron shrugged his shoulders as Alicia's husband appeared in the living room. Jarod yawned and followed Cameron into the kitchen, making a beeline for the coffeepot.

A toilet flushed in the back of the house, and Alicia pushed up from the table. "Who wants frozen waffles and peanut butter?"

Deep green waves skimmed across the beach and then receded, pulling millions of grains of sand in its wake. Two young girls and a toddler sat with their spades in hand, dumping wet sand into their buckets. Two young boys and a preteen lay atop their boogie boards, pulling their arms through the salty sea water and kicking their feet.

The scene was idyllic, and Bella sighed with contentment. Everything was finally all right with her world. She had planned a family outing to Busch Gardens for next Saturday. It would be their first family outing together in four months. Noah was beside himself; he loved the amusement park. But best of all–her daily prayer had been answered. Daniel had been more affectionate and less aloof in the last couple of weeks.

The flaps of the navy-blue sun shade over her head fluttered in the light breeze. Bella touched a weather icon on her cell phone–it was eighty degrees at ten o'clock in the morning here in Virginia Beach. A smile lifted the corners of her lips as she thought about her two selfless friends. Alicia had taken the whole morning off to accommodate Bella's need to be at the beach when it was cooler. Charley had risen early to meet them here at eight this morning.

Bella glanced over at her friends...both sprawled on their stomachs on beach towels while keeping hawk eyes on their children. Charley was particularly paranoid about sharks. If any of her three girls headed for the water, Charley would scramble up and be down by the waterline in a flash, allowing them only a couple feet into the surf.

Alicia pushed to her knees and rose in one fluid motion, pushing her blond highlighted hair behind her petite ears. Bella couldn't stop the brief flash of envy. Her body was lean and beautifully toned, her black two-piece bathing suit showcasing her rigorous workout regime. Besides being a personal trainer, Alicia taught a piloxing class once a week—a combination of Pilates, dance, and boxing. Razor-focused, she choreographed and then practiced the routine all week before her Tuesday class. Bella had attended her first...and last...class, a year ago. Panting, sweating, legs trembling, she had given up forty minutes in. She would stick to her step climber and weights—thank you very much.

"Bella, why are you staring at me?"

Bella started, her cheeks warming. "Oh...ah...sorry, just admiring..."

Alicia laughed. "Come on, let's go in the water."

Bella rose from her beach chair, her pale pink two-piece bathing suit complimenting her tanned curvaceous body. She pretended not to notice the admiring looks from two twenty–somethings as she passed by their beach chairs. She drew close to the water and paused to watch Cameron, Kelen, and Noah grab their boogie boards off the wet sand and throw themselves back into the surf. She turned and walked over to where Alicia was squatting down next to Charley's girls.

"What are you making?" Alicia said.

Hannah's eyes smiled. "I'm making a castle for my princesses." Picking up her bucket, she turned it upside down next to three other mounds of sand.

"Need any help?"

Hannah sighed dramatically. "You can't. You don't know anything about princess castles. You have *boys.*"

Bella smothered a laugh.

Alicia turned serious eyes upon Hannah. "You are right, of course. I would mess it up entirely."

Alicia stood. "Any of you girls want to go into the water?"

All three shook their heads.

"Three strikes, I'm out."

Bella put her arm around Alicia's waist. "I'll go in the water with you."

She let go of Alicia as she walked into the surf, breathing in deeply the salty air as waves lapped at her feet. Alicia dove into a wave, emerging and quickly twisting, as another wave slapped at her back. Bella waded in until she was at waist level and then halted, digging her toes into the sand for traction against the waves.

The three boys had stopped paddling out to sea. Flipping around, they plunged their arms into the water and stroked as fast as possible. A two-foot wave caught their boards pushing them towards shore. Grins split their faces, and Kelen whooped. Bella looked up as a seagull screeched above her.

She dropped her gaze as Alicia pushed through the waves towards her. "Do you want to get ice cream for the boys at the parlor on the boardwalk before we leave?"

"Perfect."

"I'm sorry we couldn't stay longer."

Bella pushed through the surf towards the shore. "Don't apologize. You have clients, and it gives me more time to prepare for my date."

"Date?"

Bella strode towards her beach chair, the warm sand clinging to her feet. "My parents are coming to the house to watch Noah. Daniel and I are going to the new Italian restaurant." She grabbed her towel. "I can't tell you the last time Daniel suggested we go somewhere without Noah…at least a year."

Alicia smiled as she reached for her towel. "I can't tell you how relieved and happy I am." She dried her face and shoulders. "I was really worried about you."

Bella sat down on her beach chair, rubbing the towel over her feet and brushing off the wet sand, her gaze resting warmly on Charley as she helped the girls with their castle. "Ever since the talk Daniel and I had after the swim meet, things have been so much better." She reached up to fold in the shade umbrella. "Won't be long before my life is perfect again."

10

Daniel opened the frosted paneled doors of the restaurant into a world of laughter and subdued conversations floating through the air. Bella smiled and eyed the elegant interior. Beautiful paintings covered the walls depicting Italian vineyards, villas, beaches, fountains, and people sipping wine at sidewalk cafes. Tasteful greenery weaved through wrought-iron railings. Red candles nestled in globes served as centerpieces for snowy cloth-draped tables. Everything looked picture-perfect.

Daniel laid a hand on the small of her back sending a delicious tingle up her spine. The hostess grabbed two menus and guided them to a secluded booth in the far-right corner near a small bubbling fountain. A waiter appeared as Daniel pulled out Bella's chair for her.

"May I recommend a wine to compliment your dining experience this evening?"

Daniel gave a slight nod. "Please."

He chose a bottle of one of the reds and two glasses. The waiter left to fill the order.

Bella slid her arm across the table and grasped Daniel's hand. "You're being very mysterious. I think it's time you enlighten me. What is this special occasion?"

Daniel squeezed her hand. "You look beautiful tonight."

Another tingle shot up Bella's arm as the breath caught in her throat. "And you have never looked more handsome." Her eyes glistened. "I love you so much."

Daniel squeezed her hand again and let go as the waiter returned. "Eat first...revelation after dinner."

Bella nodded and picked up her menu.

The candle in the globe had melted to half its height when Bella took a sip of her third glass of wine and sighed with pleasure. Normally she had no more than one glass, but Daniel had insisted. Deliciously sleepy, her eyelids drooped a bit as she looked around the restaurant and fantasized about being in her husband's arms when they returned home. Her eyebrows drew together. *Where were all the customers?* There was only one other couple in a booth near the front door.

She turned to face her husband. "What time is it?"

"Ten-thirty."

"What! We've been here three hours? We need to leave...my parents need to get home."

Daniel smiled. "It's okay. I let your parents take Noah to their house to spend the night."

Bella's eyes widened. But...you hardly ever...I don't understand...when did you ask them?"

Daniel took Bella's hand. "I need to talk to you about something important."

Bella tried to bring her foggy brain in focus. "Okay."

Daniel took a breath. "First and most important...I love you. I need you to believe that because what I have to say next is going to be hard for you to hear."

"Hard to hear?"

"Bella, I never intended for it to happen, but I am in love with Melissa. When she walked into my office nine months ago, I was instantly attracted and knew it would be a mistake to represent her. I told her my case load was full and referred her to Jessica Castings." His eyes bored into Bella's eyes. "I was thinking of you when I transferred Melissa." Daniel cleared his throat. "But a week later I ran into her at..."

Bella's alcohol-befuddled brain couldn't quite grasp the meaning behind his words. "In love with Melissa?"

"I'm sorry...you have no idea... the guilt..."

She slowly shook her head as her addled mind zeroed in on a discrepancy in his words. "Wait...*nine months ago?* You said you met her a couple of weeks before I saw you at Rudee's."

"You caught me by surprise; I wasn't prepared to tell you the truth. It was such a shock seeing you at the restaurant...and there was Noah to think about."

At the mention of her son's name, icy water doused Bella's brain, and she was instantly sober. With sobriety came the meaning behind Daniel's words and more icy water poured down her spine. Her violet eyes met Daniel's eyes, and a cry of anguish built from her diaphragm. Bella mentally strangled it, as the waiter glided up beside the table.

"Will there be anything else?"

Daniel smiled. "No, just give us a minute and we will be leaving."

He turned back to Bella when the waiter was out of ear shot. "Bella, I need you to understand…I was content in our marriage. I didn't go looking for someone else, I…"

"I want to leave…I have to leave." Her stomach was churning, and she could feel the bile building.

She jumped to her feet and raced for the restroom. She barely made it into the stall before her stomach heaved, and her dinner gushed into the toilet. She collapsed onto the cold tile, silently weeping.

The crying slowed to a halt and Bella hiccoughed a few times while staring at the open stall door. She rose to her feet on legs turned to jelly, flushed the toilet and stumbled to the sink. She turned on the faucet and scooped handfuls of water into her mouth and then spit it out. She pulled paper towels from the dispenser, wet them, and wiped her face. She looked in the mirror. Her mascara had smeared, and her nose and the skin around her eyes were bright red. She squirted soap on to the towels and scrubbed at the black on her face. Numb, Bella dropped the towels in the trash and left the restroom.

The booth they had been sitting in had been cleared, and Daniel was gone. The first stirrings of anger pushed away the numbness. He had gone back to the car to avoid a possible scene. She marched to the door and jerked it open.

The bright glow of a lamppost illuminated the license plate on her husband's car. *Justice.* Her mind turned back to the birthday brunch in April at Rudee's...*Daniel helping the beautiful Asian woman out of his car and then watching as the woman rose up on her toes and kissed her husband.* Bella's anger evaporated. Pain ripped through her gut, causing her to double over and groan. She straightened at the audible click of a car door opening. Daniel stepped out of his car. Her next breath caught in her throat. *How will I live without him?*

When Daniel drew near, Bella threw her arms around his neck and hung on for dear life. "I love you, please don't tear us apart. You said you loved me. You don't love her...it's just infatuation, lust..."

Daniel reached up and pulled her arms from around his neck and stepped back. "Not here, Bella. Let's go home."

Bella's eyes filled. "What home?"

Irritation laced his words. "I'm leaving. If you don't want to go with me, I'll call you a cab."

The tears slid down her cheek. "Why did you bring me here to tell me this? You could have told me at home."

Daniel sighed. "Because I thought with a nice dinner and the wine...."

His thumb reached up and wiped a tear away from her cheek. "I guess it was a bad idea." He turned and walked back to the car.

Bella knew when she lifted her foot and took that first step towards the car, it would be the end of her old life and the beginning of a life that yawned like a dark abyss. Her body started to tremble as she lifted her foot.

✦ ✦ ✦

As Daniel's car turned onto their street, the fear filling every pore of Bella's body suddenly made it hard for her to breathe. She turned the car fan on high and took in deep breaths. The tires bumped up the driveway and eased to a halt at the front door. She grabbed the door handle with a hand that shook. *Will this be the last time I ride in his car?*

Bella pushed the car door open and waited silently for Daniel to unlock the front door of the house. Neither had said a word on the ride back from the restaurant.

The living room lights sent out a welcome home glow that had Bella's eyes tearing up again.

Daniel closed the door and cleared his throat. "I want a divorce, Bella."

Bella's high heels faltered, her eyes squeezed shut. *This is not happening.*

"Did you hear me?"

She whipped around so fast she almost fell. "No! You can't do this to our family." Her chest rose and fell and her eyes blazed. "You made a vow to God in church! You vowed to always love me..."

Daniel walked past her to the living room couch and sat down. He put his hands between his knees and took in a deep breath. "I never should have made those vows. I was still in love with someone else."

Bella's rage deflated like a balloon, replaced by confusion. "What are you talking about...never should have married me...in love with someone else?"

"Sit down, Bella, please, and listen to me. I have a confession to make."

Bella walked to the loveseat and dropped down as her knees collapsed. She had fallen headfirst into a nightmare.

Daniel's head swiveled in her direction. "I love you, but I've never been in love with you."

Bella's heart thudded painfully in her chest.

"I told you a lie." He sighed. "To be honest…more than one lie after you saw me with Melissa. I said I had an addiction to surfing the web for Asian women, but that was untrue. I'm attracted to Asian women like some guys are attracted to blondes…normal attraction. I fell in love with an Asian girl my second year at William and Mary, a year before I met you. We were planning to attend law school together after graduation."

Daniel's eyes seemed to turn inward. "My father found out. Not that I made it a secret. He was furious…said she would ruin my career because she was Asian and an immigrant. I defied him. He said he would cut off my funds. I told him I didn't care…I loved her."

His eyes focused back on Bella. "You know my father is a very influential judge in DC. Kim was attending William and Mary on a student visa, working on her paperwork to become a citizen. He said if I did not end the relationship and marry a proper *Caucasian* girl, he would have her visa revoked."

His eyes reflected past pain. "If I hadn't agreed, Kim's life would have been ruined. And he could have done it—instantly. I had no choice; I loved Kim too much to let my father ruin her dream of becoming a lawyer and American citizen. I broke off the relationship. But there wasn't one condition—there were two. I had to marry a girl that my father would approve of."

Daniel's eyes hardened. "He gave me a time limit. I had to be married before I started law school. It was blackmail, pure and simple."

He pulled in a breath. "I knew the type of girl he wanted me to marry... I dated quite a few of the girls at school...looking for the right fit."

Each breath Bella pulled in took effort. "The right fit?"

Daniel had the decency to look ashamed. "I knew I could never fall in love again. Kim was it for me. But I wanted someone I was sexually attracted to and who had similar interests to mine."

Bella had believed that the pain she felt at Rudee's in April was the worse she had ever experienced, but now she knew that she had been wrong. The sudden pounding in her head was making her lightheaded, and spots distorted her vision. She stammered the words. "I was part of a deal...an arranged marriage?"

"Bella, I never intended for you to find out about any of this. But then the impossible happened. I did fall in love again. Melissa is the same as breathing for me. I can't live without her. And one day I hope you find a man who will make you feel that way."

"I already did." Bella struggled to breathe as the spots grew brighter. Daniel was saying her name...but from a great distance. Suddenly the spots winked out, and darkness enveloped her.

+ + +

Bella fought her way back to consciousness, first with a groan and then the blinking of her eyelids. She moved her head. Her forehead furrowed. *Where am I?* She tried to rise up on her elbows but collapsed back. *Why am I weak?* She turned her head. She was in her bedroom. The bathroom light glowed to her right. Bella rolled onto her side and pushed up to a seated position. Pain thumped inside her skull. She brought shaky hands up to either side of her head and groaned.

She gripped the nightstand and rose on bare feet. She stumbled into the bathroom, her bladder screaming for release. She flushed the toilet and stepped to the sink. She stared at the dress she was wearing, a slight frown on her lips. Her eyes widened. "No, God, no!"

Bella flipped around, her back to the sink. "Daniel!"

She pushed off the sink and rushed out of her bedroom to the front door and yanked it open. Relieved to see his car still in the driveway, Bella shut the door and glanced around. She walked to the staircase, flipped on the light, and started to climb. She found her husband asleep in the guest bedroom. The indisputable truth pressed down on her shoulders like a wet sack of cement. He would leave…and soon.

The door jamb pressed into her back as she slid down to the floor onto her rear end, her dress riding up her thighs. She pulled her knees into her chest and bent her head. *Oh, Lord Jesus, I don't understand. Why are you allowing this to happen?*

Bella looked up as her husband rolled over and onto his left side. The instinct to slip in bed with Daniel and hold him close was strong; she started to push up on her feet and then allowed gravity to settle her back on the floor. As soon as he realized she had joined him in bed he would leave and go sleep in the bed downstairs. She kneaded her forehead with her fingers trying to massage away the pain. She turned her head and watched her husband sleep, misery etched on her face.

CHAPTER

11

Blinding sunlight piercing through slats in the window blinds woke Bella. Her eyes squinted from the glare. She turned away from the window and started. *Why am I in Noah's bedroom?* Uneasiness crept through her body. *Something about last night.* She closed her eyes, trying to remember. *Date night.* She and Daniel went to an Italian restaurant. Uneasiness turned to dread. She pressed her eyelids tighter. *You don't want to remember. Go back to sleep.*

"Bella."

Bella's eyes opened. Daniel was dressed and standing in the doorway.

"We have to pick up Noah soon, and we need to talk before we pick him up."

Memories of the night before slammed into her mind, and she gasped out Noah's name.

"That's right, Noah. Why don't you take a shower and get dressed? I'll make coffee."

A heavy tread sounded on the stairs as she buried her face into the pillow. *I can't do this. God help me, I can't do this.* She jerked her head off the pillow. If she didn't get ready, Daniel would pick up Noah without her...and her parents might guess that something was wrong. She scrambled off the bed and hurried down the stairs. She glimpsed at Daniel pouring water in the coffee maker, and then she darted into their bedroom.

Forty minutes later, Bella entered the kitchen in a sleeveless white blouse with pink capris. Styled hair and perfect makeup did very little to conceal her tattered world. Daniel poured two cups of coffee and brought them to the antique wood-finished trestle table. Bella pulled out a matching wooden chair and sat down. Her hand shook as she placed a teaspoon of sugar and a bit of cream in her coffee.

"Bella, I know you're upset, but you have to pull yourself together. We have to think about what's best for Noah."

Bella's knuckles turned white on the handle of her mug. "What's best for Noah is not to have his family ripped apart."

Daniel folded his hands around his mug and stared at the dark brown brew. "I am the first one to admit you don't deserve any of this. I could tell you how sorry I am again...and I am, but...they're empty words to you right now."

Anger blazed through Bella. "You're sorry! What part are you sorry about? That you were caught at Rudee's... that you lied about your "Asian women addiction"...or how long you knew Melissa. How about that you're sorry that you dated me under false pretenses or married me when you didn't love me? I really want to know...which lies are you sorry for?"

"All of the above."

The anger ebbed away replaced by aching betray-al. "Do you realize how cruel it was to lead me on for months, letting me think everything would go back to normal? Why did you do that?"

"I…you're right, I should have told you the day you saw me with Melissa that our marriage was over, but your face at the restaurant…you looked as if I had stabbed you through the heart. And when I got back to the house it just felt too cruel to plunge the knife in deeper. The lie seemed less heartless at the time, and I thought if I gave you a few more months…pulled emotionally away from you, gradually you would handle my leaving better." He sighed. "I was wrong."

Seconds dragged by as Bella stared into her cup.

"Bella."

She looked up. "All those Saturdays you needed to be alone with Noah. You wanted an iron-clad bond with your son before you told him you were leaving." The ache in Bella's heart deepened. "I don't believe staying had anything to do with me. I was just a chess piece being moved around the board as you cemented your relation-ship with Noah."

Bella stared at her husband, waiting to be filled with seething rage, but it wouldn't come. *I want to hate him, but I can't…I love him too much.*

Desperation laced her words. "Daniel, I think if you would just talk to Pastor Burton…or we could both go for marriage counseling. I'm not perfect. Maybe there was something more I could have done to…"

Daniel reached across the table and gripped her hand, stopping the flow of words. "No, Bella." He released her hand and sat back. "You want to fix this, and you can't. It *cannot* be fixed. I'm leaving today."

Tears welled and slipped over Bella's eyelids. "No," she whispered.

Daniel voiced hardened. "We have to talk about Noah. I said we'd pick him up at ten o'clock."

With lower lip trembling, Bella started to open her mouth, then quickly shut it as Daniel's eyes narrowed.

"If you love our son, you need to pull yourself together right now. Do you want him to see that you've been crying? Do you want your parents to see that you've been crying?"

Bella shook her head and wiped her face with a napkin."

"Noah is going to be upset when I leave, but we both have to reassure him that everything is going to be fine. Make the transition as stress free as possible."

Bella's voice quivered. "Where are you going?"

"I've rented a small apartment near the law firm."

He wasn't moving in with Melissa. Maybe there was still a chance…

"Bella?"

She refocused her eyes. "What?"

"We need to leave to pick up Noah in ten minutes. You're not going if you're going to start crying the minute you see him."

Bella took a deep breath. "I'll be fine. I have to go fix my makeup."

Bella left the table, her coffee untouched. In the master bath, she repaired her eye makeup. Finished, she stared at her reflection. *Lord, help me find a way to change Daniel's mind.* She breathed in and out slowly a few times then turned and left the bathroom.

Noah rushed through the front door and pounded up the stairs to the recreation room. Deprived of his electronics for the last fourteen hours, Bella knew he was planning on making up for lost time.

She paused in the foyer talking fast. "Daniel did you see how happy Noah was when we picked him up. You can't seriously contemplate destroying his secure world… today. Wait a few days. We'll tell him gradually…let him get use to the idea.

"I'm going to pack. After I'm done, I'm going to talk to Noah. If you love your son, you will be there to support him." Daniel walked into the bedroom.

Bella's heart pounded against her rib cage. She hurried across the foyer after her husband. She watched helpless as he laid three suits across the comforter on the bed.

"Daniel, what about money, the bills? You can't just leave expecting me to…"

He pulled two more suits from the closet. "It's all been taken care of. The bills will come to me at the law firm, and I will pay them. Money will be available for you in the joint account for groceries, gas, and other essentials. After the divorce you will receive a generous amount of alimony and child support."

A stone the size of a melon settled in her stomach as Daniel disappeared back into the closet. He returned with an arm load of shirts.

"But…but we can't afford this house and an apartment. You should stay here until…"

"I was promoted to senior staff four months ago. My salary doubled."

"What…you were promoted and didn't tell me?"

Daniel dropped the shirts on the bed and turned to Bella. "Bella, you need to call a lawyer on Monday. I recommend Brad Carlow, but choose whoever you want. The divorce is going to happen whether you want it or not. You and Noah will be taken care of. I am done arguing."

Daniel brushed past Bella and climbed the stairs. On leaden feet, Bella stepped over to the bed and laid her hand on the lapel of Daniel's charcoal gray suit. She moved the hand to the shoulder and with her other hand lifted the fabric to her face and breathed deep. Her husband's cologne filled her nostrils. With hands starting to tremble, she laid it back on the bed and left the bedroom.

A contemporary Christian song burst forth from her purse in the kitchen. Bella ignored her iPhone and reached in a cabinet for the bottle of white wine. She grabbed a wine glass and splashed in a generous amount. She walked to the glass door cut into the living room wall and opened it onto the screened-in porch. She settled on a thickly-cushioned ebony wicker chair and lifted the glass to her lips, gulping down half the glass. She knew she shouldn't be drinking on an empty stomach, but all of a sudden, she didn't care–about anything.

She lowered the glass to the small wicker table, as she gazed out at a man setting a golf ball on his tee. Was he faithful to his wife? Did he have a girlfriend? What about the three golfers standing nearby, watching as he swung the club and hit the ball dead on?

Bella watched the ball sail across an impossibly blue sky, dropping quite a distance down the narrow course. She picked up her glass and took another gulp. Laughter had her craning her mind in the direction of levity. Her neighbors, the Johnsons, were sitting on their open-air deck, cooking something on their grill. Bella spotted Randy Johnson leaning over and rubbing his wife's hand. She lifted her hand and downed the contents left in her glass. Warmth and a slight tingling sensation spread through her body.

Her child's faint laughter reached her from inside the house. Her lips curved downward. She rose and entered the house, her quick stride ending at the island in the kitchen and the bottle of wine sitting atop the granite counter. She splashed more wine in the glass and took yet another gulp. She closed her fist around the neck of the bottle and strode towards the bedroom. She stopped three feet from the entrance.

A large hard-shell suitcase lay open on the bed–another sat on the floor next to the full-length mirror. Two garment bags were draped over the upholstered chair by

the window. Daniel placed a stack of shirts in the suitcase. Bella lifted the wine glass and took a drink. Her eyes
glistened as she swiveled and retreated to the screened-in
deck.

She sat the bottle and wine glass on the glass-covered
wicker table, noticing the heat and humidity for the first
time. She walked over to the porch wall and flipped the
ceiling fan on high. She settled back in her chair and lifted
the glass to her lips. She was starting to feel deliciously
languid. The golfers had moved on. She tuned out the
conversation between the husband and wife next to her
as she gazed unseeing at the houses across the course.

Bella reclined in the chair deliberately crushing any
negative thought that tried to arise in her mind. She finished her second glass and started on her third. Two golfers arrived in their cart. They jumped out and headed
for the teeing off spot. Despite the fan, she could feel the
perspiration forming on her forehead. She stood…sway-
ing a little as she nabbed the bottle of wine. She finished
off the wine in the glass. On the second try, she was able
to open the door.

Vents blowing cold air cooled her flushed face. Bella
made a beeline for the loveseat and plopped down. With
an unsteady hand, she poured more wine in her glass,
a small amount splashing onto the area rug. She took a
drink. She placed the bottle with utmost care on the end
table. She leaned back into the upper cushion and closed
her eyes.

"Bella!"

She awoke with a start.

"How much have you had to drink?"

"What?" She was having trouble focusing on Daniel's face.

"How many glasses of wine have you had?"

Daniel was mad at her. What had she done? She tried to sit up, but the room spun.

"You're drunk."

Drunk? Not possible, she never got drunk. Daniel was walking towards her. He leaned over in front of her. She looked down. A wine glass was lying on its side, a small pool of liquid soaking into the area rug. He picked up the glass without saying a word and walked into the kitchen. He pulled paper towels off the rack and returned. He squatted down and soaked up the wine, returning to the kitchen and dumping the towels in the trashcan.

That can't be good for the wood floor under the rug, I should get a towel and...

Bella winced and sank back into the cushion at the furious look on her husband's face.

"Getting drunk will not make me stay. I'm leaving and I'm taking Noah with me."

Bella froze. "What...what do you mean...taking Noah?"

"In your present condition you are incapable of taking care of our son. You have the rest of the day and night to sober up. I'll come back tomorrow morning and drop him off if you've sobered up and promise not to get drunk around our son."

Bella reached for Daniel's hand. It was hard coordinating her thoughts. "Please stay one more day. I promise not to drink like this again."

Daniel jerked his hand free. "What is wrong with you? If you cannot accept the inevitable, I *will* file for custody of Noah." His eyes narrowed. "I mean it, Bella. I'll be back around ten in the morning."

Drunk and numb, Bella stared at Daniel's back as he climbed the stairs.

CHAPTER

1 2

The café area of The Williamsburg Chapel was noisy with multiple conversations intermingling in the large space. Alicia scanned the parishioners for Bella's family while sipping coffee. Cameron and Kelen munched on donuts holes.

"Who are you looking for?" Jarod asked as his eyes followed Alicia's.

"Dan and Bella. They're usually here by now."

"Maybe they had a late night of…" Jarod waggled his eyebrows,…"and they're running late."

Alicia rolled her eyes then looked over at her sons. "Cameron, Kelen, time to head for class."

"One more donut hole, pleeezze…?" Kelen blinked twice and gave his mom his best sad puppy-dog look.

Alicia laughed. "One more, and off you both go."

She turned to exit the café area and head for the sanctuary, her husband at her side. "I tried calling and texting Bella yesterday, but no answer."

"You're doing that worrying thing again. Let it go. She'll get back to you."

Alicia sighed. "You're right. Besides there's no need to worry now. Bella was giddy with anticipation of their date Friday night. She'll probably call tomorrow." She pushed Bella from her mind.

"Alicia, Jarod, good to see you both." Pastor Burton smiled and shook their hands as they approached the sanctuary. A man in his early fifties, he had such a youthful persona he was regularly mistaken for a much younger man.

"You, too, pastor. It's gonna be a scorcher today, you stay out of the sun," Jarod said.

"Don't forget you promised me a fishing trip in September."

"Looking forward to it."

Alicia and Jarod stepped past the pastor into the worship center and looked for seats.

The grandfather clock in the entryway bonged ten times. Bella's heart rate ticked up a notch. She placed a hand on her stomach. The acid inside churned queasily. She had tried to eat something the night before, but it didn't mix well with the wine, and her stomach rejected it vehemently. This morning, she had been able to keep down a few crackers.

Heat filled her face as she remembered the day before. Daniel hadn't even let her say goodbye to her son. He had made her go in their bedroom before he left with Noah. She had sobbed out her pain and grief for hours after the front door clicked shut.

A car's engine rumbled on the driveway and then fell silent. Two doors slammed shut. Bella pulled in a steadying breath and rose from the couch as the front door opened. Noah came through the front door first. He stopped, glanced briefly in her direction and then ran up the stairs. Her heart dropped like a stone into her stomach.

Daniel dropped two empty cardboard boxes on the tiled floor and shut the door. "Sit down, Bella, we need to talk before I pack up a few more things."

Bella sat. After her crying fit had passed the night before, Bella had finally accepted that her husband was moving out of their home. Nothing she said was going to change Daniel's mind.

Daniel strode over to Bella, stopped two feet away and crossed his arms. "Because of your decision to drink yourself into a stupor, I had to tell Noah about my leaving without you. He was very upset and cried most of the day. He wanted to know if he would ever see me again. I reassured him that he would see me every Saturday. Do you have an objection to this arrangement?"

Bella shook her head.

"Once you get a lawyer, we can work out the details of the divorce and custody arrangements."

Bella mentally pushed down her rising panic. If she didn't show that she had control of her emotions, she would lose Noah, like she was losing her husband.

Daniel's eyes narrowed. "After I finish packing, we are going upstairs and reassure our son that my leaving has nothing to do with him. We will present a united front for our son. Agreed?"

Bella nodded her head...afraid to speak, lest she say the wrong thing. Daniel turned and picked up the boxes, then disappeared into his study. She sat in agony for the next hour until Daniel emerged first with one box and then with the second one, setting them by the door.

He walked towards her. "For God's sake, wipe that look off your face, you'll send Noah into an absolute panic."

Bella made an effort to smile. It was torture.

"Let's go."

Bella rose on legs that shook and followed Daniel up the stairs. He glanced in the entertainment room, but Noah wasn't there. He continued on to Noah's bedroom. The door was shut. He grasped the knob and twisted it. It didn't bulge.

"Noah?"

"Go away."

"Your mom and I need to talk to you."

"No."

Daniel heaved a sigh. "If you don't want to say goodbye to me, I understand. I'll see you next week."

There was an anguished cry from her son, and the door was unlocked and thrown open. He threw himself at Daniel. "Don't go, Dad, please don't go."

Daniel wrapped his arms around his son and held him until Noah pulled back, tears streaming down his face. "Please, Dad."

Daniel led his son back into the bedroom and sat him on the bed, sitting down next to him. He looked over at

Bella and canted his eyes to the other side of Noah. She took the hint and sat on the other side of her son. "Noah, we talked about this last night. I'm not leaving you. I just won't be living in this house."

Noah's hazel eyes reflected his misery as he turned to his mother. "Why, mom, why can't dad live here?"

Bella mentally scrambled for something to say to ease her son's pain. She placed a hand on the dark curls on the side of her son's head. "Honey, this is hard to understand, but this arrangement will work out better for all of us."

"But, you're not mad at each other. You never fight. You're not like Sam's parents. Sam said his mom and dad fought and yelled all the time before his dad left and they got a divorce."

Noah pulled his head away from his mom's hand and turned his wet face to his dad, eyes wide. "Are you getting a divorce?"

Daniel closed his eyes briefly and then opened them. "I won't lie to you, Noah. Eventually, we will be divorcing."

Noah's face crumbled. "No, Dad, please don't divorce mom."

Daniel's hand gripped his son's shoulder. "Noah, I love you. This doesn't have anything to do with our relationship. That will not change."

"But I don't understand, you're not mad at each other, why…"

Bella grabbed her son's hand. "It's a bit too complicated for you to understand right now, but one day you will. Right now, all you need to know is that we both love you, and you will be our first priority."

Daniel stood, drawing Noah up with him. "You'll need time to adjust, but soon you'll see that this decision will work out for all of us."

Bella winced at the lie.

"I have to go, buddy. Can I count on you to take care of your mom?"

Noah nodded his eyes bleak. Daniel pulled him into a hug and kissed the curls atop his head. "I'll call you every day. You won't believe the surprise I have for you next Saturday when I pick you up." He smiled down at his son. "Can you walk me to my car?"

Noah nodded again, his face a mask of hopeless defeat. He followed his dad down the hallway to the stairs. Bella continued to sit on the bed suddenly numb with grief. After the front door shut, she rose and walked to the window. She parted the blinds and looked down at the driveway. Daniel was putting the boxes in the trunk of his car as Noah looked on. He shut the trunk door and turned to Noah, grabbing him in a hug. He squeezed his shoulder and opened the driver's door. Noah backed away as the car's engine came to life. Daniel backed the car down the driveway waving at his son before he moved on down the street.

Bella drew back from the blinds. She should go and comfort her son, but all she wanted to do was curl up in a ball and shut out the world. Earlier that morning, she had dumped every bottle or can containing alcohol in the trashcan in the garage. She hadn't wanted to be tempted to drown her pain again…because it would be too easy to do just that.

The front door opened and closed, and Noah's light tread sounded on the stairs. She forced a smile and stood in the doorway of his room. "Are you hungry, honey?"

"No." The two letters came out dull and flat.

"How about a video game or DVD?"

Noah shook his head, walked to his bed and threw himself onto the Star Wars comforter burying his face in his pillow. The muffled sobs broke Bella's heart. *How could Daniel do this to us?*

She lay down next to her son, head next to his on the pillow and ran her hand up and down his back. Minutes went by and gradually the crying stopped, Noah's breathing evened out and Bella knew he was asleep. She wrapped an arm around her son and followed him into a thorough slumber.

13

A loud battle cry awoke Bella. She jerked upright on the bed before the meaning of the fighting penetrated her brain. Noah was playing a video game–extremely loud. She swung her legs out of bed to tell him to turn the volume down when two things struck her. The game was loud because she had been sleeping in the guest bedroom upstairs, and *Noah was playing a video game.*

She sighed with relief. He wasn't moping in his room. She yawned and thought about going back to sleep…just curl up under the covers all day. Unable to bear sleeping downstairs without her husband, Bella had retreated to the guest bedroom, which did little to prevent her from tossing and turning all night. Her husband's scent still lingered on the pillow from three nights before. She swiveled her head towards the windows. Sunlight pushed at the closed white mini-blinds. *No, I can't stay in bed; I have to think about Noah.*

Bella picked her cell phone off of the antique-white end table. Ten-thirty! She never slept this late. She pushed aside the white comforter and dug her toes into the plush off-white carpet. She stepped down the hallway to the entertainment room. Her son, clothed in Star Wars pajamas, sat on the sofa with the control in his hands.

Bella forced a cheery tone. "Morning, honey. Do you want me to make pancakes?"

Noah stared at the television screen as he answered. "Nah. When you didn't wake up, I ate cereal."

Bella cringed. "Sorry, honey. I didn't realize it was that late."

No answer.

"I'll be downstairs if you need me."

Bella stepped down stairs–cautiously. She was still groggy from being sleep-deprived. In the kitchen she prepped the coffee machine. After adding the coffee and turning on the machine, she rubbed her forehead. A slight throbbing had started behind her eyes. She stared out the window. Her brow furrowed. What day is it? Her iPhone was upstairs. She groaned internally, as she headed back to the stairs.

A mug of coffee in her hand, Bella sat on the living room sofa and stared listlessly at her phone. It was Monday. She pressed an icon, and her daily calendar opened. Her violet eyes widened. She and Noah were supposed to meet her mom for lunch in one hour. She slowly shook her head. *I can't.* She texted her mom a brief message about being unable to meet with her for lunch. She took a sip of her coffee, waiting. Her phone dinged, her mom texting back on when she would like to reschedule. Bella texted back for the same time next Monday. She set her phone on the cushion beside her. She ignored the confirming ding from her mother.

The Star Wars battle had ceased. She hoped Noah was okay, but she didn't have the energy to climb the stairs again. As she raised the white ceramic mug to her lips, her hand froze. Right in her line of sight were the family pictures on the mantle. Bella stifled a sob, as her eyes moistened. She set the mug down and rose from the couch. Walking to the fireplace, she lifted the picture of her and Daniel staring into each other's eyes, off the mantle. *Eyes full of love.* Her tears made no sound, as they dropped onto the framed glass.

In one fluid motion, she dropped to the floor and closed her eyes. *Why, God? Why have you allowed this to happen? I don't know how I'm going to get through each day without him.*

"Mom?"

Bella's eyes shot open. Noah stood a foot away, concern stamped on his face. "Are you okay?"

Bella knuckled her tears away and pushed to her feet setting the picture back on the mantle.

"I will be honey, a little sad about your dad leaving."

"Did you want him to leave?"

Bella brushed a hand across her son's curls. "No."

Her son's face fell. "Then why did he leave?"

Bella gathered Noah in her arms. "That's his story to tell you, and he will one day. All you need to know now is that we both love you."

She pulled back. "How about lunch? You can have your favorite sandwich…peanut butter and banana."

"I'm not hungry. I'm going back up to my bedroom."

Bella watched helplessly as Noah, made his slow way to the stairs.

✦ ✦ ✦

Alicia drummed her fingers on the dining table as she stared off into space. The dinner plates and utensils rattled as the boys put them in the dishwasher.

"A dollar for your thoughts?"

She smiled up at her husband. "I thought it was a penny?"

"Inflation."

She looked toward the boys.

"It's noth…"

Music burst forth from her cell–loudly.

"Jeez, hon, get your hearing checked." Jarod stuck a finger in each ear and retreated to the soccer game playing out on the television screen in the living room.

"Hey, Charley."

"Just calling to coordinate our lunch in your neck of the woods this Saturday."

It's not this Saturday. Remember, Bella and her family are going to Busch Gardens."

"Are you sure? I had it in my phone as this Saturday?"

A splash sounded from the kitchen. "Hold on." Alicia jerked around in her chair. Both boys were giggling. Soapy water covered the counter and floor. Her eyes narrowed. "You, boys, think that's funny? If it's not cleaned up in two minutes, I'm going to think it hilarious when you go to bed thirty minutes early."

The giggles came to an abrupt halt as Cameron grabbed a handful of paper towels off the holder.

"Sorry, Charley."

"Hannah's going to bed early because she wanted her baby sister to look more like a fairy princess."

"What did she do?"

"Dumped a container of glitter over her head. She sparkled pink from head to toe."

Alicia barked out a laugh.

"Poor baby...took me an hour to de-glitter her."

"De-glitter?"

"A made-up word to suit the occasion." Charley hesitated a moment. "I'm trying not to think the worst, but I tried to call and text Bella yesterday and Saturday about our lunch, and she's never called me back. It's like déjà vu.

Alicia sighed. "I know. I was just thinking about her. She wasn't at church yesterday. I can't think of the last time she wasn't at church."

"You don't think Daniel..."

"I don't know. She was happy Friday. She talked about her and Daniel's date practically the entire drive back to Williamsburg. Doesn't make sense."

Charley sighed. "Well I guess we can do like we did in April. Give her a few days, and if we haven't heard from her, do a tag team cell phone barrage."

"Okay. I'll talk to you later. I have to go see how well the boys cleaned up the soapy water off the floor."

Still fuming, Alicia marched to the back of the grocery store, with Kelen in tow. It was seven in the evening on Wednesday, and she had just picked Kelen up from a friend's pizza party when her husband called her. Cameron had tripped over his big feet with an open gallon of milk in his hand and… let's just say clean-up would take a while. That gallon of milk had been only hours old from her trip to her neighborhood store that afternoon.

Getting back on the road with Kelen, she had stopped at the first store she had come across. Of course, never having been in this particular store, she had no idea where the milk was, but after turning down two wrong aisles, she struck pay dirt. She scanned the selections and then pulled open the glass door and grabbed a gallon jug of two-percent. She turned, took two steps, and repeated Cameron's mistake.

Stunned by what she saw nearby in the store, Alicia's nerveless fingers loosened on the jug's handle. The container dropped to the floor; the top popped off, and milk splashed the chrome of the refrigerated section and pooled on the tiles, as she stood rooted to the floor–her mouth agape, but not because of the spill.

Charley was spot on...*Déjà vu*. Daniel stood frozen two yards away, his hand holding the hand of the woman from Rudee's restaurant. Too furious to notice the features of the woman before...she got a good glimpse this time. She was absolutely stunning, with long black hair, dark brown doe eyes, a slight almond shape, perfect nose, and full lips. At the moment, her doe eyes reflected puzzlement at the woman responsible for the spill, for obviously she didn't remember that they had crossed paths at Rudee's and that this woman was Daniel's wife's best friend.

Daniel recovered first. He tugged on the woman's hand and led them back the way they had come. Alicia became aware of the strident pounding of her heart as she glanced down in consternation at the mess on the floor. She looked around for a store clerk. A middle-aged man came around the corner, leading an employee pushing a cart with mop and bucket. She stepped out of the pool of milk and joined Kelen on a dry patch of floor. The clerk plopped the mop head down in the center of the spill.

Alicia's face warmed with embarrassment. "I'm sorry, I'll pay for the milk."

The clerk looked up with a sympathetic smile. "It's okay, ma'am. Go ahead and get yourself another gallon of milk."

"I've, uh, changed my mind." She grabbed Kelen's hand and rushed to the front of the store.

Alicia hurried to her car and unlocked the doors. She jerked on her seatbelt, made sure Kelen was strapped in and drove out of the lot onto the side street, taking deep breaths as she tried to slow down her heart rate. At the light, she took a right heading for Governor's Land. She pushed the button on the steering wheel to activate her Bluetooth and said a name when asked.

"Hey, honey, what's up?"

Alicia concentrated on making her voice sound matter of fact. "I'm making a quick stop at Bella's and then I'll be home."

"Okay, did you get the milk?"

"Not yet."

"Don't forget."

"Won't…love you, bye." She pressed the disconnect button.

"Why are we going to Noah's house?"

Alicia started at the sound of her son's voice. "I need to talk to Noah's mom."

"Who was that lady with Noah's dad?"

Alicia groaned inwardly. "I don't know."

"Why was he…"

"Kelen, I can't answer your questions right now, but I will tomorrow okay?"

"Okay."

Kelen fell silent. Alicia chewed on her bottom lip, her heart still thumping too fast. What was going on? What happened? Did Bella know? Is that why she hadn't returned her calls and missed church? These questions and others chased each other like a dog trying to bite his own tail during the ten-minute ride.

Alicia pulled into Bella's driveway and shut off the engine. She took a couple of steadying breaths. "Kelen, you stay in the car. I'll let you know if we're going inside."

She closed the driver's door and walked to the front door. She pressed the doorbell. Footsteps pounded towards the door, which was jerked open by Noah. The eager look on his face morphed into profound disappointment. Alicia had the answer to one of her questions.

"Hey, buddy, it's good to see you."

Noah threw his arms around Alicia and started to cry. She bent over his curly head and whispered soothing words in his ear. After a couple of minutes, he pulled back and wiped his face. Alicia looked up to see Bella standing a few feet away, wiping her eyes.

"Hey, guess who's with me? Kelen has been begging me to bring him by so he can play your new video game."

Alicia turned and walked to her car. She opened the back door and whispered urgently. "Kelen, don't mention seeing Noah's dad, okay?"

Kelen's troubled eyes looked into her eyes. "Why is Noah crying?"

"I'll find out from his mom. Not a word about his dad, okay?"

Kelen nodded and jumped out of the car. He stopped a foot in front of Noah and put his right hand up for a high-five. Noah smacked his palm, and both boys headed to the stairs.

Alicia turned to Bella who stood on the tile floor, her face as pale as the spilled milk on the grocery store floor.

Dark shadows underscored her lower eyelids. Alicia walked over and hugged her. "I'm sorry, Bella." She could feel her friend's body trembling in her arms.

Bella stepped back. "How did you find out?"

"Let's go sit down. Can I make you some tea and honey?"

Bella shook her head as Alicia led her by the hand to the loveseat. Alicia's eyebrows rose as she glanced into the kitchen. Dirty dishes, pots, utensils, and glasses covered every inch of the counters and stove. She eased Bella down on the gray cushion and sat down next to her, still holding her hand.

Bella's eyes were twin pools of despair. "When did you find out?"

Alicia squeezed her hand. "I haven't found out anything."

"But…"

"I ran into Daniel tonight." She sighed. "He was with the woman from Rudee's."

Bella uttered a cry of despair and covered her face with her free hand.

Alicia gently pulled the hand down from her face. "Tell me what happened."

Bella wiped a hand under her nose. "I didn't want you to know…I didn't want anyone to know…not yet. I've been hoping Daniel would come to his senses and… come home."

A chill filled Alicia's chest and spread down to her gut. "Tell me everything, Bella, now."

Alicia could tell that it was the last thing Bella wanted to do…but finally her shoulders slumped in defeat. "Friday night Daniel told me he wanted a divorce."

Alicia gasped.

"He took me to this Italian restaurant and…"

It took her twenty minutes to talk about the events of the last six days. As her words came to a halt, Alicia tried to harness her multiple emotions, before they suffocated her. Rage, grief, despair, compassion, and alarm all clogged her chest, making it hard to take a breath. But it was the alarm moving from her chest to her brain that forced her to ignore all other emotions. Her friend was in serious denial.

"Bella?" Bella looked up from the hands in her lap. "He isn't coming back."

She shook her head. "That's why I didn't want to tell you. I knew you would be negative…tell me I had to let my marriage go…move on with my life."

"No, Bella, you can't get over it like a cold or the flu. It will take a long time. But denying what has happened won't change the outcome."

Bella's lips quivered. "Now you sound like Daniel."

"What do you mean?"

"He called today to ask if I had decided on a lawyer. I told him I wasn't going to hire one…that I wouldn't need one when he came to his senses." Bella rubbed a finger across her bottom lip. "He was furious."

Alicia changed tactics. "What makes you think he'll come back?"

"He…vowed to God to stay with me forever. That vow can't be broken. And God is faithful. He'll send him back to me." Her voice became a whisper. "He has to."

Alicia heaved another sigh. "Bella, a marriage vow can be broken and has been many times. What about the McAllisters and the Robertsons at church? They are awesome Christians, but both of those marriages ended in divorce."

Bella blinked away tears and shook her head. Alicia chewed her bottom lip. This battle wouldn't be won in a night, and she needed to get Kelen home. "How about I take Noah with me for a sleepover?"

"I don't…"

"Bella, your son needs to get away from this oppressive house. Have you taken him anywhere in the last three days?"

Bella's face flushed, and she shook her head. "I didn't want anyone to see me like this." She gave a quick nod. "Thank you. Moping in his bedroom isn't good for him."

Bella squeezed her friend's hands and stood up. She shouted up the stairs. "Kelen, Noah come on down."

The boys bounded down the stairs. "Kelen, how would you like it if Noah spent the night with us?"

Kelen's face lit up. "Yeah!"

"Noah?"

Noah nodded then looked at his mom. "Sure, honey. I'll see you tomorrow. Have a good time."

Alicia said, "You boys head to the car." They rushed to the door.

"What about pajamas and…?"

"I have extras of everything." She pulled Bella in for a hug and whispered in her ear. "I love you…and clean your house tomorrow…you'll feel better."

Bella nodded then waved as Alicia shut the door behind her.

Alicia put the key in the ignition. "I have to stop and get milk. Who wants ice cream?"

Cheers erupted from the back, as Alicia wiped her suddenly wet eyes. She pulled onto the street, heading back to the grocery store.

Thirty minutes later, Alicia waited until the boys slammed shut her car doors and ran toward the front door of her vinyl siding-clad, one-story home before hitting the Bluetooth connection on her steering wheel.

"Hi, Alicia."

"Could you hire a sitter and come to my house tomorrow at one-thirty?"

"I…ah…I think so. What's wrong?"

"Everything. It's Bella. I'll fill you in tomorrow when you get here, and then we're going to her house at three."

"Okay."

"I'm sorry, I have to run before the ice cream melts." She disconnected the call as her husband appeared in the doorway. He started down the walkway. She opened the door and handed him the bags containing the milk and ice cream.

His eyebrows rose. "Spur of the moment sleepover. Something I need to know?"

"I'll tell you after the boys are in bed."

He turned with the bags as Alicia locked the doors. "I get the feeling you were right to be worrying."

The doorbell rang, and Alicia strode to the door to answer it. Charley stood on the stoop in black leggings and a vibrant pink shirt. Black earrings dangled almost to her shoulders. Alicia pulled her into a fierce hug. She swiped at her eyes when she let her friend go. "Thanks for coming on such short notice."

Shouts and cheers rang out from Kelen's bedroom.

"Is one of those voices Noah?" Charley asked.

Alicia nodded. "Make yourself comfortable. I'll be right back."

She walked into the kitchen and picked up two glasses of iced green tea. She entered the living room and handed one to Charley. She settled across from her on the brown leather loveseat. "I just got home thirty minutes ago. Noah and Kelen went with me to work and stayed in the Kid's Zone at the athletic club." Alicia took in a breath. "It's bad, Charley."

Charley's hands tightened on her glass. "What happened?"

"Remember when I told you on the phone about Bella's date with Daniel Friday night?"

Charley nodded.

"It had been months since Daniel had taken her out on a date...just the two of them. And that...that bas..." Alicia quickly gulped her tea to prevent a repetition of the word that had slipped out at Rudee's restaurant.

Charley tensed. "What happened?"

Alicia's eyes hardened. "Daniel took his wife to this nice restaurant, plied her with wine, and then asked for a divorce."

Charley's jaw dropped. "He did not!"

"He did, and it gets worse. Because of all the guilt he was feeling, he decided to *explain* in detail why he wanted a divorce."

Alicia's hands started to tremble. "One of the things he told her was that he had never been in love with her... that he was blackmailed into marrying her because of his father."

Shock changed Charley's face into a mask of disbelief. She parted her lips, but no words emerged. She raised her glass to her lips with a hand that shook. She took a drink, eyes moist. "How could anyone be so cruel?"

Alicia's mouth formed a thin line. "It wasn't enough to crush her hopes and dreams for their perfect little family...he had to destroy her."

"When did she call and tell you?"

"She didn't. Last night I ran into Daniel with that woman from Rudee's. I went straight to Bella's house."

"Oh, my dear Lord in Heaven!...Bella must be beyond devastated," Charley whispered.

"She is, but she's also in denial. She's convinced Daniel will eventually come back to her and Noah." Alicia's lips drew into a hard line. "I, for one, don't understand why she would want him to."

"My poor Bella." Charley shook her head.

Alicia sighed. "I saw this coming from the moment I looked through that window at Rudee's. I could tell Daniel was in love with that woman."

She rose off the loveseat. "Charley, I need to get out of my work clothes, take a quick shower, and then we'll go see Bella." She walked down the hallway to Kelen's bedroom to tell the boys that they all would be leaving soon to take Noah home.

+ + +

Alicia turned left into the entrance to Governor's Land. She glanced in the backseat to make sure the boys were occupied with the video games she had them bring. She lowered her voice. "Charley, what are we going to say to Bella to convince her that Daniel is not coming back?"

Charley took in a breath and then let it out slowly. "We're not going to say anything."

"What?" Alicia's green eyes darted in Charley's direction and then back to the road.

"Alicia, I love your 'take charge...bring it on' persona...defender of the weak and downtrodden...white knight with the lance charging the black knight. I'm sure if you had had the chance you would have given 'you know who'..." Charley looked over her shoulder into the backseat. "...a piece of your mind last night. You're also a 'fixer,' and though I love you for it...you can't fix this."

Alicia swiped at her suddenly wet eyes.

"Nothing you say is going to change Bella's mind. All we can do is be there for her...love on her...and when she finally accepts the truth–because I also believe that 'you know who' is not coming back–be a soft place for her to land."

Alicia gave a shaky laugh. "You are right...again. And I love you for being the kind, sensible, calming influence both Bella and I need."

She guided her car up Bella's driveway and shut off the ignition. Both boys jumped out of the car. Charley opened her door. "Where's Cameron today?"

"He's at Busch Gardens with a friend," Alicia said as she emerged from the car and pressed the key fob to lock the car doors.

"I love Busch Gardens." Charley walked through the door the boys had left wide open.

Alicia shut the door and looked around. Bella was no-where to be seen. She walked across the foyer heading for the kitchen. Not in the kitchen. She reversed direction and headed into Bella's bedroom calling out her name. No answer. She came back out to the foyer and looked up the stairs.

"Hey, Noah is your mom upstairs?"

"I'll go look," came the shout from upstairs.

Footfalls rushed around upstairs.

"She's not up here."

Alicia's brows knit together. "Where is she?"

"Did she know what time you were coming?"

"Yeah, I called her this morning and told her."

"We should check the garage for her car."

Charley and Alicia cut through the formal dining room to a short hallway. They passed the laundry room to the right. They entered another short hallway that led to stairs off to the left and the door to the garage. Charley opened the door and looked in. Bella's one-year-old Volvo occupied one half of the garage. She shut the door.

"Do you think she went for a walk?"

"No. She told me yesterday, she didn't want anyone to see her looking like a wreck."

Charley chewed her bottom lip. "This doesn't make sense, where could she be?"

Icy tendrils slithered up Alicia's spine and branched out to her extremities. "Oh, no, God, please not Bella."

"Alicia, what's wrong, you're as white as a ghost!"

Alicia's heart beat a tattoo against her ribs. "One of my sister's best friends committed suicide a few months ago because her husband left her for another woman. She left behind a four-year-old son."

Alicia's head turned and looked up the stairs beside her. Blood thrummed in her ears. "Bella!" She took the stairs two at a time and yanked open the door. Bella lay sprawled on the bed face down.

"Bella!

Alicia ran to the bed, and shook her friend's shoulders, while repeating her name. No response. She shook harder and was rewarded with a groan.

"Bella, can you hear me?"

A moan and movement. "Bella wake up!"

Bella pushed up on her elbows and swiveled her head to the left, mumbling, "Alicia? Charley?"

Alicia's adrenaline rush abated. "Yes, it's us."

Bella maneuvered to a seated position, legs dangling over the edge of the bed. She yawned and shook her head as if to clear it. She stared at her friends.

"Bella, what's wrong. What are you doing up here?"

Bella closed her eyes and rubbed her forehead with the fingers on her right hand. "I…um…I think I came up here to take a nap."

Alicia frowned. "Up here? It's hot as blazes without the air conditioning on."

"I haven't been able to sleep since Daniel left. I can't look at our bed much less sleep in it. I've been going to bed in the other guest room, but no matter how hard I try, I can't get to sleep at night. I thought maybe I would try to get a quick nap up here before you came."

"I wouldn't call that a nap. More like you were unconscious."

"Yeah, I'm pretty sleep deprived."

"Can we go down to the living room and talk…I'm sweating to death up here."

"I see you brought reinforcements." She gave Charley a weak smile.

Charley reached down and gave Bella a fierce hug. "I'm sorry, Bella."

Bella nodded and stood up. She took a step, wavered a bit and then got her bearings. Alicia let her go first down the stairs. Leaving the hallway with the laundry room, Bella entered a doorway to her right that led to the kitchen. Alicia was glad to see that Bella had heeded her advice and cleaned her kitchen. She needed to focus on other things beside Daniel.

"I have iced tea, would you like some?"

Alicia and Charley glanced at each other and nodded.

They both took a sip of tea from the glasses Bella handed them and walked to the couch and sat down. An awkward silence filled the room.

Bella broke it. "How was Noah?"

Alicia smiled. "He was fine. He and Kelen had a blast together as always."

Bella heaved a sigh. "I'm glad. I'm worried about what Daniel's moving out is doing to him."

Alicia took another sip of tea and cleared her throat. "Bella, you and Noah both need to get out of this house. Something to take your mind off of…"

"I know, but I just don't have the will or the energy." The fingers of one hand rubbed the knuckles of the other hand.

"Why don't you take him to Busch Garden's tomorrow? You love the amusement park."

Bella sighed. "Daniel's taking him on Saturday."

Irritation crept into Alicia's voice. "So what? There's no law that says Noah can't go two days in a row."

Bella shook her head. Alicia flicked a glance at Charley.

"Bella, how about while Noah's with his dad, you and I go for a spa day? The whole works…massages, facials, pedicures and manicures," Charley said.

Bella's eyes filled. "I did that last Friday before my date with Daniel."

Charley grimaced. "I'm sorry, Bella…I didn't mean to bring up a bad memory."

"I know." She rubbed her knuckles harder. "I pray Daniel doesn't take too long realizing he's made a horrible mistake and come home."

Alicia opened her mouth but shut it when Charley's eyes shot her a warning. "What can Alicia and I do to help, Bella?"

Her eyes reflected pain. "Noah still has three more weeks until school, if you or Alicia could pick him up once in a while for a play date to get him out of the house that would be a big help." She looked down at her hands. "It's getting more difficult each day to put on a brave face." She lifted her head, mouth trembling.

Alicia's heart clenched as she stared at her friend's pale, drawn face. All vestige of Bella's vibrant, sunny persona was gone. , Alicia plastered on a bright smile. "Jarod, I, and the boys are going to Lake Gaston this Sunday for a week. We've rented a house on the lake. We'd like to take Noah with us."

"No, I don't want to inconvenience your family trip."

"Bella, please, he's like a third son to me and Jarod… and a brother to the boys."

Bella hesitated a moment. "But Noah would have to be back by Saturday morning for his time with Daniel."

"You just let us know what time on Saturday." She clapped her knees. "Okay, it's settled. I'll text you about what time I'll pick up Noah. And when we get back from the lake the three of us are going to lunch."

Bella gave a wan smile.

Charley's voice was gentle. "Bella, have you told your mom and dad?"

She shook her head.

"Bella, you have to tell them."

She nodded. "I will, after you leave. My mom has already called twice today, and I have to call her back."

Charley placed her glass of tea on the end table and stood. She stepped over to Bella and grasped her hand. "Please, answer my text and phone calls."

Alicia stepped over and took her other hand. "Mine, too. Otherwise, I'll jump in the car and come over."

Bella gave a weak laugh. "Okay." Her eyes teared up again. "You both are the best." She stood up and hugged her friends.

All three pulled back and cleared their throats.

"Can I say a quick prayer?" Charley asked.

Bella nodded.

All three grasped hands and bowed their heads as Charley started to speak. "Oh, God, we come to you with heavy hearts today. Our friend, Bella is hurting. Please keep her close within your strong arms. Give her the strength to weather this storm and remind her each day to trust in you and not lean on her own understanding. Amen."

Bella and Alicia repeated the 'Amen' as they dropped each other's hands.

All three walked to the staircase.

Alicia spoke up the stairs. "Kelen…time to go."

Both boys thundered down the stairs.

"Ah, mom. Do we have to go now?" Kelen begged his mother.

Alicia ruffled her son's blond hair. "We do, but guess what? Noah's going to the lake with us."

Both boy's eyes widened, and grins split their faces.

"Say goodbye."

"Bye, Noah. See you on Sunday."

"See you, Kelen."

Alicia walked to the door and opened it. Kelen shot out the opening. She turned to Bella. "I'll see you on Sunday."

Alicia followed Kelen out the door with Charley right behind. They turned to wave but Bella had already shut the door.

Alicia bit her lip as she turned right onto Route 5. "Charley, I'm really concerned about Bella."

"Me, too. She's…" Charley searched for the right word.

"Delusional."

"That's a bit harsh, but…yes. It's not only that she can't accept that Daniel's not coming back…she's clinging to that hope like it's the only lifeline she has. We are going to have to be very careful with what we say around her." Charley glanced over at Alicia's fear reflected in her eyes. "Never in a million years would I have considered Bella suicidal, but now…"

Alicia's hands gripped the wheel harder. "Once she realizes that Daniel is never coming back…"

Charley's voice quivered. "We have to convince her she can have a full life without him."

Both women fell silent for the rest of the ride back to Alicia's house. Jarod's black mid-size truck was pulling onto the left side of their driveway as Alicia approached. *Well, Jarod, you thought I was worrying too much about Bella before…you ain't seen nothing, yet.*

16

Two golfers came into view through the kitchen window as Bella stood at the sink, twisting the small apple back and forth through the stream of water. She watched one of the golfers push a tee into the green, place his ball on top of it and then point his club down the course. She grabbed a paper towel off of the rack and dried the apple. She switched her view to the oven clock. Eight-thirty. She needed to get Noah to the bus stop. It was hard to believe this would be his last year at Matoaca Elementary School.

Bella added the apple to the sandwich and chips in the *The Force Awakens* themed lunch bag. She strode over to the back pack sitting on the kitchen table and put the bag in the middle section. Pulling the zipper to seal up the book bag, she hefted it and carried it over to the front door.

Her voice carried up the stairs. "Noah, time to go."

As she waited on her son, she thought back over the last three weeks. For the first two weeks, Daniel had badgered her about hiring a lawyer. His calls alternated between trying to reason with her and threatening consequences if she didn't hire an attorney. Then the calls stopped. He hadn't said anything about a lawyer in the last week, not even when he picked up Noah on Saturday. And he had actually spoken to her, which he hadn't done the last two Saturdays. He had asked how she was doing. He seemed genuinely concerned.

Noah had told her that when he was with his dad on Saturdays, Daniel talked about how much he missed seeing Noah every day. Bella's heart had gladdened at those words. She was positive that he was starting to regret his decision to leave his family. The fact that he had stopped bugging her about hiring a lawyer was another good sign. All she had to do was wait out this infatuation with Melissa…and then he would come home.

Noah bounded down the stairs. "I'm ready."

"Okay, let's go."

Noah could have gone by himself, but she wanted to be there, as he got on the bus for the first day of school. She had made an effort to look presentable–for the walk to the bus stop a block away. For the last three weeks, she could have cared less about her appearance, only making the effort when she had to go to the grocery store once a week.

She shut the dark green door behind them and reached for Noah's hand as they walked, knowing it wouldn't be long before he would be too embarrassed to have her hold his hand.

They arrived at the bus stop before anyone else, and Noah dropped her hand. *Won't be long now.* Noah waved as a boy his age rushed out of the house on the corner. As they jabbered, Bella pulled in a deep breath of the warm morning air and looked around. She could feel herself unwinding…a bit. She had refused all lunch invitations and social events from her friends and family. She couldn't bear the thought of inane conversations while her life lay in ashes around her feet.

Two mothers with younger children walked up as the bus turned the corner and came to a halt, brakes screeching. Bella wanted to give Noah a hug but held off. She didn't want to embarrass him.

"Have a good day, honey."

"Bye, mom." He climbed the steps and disappeared inside.

Bella hurried back the way she had come before one of the other moms could draw her into a conversation. As she cleared the trees that screened her property from the neighbor's, she saw a strange man in a suit standing in her driveway. Her footsteps slowed.

"Are you Bella Stanford?"

"Yes, who are you?"

The man handed her a large envelope. "Ma'am, you've been served."

He turned and walked to a car parked across the street. Bella remembered noticing the car as she walked to the bus stop with Noah.

Bella looked down at the envelope. What is this? *What did he mean I've been served?* And then suddenly she knew and could barely breathe. She stumbled to the brick steps and sat down hard. She whimpered through the hand covering her mouth. "Please, God, no, oh, please, oh, please…"

She tore open the envelope with trembling fingers and pulled out the papers. She read the three prominent words at the top of the first page and wailed in agony. The pages fluttered from her nerveless fingers to the pebbled driveway. The words in bold black type at the top of the first page stood out against the stark white sheet of paper: COMPLAINT FOR DIVORCE.

Bella, you have to go." Alicia paced the length of Bella's living room and back again. "If you don't show up for the hearing tomorrow, the court will make the decision for you on the divorce settlement and custody of Noah."

Bella shook her head stubbornly.

Alicia glared at her friend with exasperation mingled with irritation. For the last six months, she, Charley, and Bella's parents had tried to convince Bella to hire a lawyer. After she received the complaint for divorce from Daniel, they were sure that Bella would finally accept the fact that her husband would not be returning. But she had only dug her heels in more deeply. Like a litany, Bella kept repeating to her and Charley, that according to the Bible, a marriage could only be dissolved for one reason—adultery—and since neither she nor Daniel had committed that sin, there was no legitimate cause for a divorce.

The only saving grace in this whole divorce debacle was that Daniel promised not to take advantage of his wife's lack of counsel. Bella and Noah would be taken care of financially, and Bella would retain full custody of Noah with visitation rights granted to Daniel.

Alicia halted before the bank of four windows facing the golf course. The course was covered in a blanket of snow. The bare limbs of the few trees dotting the golf course whipped back and forth each time a gust of frigid air engaged the branches. She rubbed at the headache starting to pound at her temple. *How do I convince her?*

She slowly pivoted back to her friend. Bella sat on the couch with her head in her hands...weeping–something she had been doing a lot of in the last few months. The feeling of helplessness that had begun almost a year ago at Rudee's restaurant flooded her body.

Bella had given Alicia a key to her home when she first moved into the house in Governor's Land in case of an emergency. Extremely worried about her friend, Alicia had started carrying the key on her key ring and letting herself into Bella's house any time she knocked, and Bella didn't answer.

Alicia's thoughts traced backwards to a few weeks earlier. When there had been no answer to her knock, Alicia had let herself into Bella's house. From the second floor, she could hear Bella crying and Noah trying to reassure his mom, telling her everything would be fine, that he liked Melissa and his dad was really happy...which made Bella cry harder.

Noah had had to mature in a way no ten-year-old should have to. Alicia's eyes widened. *Ten.* It was March. Noah would be *eleven* in a couple of weeks. *I need to start planning a birthday party and think about...*She shook her head. *Bella is my priority right now.*

She sighed inwardly and walked over to her friend, sitting down next to her, wrapping an arm around her shoulders. "Bella, you have to go to court tomorrow."

She pulled back wiping her eyes. "I can't."

"Why?"

"Because it would mean I accept the divorce, and I don't...and I..."

Alicia squeezed her shoulder. "What, Bella?"

Her eyes were pools of grief. "I don't understand why God is allowing this to happen to me. I know he loves me."

"He does, Bella, he loves you so much, but we are all sinners with a free will given to us by God. Daniel exercised his free will. God isn't going to force him to change his mind anymore than he would force you to change your mind or me to change mine. We can only do that ourselves."

"But the marriage vow..."

"Made by a man...not God."

Alicia's hands gripped her friend's shoulders and locked eyes with her. "Bella, the divorce will be granted tomorrow whether you go or not."

Bella's lips barely moved as she whispered on a grief-stricken breath. "I know."

Alicia started to open her mouth and then shut it when Bella continued. "But I can't bear witness to the death of my marriage."

Alicia straightened her shoulders and grasped her friend's hands. "I'm proud of you. This never should have happened to you, but you fought the good fight. You stood up for your marriage vows and a fulltime father for your son. No one could have been a better champion for what is right...what is moral."

One corner of Bella's lips quirked up. "They can put that on my tombstone."

Alicia smiled. "That's the first hint of humor I've heard from you in months." She stood up. "I better go; the boys will be getting off the bus soon. I'll come by tomorrow for moral support."

"No, I want to be alone."

"Bella…"

"Alicia, I…I won't be fine, but I promise to be okay for Noah."

"I'll call you the day after." She squeezed her friend's hand and walked to the door. She opened it, but before shutting it behind her, she sent a glance in Bella's direction and froze as her heartbeats accelerated. The features of Bella's face seemed to reflect the thoughts of a condemned prisoner as he is placed in the electric chair and the black hood begins to descend over his head…*I sit here adrift between life and death.*

Alicia shut the door and sent a prayer heavenward.

Getting awake was akin to trying to surface through gelatin. Bella's eyes sluggishly opened in the dark room. The nightmare was fading, but the image of her son lying in a pool of spreading blood remained. She tried to shove off the covers, but the signal sent from her brain wasn't reaching her arms. She pulled in a shallow breath. *I have to check on my son!* With a herculean effort she pushed off the bed…and collapsed on the carpeted floor.

Bella lay on the floor, butterflies beating against her ribcage in a feeble attempt to escape. She gasped for air. She shook her head and groaned. She turned to the nightstand and grabbed the edge. As she began to pull up on to her knees the nightstand tipped, and the water glass and pill bottle hit her in the forehead before falling to the carpet. She let go and fell back, moaning.

She tried to swivel her head toward the dim light, but it was hard…so hard. The glow from the nightlight outlined the railing outside the bedroom door. Bella scooted on her belly over the threshold of the bedroom towards the railing. She grabbed a railing slat in a two-handed white-knuckled grip and grunted as she pulled up to her knees. Still breathless, Bella drew a quivering wrist across her sweaty forehead. Minutes passed, as she pressed her face against the slats, waiting for the fog in her mind to lift, but nothing happened.

Her eyebrows pulled together in puzzlement as she looked down. *Where am I?* She tried to concentrate. *Noah.* Bella grasped the top of the railing and pulled with all her might. She managed to get one foot beneath her and then the other. On shaking limbs, she rose teetering as she grasped the railing.

Her hands clung to the railing as she stumbled towards the hazy glow against the baseboard. She reached the end of the railing and looked to the left. The glass doors of the entertainment room wavered nauseatingly in front of her. *Wrong way...I went the wrong way.*

Bella tried to execute a wobbly turn to her right, but her left foot landed on nothing but air. She tried to move her foot back to the solid wooden surface of the hallway floor, but her brain again misfired. Precariously off-balance, her body weight conspired with gravity pulling her backwards. Instinctively, she tried to grasp the railing harder, but it was no use, her hands slipped off. Pain exploded in her hip and shoulder. She screamed. Pain shot through her other shoulder, and a starburst exploded in her head...followed by nothing.

19

The incessant vibration of her iPhone awoke Alicia from a restless sleep. She looked at the screen... Noah. She glanced at the digital clock as she answered with her heart in her throat. "What's wrong, Noah?"

Sobs answered her.

Alicia shot out of bed onto her feet. Her husband stirred. "Noah, tell me what's wrong!"

"It's...it's my mom...she fell down the stairs. I tried to call my dad, but..."

"Noah, I'm calling 9-1-1. I'll call you right..."

Jarod sat up abruptly. "No, I'll call; you stay on the line with Noah." He grabbed his cell off the nightstand.

Alicia took a deep breath. *She had to be calm for Noah.* "Noah, I'm going to stay on the phone with you as I get dressed and drive over. Where is your mom?"

"At the bottom of the stairs." His sobs were lessening.

"Jarod, Bella fell down the stairs." Alicia said as she raced into her closet. "Noah, is she conscious?"

"No."

"Can you tell if she's breathing?"

The few seconds of silence were torture.

"Her chest is moving up and down."

Alicia's relief was so profound, she almost collapsed to her knees.

"Alicia, the ambulance is on the way. The dispatcher needs to talk to Noah."

Alicia rushed out of her closet with a pair of sweats. "Noah, the dispatcher with 9-1-1 needs to talk to you about your mom. Hang up so they can call you, okay, honey? I'll be there in twenty minutes."

Noah's voice trembled. "Okay."

Alicia threw her phone on the bed as she jerked her pajama top over her head. She grabbed a bra out of her dresser drawer, hooked it and yanked down the pajama pants. She threw on the sweats and grabbed her phone as she tried to control a sudden outbreak of shivering. Jarod pulled her into a quick hug. "I'll be praying."

Alicia swallowed, nodded, and darted out the bedroom door.

Red lights blinked in the near distance, as Alicia pulled onto Bella's street. She parked beside the curb, rushed from her car, past the ambulance parked in the shoveled driveway, up the front steps and into the house. She was vaguely aware of the shriek of sirens behind her as she stood frozen a foot inside the door. Two emergency techs were strapping Bella to a gurney. She had a brace covering her neck. Noah looked up, caught sight of Alicia, tears rolling down his face. She opened her arms, and he ran into them.

The sound of the siren was deafening. Gripping Noah tightly, she looked over her shoulder as a police car slammed to a stop beside the ambulance, and two police officers stepped from their vehicle into the pool of light cast by the motion detector over the garage. She pulled Noah with her away from the door. The techs finishing strapping Bella to the gurney and wheeled her to the front door.

The policemen helped the EMTs lift the gurney down the steps and into the ambulance, one tech jumping in the back with Bella. Words were exchanged between the other tech and one of the police officers before he jumped into the driver's seat. He backed the vehicle down the drive and turned onto the street, siren blaring.

The two officers walked up the steps and into the house, shutting the door behind them.

"Did they take her to Sentara?" It was the closest hospital.

The taller of the two officers answered. "Yes, Ma'am. I am Officer Garcia, and this is Officer Knapp. The other officer gave a half-smile. "Were you here when Mrs. Stanford fell?"

"No. I arrived just before you did."

He turned to Noah his voice gentle. "What's your name, son?"

"Noah." He pressed closer to her side.

The officer's eyes reflected compassion. "Noah, I need to ask you some questions about your mom."

"Please, can they wait? We need to get to the hospital." Noah shivered beside her in the cold air of the entrance hall.

"Your name, ma'am and relation to Noah?"

"Alicia Kenner. I'm his mother's best friend. Noah hasn't been able to reach his father. I called his mother's parents on the way over. They're meeting us at the hospital."

"Okay, Ms. Kenner. You go on ahead. We'll meet you in the emergency waiting room. I can question Noah there." He smiled reassuringly.

"Thank you, officer."

"Noah, what's your dad's address?"

"13786 Richmond Road."

"We'll send a car and inform him of the situation."

"Thank you." She turned to Noah. "Run upstairs and get dressed, honey."

✦   ✦   ✦

Making sure Noah was strapped in, Alicia pulled away from the curb. A snowman sitting in the yard next door glistened in her headlights.

Alicia's heart thrummed in her ears. "Noah, would you like to say a prayer for your mom?" Her eyes darted to the right. She could barely make out the pale oval of Noah's face in the darkened interior. He shook his head. "That's okay, I'll say one."

As she prayed out loud, the thrumming in her ears lessened. And as Noah echoed her amen, a sudden calmness infused her. Was God telling her Bella would be alright? Whatever the reason, Alicia eased a grateful sigh through her lips.

✦   ✦   ✦

The emergency doors whooshed open, and Alicia and Noah hurried inside. The harsh artificial light glared down on the occupants of the waiting area. A dozen people reclined in gray vinyl chairs around the room sleeping, silently staring at nothing, or talking in low voices to companions. The calm she had felt in the car evaporated as she glimpsed the faces of Bella's parents. John rose from his chair, and Noah ran into his grandpa's arms. Alicia strode over to Ginny, enveloping her in a strong hug. Bella's petite mother started to weep.

"They wheeled her in fifteen minutes ago. She looked… her face was white as a sheet. The nurse said the doctor would come and talk to us after assessing her condition." Her words were muffled with her face pressed against Alicia's shoulder.

Ginny wiped her eyes as she pulled out of Alicia's arms. "Do you know why she fell down the stairs?"

Alicia shook her head. She glimpsed the two police officers standing by the plain reception desk respectfully giving Noah and his grandparents a few moments before starting the questioning. She cleared her throat and turned to John. "Those officers standing by the desk need to question Noah."

"Now?" John rotated his head towards the desk.

Alicia nodded.

John looked down at his grandson. "Buddy, you sit down next to your Nana. I'm going to talk to those officers."

Noah nodded and sat down in his grandpa's vacated seat. Ginny sat beside him with a protective arm around his shoulders.

"I'll be right back. I need to call Charley."

Ginny nodded.

Alicia removed herself to a row of red vending machines along one of the walls of the large emergency room, away from the occupied chairs. She pressed Charley's number into her phone.

"Oh, no, Alicia...what's wrong?" Her sleep-laden words rush into her ear.

"It's Bella." Alicia tried to blink away the sudden wetness in her eyes.

She heard a sharp intake of breath through the phone.

"She fell down the stairs at her house. I'm at the Sentara hospital with Noah and Bella's parents."

"Oh, sweet Lord. How did it happen?"

"I don't know."

"I'll be there as quick as I can."

"I shouldn't ask you to come, because you're an hour and half away, but I'm scared, and I really need you here while I wait."

"Of course. Love you. I'll be praying. See you soon."

Alicia pressed the red icon and wiped away the tears. *I have to stay strong for Noah.* John was walking towards Noah with the two officers. She took a step and then hesitated. She wasn't family. Would she be allowed to be party to the questioning? She took a breath, squared her shoulders and strode over to the small group. Officer Garcia's dark eyes looked over at her. He started to say something, thought better of it, and instead took a seat next to Noah.

Taking that as permission to stay, Alicia sat down beside John. Officer Knapp, short, stocky, with a receding hairline, sat nearby with a small laptop open on his knees.

"I'm very sorry about your mom, Noah." His brown eyes were reassuring, and his voice low and soothing.

Noah stared at the officer, his body tensing.

"It's okay. I just need to know what happened to your mom."

"She fell down the stairs."

"Do you know why she fell down the stairs?"

Noah shook his head.

Officer Garcia smiled. "Okay. Can you tell me everything you saw and heard from the minute you woke up?"

Noah shifted uneasily in his chair. "I heard her scream. It scared me. Then I heard a loud thumping noise. I got out of bed and ran into the hallway. I didn't hear anything, and I couldn't see anything, so I turned on the light."

"What did you see when you turned on the light?"

"Nothing."

"Okay, what did you do next?"

"I ran into her bedroom, but she wasn't there. Her pill bottle and glass were on the floor."

Alicia's eyebrows pulled together. *Pill bottle?*

Officer Garcia's eyes stayed focused on Noah. "Do you know what the pills are for Noah?"

Noah nodded. "I asked her, and she told me sometimes she can't sleep. The pills help her sleep."

Alicia's eyes widened, and she glanced over at Ginny. Her facial expression reflected her own shock that Bella had been taking sleeping pills.

"Okay, Noah. What did you do next?"

"I ran towards the stairs and that...and that's when..." Noah's eyes welled.

Ginny squeezed Noah's shoulder tighter.

Officer Garcia gave Noah's hand a squeeze.

"I saw her...I saw her at the bottom..." Noah started to cry.

"Noah!"

Alicia looked up as Daniel rushed over. Her eyebrows peaked. She had never seen Daniel disheveled. He had always been impeccably groomed around her–even at the swim meets. But tonight, his curly hair sat atop his head in a wild halo, and he wore a wrinkled polo shirt under his coat. His face reflected guilt.

Noah jumped out of the chair and wrapped his arms around his dad sobbing out what happened.

Daniel dropped to one knee to better hug his son. "I'm sorry, Noah."

"I tried to...call...you."

"I know, buddy. I'm sorry. I forgot to bring the phone into the bedroom from the charger in the kitchen."

Daniel rose to a standing position keeping an arm around Noah. He surveyed the faces in front of him, his gaze settling on Officer Garcia. "What happened?"

"We had just started questioning Noah about what happened."

"What? Now? Here?" Daniel's voice rose in anger.

"Your father gave permission to…"

Daniel's eyes narrowed. "He is not my father. He is my ex-father-in-law…"

Alicia heard the particular emphasis on *ex*.

"I am Noah's father, and I do not give you permission to question him now. He has been through a horrible traumatic event, and I'm taking him home with me."

"But, Daniel, he needs to stay. His mother…" Ginny pleaded.

Daniel's eyes flashed at Ginny. "He does not need to stay here, waiting and worrying about his mother for the next five hours. You have my phone number and you can text me with updates. I'm taking him to my apartment to get some sleep. I will bring him back when Bella can have visitors."

Daniel turned to Officer Garcia. "I will call you in a few hours to set up a time to interview my son."

Officer Garcia looked at Daniel, seemed to come to some sort of decision, and then gazed down at Noah. "I'll see you later, Noah. Thanks for your help."

Noah nodded as he wiped away tears. Officers' Knapp and Garcia nodded briefly to Alicia, Ginny, and John and then turned and strode to the emergency room doors.

Daniel cleared his throat and looked at John and Ginny. "Thank you for taking care of my son."

"Noah called Alicia. She went to the house and brought him here," Ginny said.

Daniel gave a curt nod. "Thank you, Alicia."

Noah stepped over, and Alicia hugged him. "We'll keep a good eye on your mom. I don't want you worrying, okay?"

Noah nodded as his grandparents rose to hug him.

Without another word, Daniel pivoted Noah toward the exit. Alicia watched them leave, her heart sinking into her stomach. Bella had to pull through. Noah couldn't lose his mom.

✝   ✝   ✝

Alicia's eyes snapped open. Charley was lightly gripping her hand. She reached her arms up enveloping Charley in a fierce hug, silently weeping.

Charley pulled back, her eyes moist. "Any word?"

Alicia shook her head as she felt around in her purse for a tissue.

"How long has it been?"

"Two hours. We asked at the desk a little while ago, and all they would tell John is they were running tests." She wiped her eyes.

Charley looked around the room. "Where's John and Ginny?"

Bella's parents had insisted on Alicia and Charley calling them by their first names from the moment they met them their freshman year at William and Mary. They were as close to Bella's parents as their own. Bella's house had been their home away from home while at college. Charley's parents lived in Raleigh, and her parents lived in Leesburg.

"The cafeteria opened at six-thirty; they went to get coffee."

Charley heaved a sigh. "This is a horrible blow for them. They've been worried sick about Bella's emotional state for the last six months...and now this."

Alicia glimpsed Bella's parents walking through the doorway into the emergency room. "Here they come."

"Oh, Charley, we're glad you're here." Ginny handed Alicia a cup of coffee before drawing Charley into a one-armed hug.

John gave her a hug after Ginny released her. He pulled back and smiled. "It's good to see you, it's been awhile."

The three women sat down in the vinyl chairs. Alicia sipped her hot coffee.

John looked down at Charley. "What do you like in your coffee?"

"No, don't make another trip for me. I can go."

John's smile disappeared. "Please, it helps to distract me. Just sitting here helpless is driving me crazy."

Charley nodded. "Cream, no sugar."

She turned to Alicia as John started to walk away. "What happened?"

"Noah told us that..." Alicia froze. A man, who looked to be of Indian heritage, clad in sage-colored doctor's scrubs, was walking toward them, the doors to the treatment room swinging shut behind him. *Lord, please, not bad news...not bad news.*

John halted in his tracks as the doctor approached. "Mr. and Mrs. Claremont?"

Both John and Ginny visibly tensed. Alicia held her breath.

John answered, "Yes."

"I'm Dr. Kodura. We're still running tests, but I wanted to update you on the condition of your daughter. She has a broken scapula and wrist…and major soft tissue trauma to her right hip, but no fracture. She has a concussion, but no brain swelling–a good sign. She is still unconscious." The doctor paused and took a breath. "Her lab results indicate high levels of Zolpidem Tartrate."

Alicia was sure her face reflected the same puzzlement reflected on John, Ginny, and Charley's faces.

"It's the active ingredient in certain forms of sleeping pills. One of the first things we do with a fall is order a drug screen."

Ginny hissed in a breath.

Dr. Kodura gave an encouraging smile. "It is my opinion that further tests will show what we already know. I believe your daughter will make a full recovery."

Ginny burst into tears. Alicia turned in her seat and hugged her. Charley murmured, "Thank you, Jesus."

John held out his hand. "Thank you, doctor."

Ginny's voiced quivered. "Can we see her?"

"It will be a couple more hours for the rest of the tests to be finished, and then she'll be moved to a room."

As he turned to go, Alicia spoke up, "Do you know when she might wake up?"

"Hard to know with a concussion, and it will take some time for the effects of the sleeping pills to wear off. Best guess, between four and eight hours."

He left with a determined stride back through the large, gray, swinging doors.

John heaved a relieved sigh. "Well it looks like we have a lot more waiting to do. How about breakfast in the cafeteria...my treat."

"No, John."

"No arguing, Alicia. Let's go."

Alicia reached for Charley's hand as they walked down the long hallway. She hadn't walked hand in hand with a friend since she was in elementary school, but she needed the strong grip of Charley's hand to help steady her fraying emotional state. They entered the open doorway of the cafeteria and lined up at the first station to get trays and utensils.

John kept the conversation light and focused on Alicia and Charley's children until everyone had finished their meal. He placed his fork on his plate and cleared his throat. "Let me be blunt—Ginny and I don't want to lose

our only child. We...need your help...we're at a loss..."
His words faltered.

Charley reached over and briefly squeezed John's
hand. "We will help anyway we can."

She looked around the table. "Can someone tell me
when Bella started taking sleeping pills?"

"We didn't even know she was taking the pills. Noah
told us tonight," Ginny said.

"Where is Noah?"

Alicia's lips formed a thin line. "His dad took him back
to his apartment."

Charley frowned, but stayed silent. John stirred in his
chair. "I can barely think the words much less say them,
but Bella is emotionally unstable and...I don't know how
to help her."

Ginny wiped a tear from the corner of her eye. "I've spent
more time at Bella's house than my own home in the last six
months. And the only thing that kept her from completely
falling apart was her steadfast belief that Dan would eventually come home to her and Noah." She looked around the
faces at the table, fear stark in her eyes. "Within twelve hours
of the divorce being granted she fell down the stairs after
taking too many sleeping pills–she could have died."

John's face had turned an alarming red. "This is all that
son of..."

Ginny gripped her husband's arm. "John..."

Alicia gave John a grim smile. "John, it's a good thing
we have Ginny and Charley, otherwise you and I would
probably be in jail for assault."

John gave a rueful laugh, the beet red hue of his face fading.

"How do we help my precious girl?" Ginny's voice broke.

Alicia pushed her plate forward and folded her hands atop the white vinyl table. "Number one and most important, she needs to see a therapist. Six months of supporting, loving, and trying to talk sense into her hasn't worked. Bella didn't just love Daniel; he was her obsession." She shook her head. "I had no idea that her whole world was wrapped up in him."

John glanced at his wife. "Ginny knew."

She shook her head. "Not really. Bella just seemed to go a bit overboard to please him."

"She can't live alone." Three heads swiveled towards Charley.

"Alone? What do you mean? She has Noah," Ginny said.

"Do you think Daniel is going to let tonight slide… especially when he finds out about the pills? He's going to petition for temporary custody, and he may go for permanent."

Ginny gasped. "Oh, no, he wouldn't!"

John slumped in his seat. "Charley's right. Once he finds out about the pills…" He shook his head.

"Bella cannot live alone." Charley's intense gaze enveloped the table. "Tonight, she may have taken a few extra pills to obliterate thoughts of the court decision…but when a long, looming future without Daniel truly sinks in…"

Alicia tightened her grip on her coffee mug as her hand began to tremble. "My worst fear for the last six months." She swallowed hard. "And if Daniel gets custody, even temporary…"

Tears were flowing freely down Ginny's cheeks.

John gripped his wife's hand. "She's coming home with us. It will be awhile before she can live on her own anyway because of her injuries."

Ginny implored the other three. "But what can we do to help her get over Daniel?"

"While she's convalescing with you…you have to convince her to see a therapist. None of us are trained in how to help someone get over severe depression." Alicia's eyes darted from John to Ginny and then to Charley. "Each of us tried everything we could think of, and nothing has worked."

Charley looked around the table. " 'Where two or more are gathered…' let's say a pray for Bella."

Alicia nodded and bowed her head.

"Lord, Jesus, we come to you with very heavy hearts. Please, Lord help Bella to heal physically, but more importantly please help her to recover from her depression and grief over the end of her marriage. Help her to see that she has loving parents and friends to lean on. Help her to be strong for her son, who needs his mother in his life." Charley paused, wiping her eyes. "We all love her. Please bring Bella back to us. Amen."

John let go of his wife's hand, pulled a hankie out of a pocket and wiped his eyes. "Thank you, Charley." He cleared his throat and looked at Charley and Alicia. "Now both of you go to Alicia's house and get some sleep, I'll…"

"No, we have to stay."

"You heard the doctor…four to eight hours. Get some sleep, we'll call when she wakes up."

"But you need sleep, too," Charley said. "How about we do shifts?"

Ginny shook her head. "I'm not leaving this hospital until I talk to my daughter."

John smiled. "Stubborn as the day is long. Now go, you two."

Bone weary, Alicia nodded. "Okay, I could use a nap, but call as soon as she's awake."

Ginny nodded as Alicia and Charley pushed back their chairs. Alicia turned toward the hallway and the walk back to her car, Charley beside her.

✦   ✦   ✦

"Hon. Honey, wake up."

Alicia blinked her eyes. Jarod was standing over her. Her eyebrows drew together…*something she needed to rem…*

"John just called from the hospital. Bella's awake."

She threw off the comforter.

"What time is it?"

"Two-thirty."

She stepped onto the carpet. "I've got to go to the hospital. Is Charley up?"

Jarod shook his head.

"Okay, I shouldn't be too long. A couple of hours. Bella won't feel like talking."

Jarod squeezed her hand. "Take all the time you need. I'll throw some chicken and corn on the grill for dinner."

Alicia's brows shot up. "It's still winter…and it's freezing out."

"Kidding. I'm making my famous chicken gumbo."

"Yum, can't wait."

Alicia turned the key in the lock of the front door. She and Charley slid into the cold interior of Alicia's car, their breaths misting in the chilly air.

Charley yawned. "Can I move in? That's the most sleep I've had in a month. And now I'm starving."

Alicia handed her a granola bar, banana, and a bottle of water.

"Well it's not swordfish, but I guess it will do."

Alicia sighed as she turned the key in the ignition the engine rumbling quietly to life. "It feels like a lifetime ago that we met at Bella's club for lunch." She backed down the driveway and onto her street.

After a short drive, she and Charley hurried through the entrance doors of the tastefully decorated main lobby of the hospital and up to a highly polished reception desk made of dark wood. The receptionist looked up.

Alicia smiled. "Hello. Can you tell me what room Bella Stanford is in?"

The reception tapped the keys on her computer, waited a few seconds and then looked up. "Room 342."

"Thank you."

Alicia and Charley walked over to the bank of elevators. Alicia started to press the up button.

"Wait. I want to go to the gift shop first," Charley said.

"Good idea."

The friends walked into the gift shop next to the elevators. Charley sucked in a breath. "Oh, wow, look at that scarf."

On a pewter-colored pole next to a display of bracelets and necklaces, hung four scarves. One stood out from the rest in vibrant shades of teal, yellow, and the exact violet shade of Bella's eyes.

Alicia walked over and removed it from the display. "Perfect and it's only…" Her jaw dropped. "Fifty dollars!"

Charley whipped the scarf from Alicia's hands and strode to the cashier. "Wait, don't you think…"

Charley handed the scarf to the cashier and turned her head slightly. "How much cash do you have with you?"

"Not enough."

Charley's eyes narrowed. Alicia sighed. "Okay, about ten dollars."

"Great, hand it over."

"Charley, I can't let you pay…"

Her eyes narrowed further.

"Okay, fine." Alicia fished in her purse pulling out a ten-dollar bill and handing it to Charley.

Charley shoved the bill in her purse and handed the clerk her credit card. She gave Alicia a one-armed hug.

"I've told you a million times, what you give is more of a sacrifice than what I can give. You are on a tight budget, and I...well...God blessed me with an extraordinary gift. And to whom much is given...much should be given away."

Alicia laughed. "I think you've got the quote wrong."

Charley accepted the receipt and the cheery gift bag from the clerk. "What quote? I just made that up. Besides, you are even more generous than I am with your time spent in hospital visits to church members and the meals you make for those in need."

Alicia could feel tears threatening. She hugged her friend. "I love you."

"Right back at you."

Alicia exited the elevator with Charley and followed the numbered signs to Bella's room. She could feel her heart thudding in her chest when she raised her fisted hand to knock on the door. She rapped two times. Ginny opened the door, stepped out into the hall and shut the door. "We need to talk before you see Bella."

She led the way down the hallway to a waiting room decorated in burgundy and gray. A young mother looked up from the children's book she was reading to a golden-haired toddler. Ginny took a sit in a cushioned burgundy chair. Alicia and Charley sat down on either side of her. Alicia's heart ramped up its beats while she held her breath.

Ginny pushed limp strands of blonde hair streaked with gray behind her ear. "Bella woke up in a lot of pain. They were waiting until the sleeping pills were out of her system before giving her pain medicine. Now she's pretty heavily sedated…she won't be too coherent."

Alicia released the breath as her rapid heartbeat slowed. She nodded.

Ginny pulled in a deep breath. "Daniel called us. He… he filed for temporary custody today, and I'm sure it will be granted."

Charley's face reflected abject misery. "I knew this was coming…my poor Bella."

Alicia wiped away the wetness on her cheeks only to find them immediately damp again.

"John and I aren't going to mention the custody issue until she's ready to leave the hospital. She needs to be as strong as possible when she finds out." Ginny wiped at her eyes.

Charley grasped Ginny's hand. "I'm sorry. I will be praying for you and John as well as Bella. I'll come by and visit as much as possible."

"Please pray, too, that Daniel doesn't file for permanent custody." She stood up. "Only two visitors are allowed in the room at a time. John and I will go get something to eat while you visit with Bella. She doesn't remember falling down the stairs, but she knows that she did." A warning note entered her voice. "We haven't mentioned the pills as the cause, yet."

"We won't say a word about it," Alicia said as she followed Ginny back to Bella's room.

Ginny paused at the door. "Bella looks pretty bad. It's going to upset Noah. We told Daniel to wait and bring Noah tomorrow when she might be coherent enough to reassure him that she'll be okay."

She ducked through the door returning with John. They walked off toward the elevator. Alicia and Charley slipped through the door. Alicia sucked in a breath. Bella lay as still as a statue under the light blue blanket. Her face was swollen. There was a massive bruise on her forehead and another on her left cheek. Her right arm was encased in a sling, and her left arm in a pale pink half-cast.

Alicia approached the bed. Bella's eyes were closed. Her fingers reached over and lightly caressed her friend's hair. She was afraid to touch any other part of her body. Bella's eyes fluttered open. Alicia smiled. "Hi, Bella, Charley and I came to visit."

Charley reached over and grasped the fingers poking through the cast. "Hey, sleepyhead."

Bella started to smile, but it quickly turned to a grimace.

"We just want you to know we love you." Charley squeezed the fingers.

Bella's lips moved but no sounds emerged from her mouth.

"Hush, no need to talk."

Bella nodded.

"We're going to sit with you for a little while. If you feel sleepy, go ahead and nod off."

Alicia and Charley removed their coats and sat down in the chairs that John and Ginny had vacated next to the bed. Bella turned her head slightly, mouthed 'I love you,' and then let her eyelids slowly drift shut. Alicia covered her mouth with her left hand. Her shoulders shook as she silently wept. Charley pulled her into her arms, their foreheads touching.

CHAPTER

21

Bella emerged from the hospital bathroom. It had taken over an hour to apply her make-up. She wanted to be presentable when Daniel brought Noah. At least she no longer had to try and cover up the bruises on her face. They had finally disappeared after her nearly two-week stay in the hospital. Her mother had washed and styled her hair for her yesterday, and it still looked good.

She slipped onto the bed, grimacing slightly at the sudden pain in her head. The doctor said as long as she got plenty of rest in the next few weeks, the pain should go away. He was pleased that the scapula and wrist were healing quicker than he had estimated. She would be able to dispense with the sling in a week and have the cast removed in three weeks.

Bella used the remote to raise her bed to a sitting position. She couldn't wait to get out of the hospital and go home tomorrow. Her parents had asked her multiple times to move in with them while she healed, but she had refused. She didn't want to upset Noah's routine. Guilt washed over her as she recalled snapping at them when they brought up the subject of a therapist again yesterday.

Thoughts of her parents evaporated as she closed her eyes and tried for the hundredth time to remember the events that led to her fall. After a few minutes, she sighed in frustration. The last thing she remembered was climbing the stairs to bed.

"Mom!"

Bella rotated her head as her mouth pulled open in a wide grin. "Noah."

Noah rushed to her bedside and carefully hugged her, pressing his cold face against her cheek. "I've missed you, buddy."

"Me, too, Mom."

"How was school today?"

"Okay."

Bella smoothed back his wavy bangs as he took a seat. She cleared her throat. "How's your Dad?"

"He's good."

"You haven't mentioned him at all while I've been in the hospital." Bella couldn't stop the little flair of hope. "Is there…an issue with your dad and Melissa?"

Noah shifted uncomfortably in his chair and stayed silent.

"It's okay, buddy, I'm fine. You can tell me."

With indecision written all over his face, Noah stared at his mom. "I don't know if…I don't want to upset you."

The flair brightened. "It's okay…shoot."

"Dad and Melissa are getting married in a couple of weeks. I'm going to be the best man."

She caught her breath as her gut clenched tight in pain.

Bella slowly exhaled. "Oh." She looked away from the sudden pity reflected in her son's eyes. She squeezed his hand and forced a smile. "Guess what? I'm getting released tomorrow. The doctor told me today."

A smile lit Noah's face. "That's great, Mom."

"Do you think your Dad can bring you home after work tomorrow?"

"Hold on. I'll go ask."

As soon as Noah left the room, Bella bent over and grabbed her aching stomach. Tears dropped silently on her hands. The pain was *unbearable*.

"Bella."

Bella looked up to find Daniel standing in the doorway. She struggled to breathe while staring at the man she still loved with every fiber of her being…the man who would soon be someone else's husband. He walked over to a chair and sat down. "We have to talk."

Bella wiped away the tears. "Where's Noah?"

"He's in the waiting room."

"Why?"

He ignored the question. "I shouldn't be the one to tell you this." His lips pulled into a tight line. "Your parents should have told you days ago."

"Told me what."

"Noah's not coming home tomorrow."

Bella stared at Daniel, not comprehending. "Why not? I'm going home."

"The court granted me temporary custody of Noah."

"Temporary…what are you…?" Sudden pain beat at her temple.

"Noah's safety is my number one priority, and it should be yours, too."

"It is. What has that got to do…?"

"I'm not going to take a chance that Noah could be hurt because of your irrational behavior."

Bella straightened in bed, her eyes flashing. "I would never hurt Noah. What are you talking about?"

Daniel's eyes narrowed. "Do you honestly believe overdosing on sleeping pills and falling down the stairs, almost killing yourself, was rational?"

Bella literally felt the blood drain from her face as a gasp sounded from the doorway.

"Daniel…no."

Bella barely registered her parents as she tried to wrap her brain around what Daniel had revealed.

Her ex-husband rounded on her parents. "I thought she knew about the temporary custody until Noah asked me a few minutes ago if I was taking him home tomorrow after work." His words were clipped with anger. "I told Noah he would be living with me for a few months while his mom healed from her injuries. I did not want to upset him further by telling him about the change in custody because his mother overdosed on sleeping pills and fell down the stairs."

Bella shook her head. "But I don't remember taking any sleeping pills. Are you sure?…I mean I've only taken an occasional pill when I couldn't sleep. The last one I took was weeks ago. No...it's a mistake."

"Honey, the doctors found a large amount of the drug in your system after you fell." Ginny's eyes, full of sorrow, stared into her daughter's shocked eyes.

"Noah is the one who found you at the bottom of the stairs." Daniel said.

Bella brought the fingers of the hand in a cast up to her open mouth. She whispered through her fingers. "Noah found me?"

John walked over and squeezed her hand. "Yes, honey."

Bella's reproachful eyes landed on her mother. "You said Alicia came by and found me."

Ginny's face flushed with guilt. "You have a concussion. We didn't want to upset you."

Daniel rubbed fingers across his forehead and sighed. "Bella, this is temporary. If you agree to talk with a therapist on a regular basis and pull yourself together, Noah can come home in a few months."

"A few months?" Bella's eyes welled.

"I'll bring him by for visits on the weekends." Daniel took a step back. "I'm going to get Noah. He can visit with you a bit longer." He turned and walked through the door.

"Bella, we..." Ginny implored.

Bella's eyes flashed with anger. "You need to leave... both of you."

John put an arm around his wife's waist and pivoted her to the door. At the threshold he glanced back. "We're sorry. We thought we were doing what was best."

A minute later, Noah walked into the room, and Bella plastered on a smile.

Alicia turned the key in the ignition, and the engine fell silent. She lifted her hand off the steering wheel and tried to control her slight trembling. Adrenaline coursed through her body. Taking in one deep breath after another, she mused, *This must be what it feels like before you go into battle.* There was no question in Alicia's mind that a major battle was about to erupt in Bella's hospital room.

Ginny had called. She wanted Alicia and Charley to come to the hospital today to help convince Bella to move in with her and John. Bella was upset that her parents hadn't told her about the temporary custody and that she had to learn this from Daniel. She had refused all along to discuss living with them and then yesterday asked them to leave her room after Daniel's revelation.

Alicia stared through the windshield. She was afraid if Bella went home, she would swallow a handful of sleeping pills to shut out the world–maybe forever. Alicia's heart thudded in her chest. After pulling in a shaky breath, she exited her car.

The hospital entry doors slid open, and Alicia stepped through. Exiting the elevator on Bella's floor, Alicia's nostrils flared when an orderly passed, rolling a bucket containing a strong disinfectant. She walked down the hall to Bella's room, wishing again that Charley could have been here with her, but one of her daughters had the flu. A sudden, overwhelming feeling of helplessness made her weak at the knees. She backed up against the light gray wall for support. She closed her eyes. *Lord, Jesus, give me strength...for Bella.* She pulled in a deep breath and steeled her spine with resolve. Pushing off the wall, Alicia knocked on Bella's door.

John opened the door and silently ushered her into the room. Bella was dressed and sitting up in bed wearing a mutinous look on her face. "I suppose you knew about the custody too."

Alicia nodded.

"And you thought that I was too fragile to accept the truth."

Alicia glanced over at Ginny, who was standing stiffly by the window. "No. But the doctor said that stress and concussions don't mix well."

Silence filled the room.

Bella cleared her throat. "If you came here to side with my parents don't waste your breath."

Heart still beating faster than normal, Alicia walked over and sat on the bed next to Bella. "What do you want, Bella?"

Bella stared straight ahead avoiding eye contact with the three people in the room. "I want to be left alone."

"To do what?"

"That's my business."

Alicia reached for Bella's hand, but she pulled it away.

"Bella, look at me."

Bella's lips tightened as she continued to stare at the wall.

Alicia's voice hardened. "Stop being the victim and look at me, Bella."

Bella's head turned, her violet glare furious. "I'm not a victim. You didn't…"

"And what if we had told you a week ago…every time Noah walked through that door you would have been miserable, knowing he wasn't coming home with you. We gave you two weeks of happy visits with your son."

Bella's stiff posture relaxed a tiny bit and the fire in her eyes dimmed.

"Bella, you need to recognize what this emotional outburst really is. You're covering heartbreak with anger and taking it out on us because you won't take it out on the person who most deserves your rage–Daniel."

Bella opened her mouth, but Alicia stopped her before she could protest. "Noah needs his mother. And not the one he had for the last six months. If you go home, you'll sit in that house, take those sleeping pills, and wallow in the misery of losing your husband and son. You won't see a therapist, and you won't get your son back."

Alicia saw the truth of her words flash for a millisecond in Bella's eyes and then was gone.

"Bella, you need to decide right now. Do you want your son back, if that means Daniel is never coming home?"

Ginny gasped.

Bella's hesitation spoke volumes before she managed to spit out, in a voice full of righteous indignation, "How could you ask me that?"

"Because I believe–to you–Daniel and Noah are a package deal."

She sputtered the words, "That's not true!"

"Then prove it. Prove that you will do anything and everything to get Noah back. Move in with your parents and see a therapist."

Muffled conversation from the nurses' station drifted through the doorway. Ensuing silence filled the hospital room. Alicia rose from the bed and went to stand next to Ginny draping a supportive arm around her shoulder.

Bella sighed heavily. Her eyes met Alicia's. "You're right. Before my parents got here, all I could think about was going home, taking a sleeping pill, and crawling into bed." Her eyes shifted to her mom's eyes. "I need help... your help. I'll go home with you."

John cleared his throat. "And see a therapist?"

Bella nodded.

Ginny pulled away from Alicia and hurried over to her daughter. She reached down and hugged her. "Thank you, honey."

Alicia closed her eyes and breathed in deeply. *Thank you, God.*

23

A mare thundered down the length of the pasture, mane and tail streaming out behind her. Alicia smiled as the horse reached the fence line, rose on hind legs for a couple of seconds, and then dropped her chestnut forelegs to the ground. She whipped around and galloped back the way she had come, deserting her other two companions. Alicia drove her vehicle up to the huge white barn and stopped the car, reserving a moment to take in the tranquil family scene through the windshield.

John, Ginny, and Noah leaned against the paddock fence as they watched Bella circle the enclosure on her favorite dapple gray mare. Alicia could see the smile on Bella's face and breathed a sigh of relief. This was her first glimpse of Bella since the confrontation in her hospital room over a month ago.

Three days after Bella's release, Alicia's teenage son had contracted mononucleosis, nicknamed 'the kissing disease.' Monday he could go back to school after a month's absence. A smile drifted across her lips as she remembered how vehemently Cameron had denied kissing any of the girls he hung around with. Alicia pulled her jacket tighter across her chest as she walked towards the group. The temperature was in the fifties, cooler than normal for the end of April.

John caught sight of her and waved. Although she hadn't seen Bella before today, she had talked to her regularly, and Bella seemed more upbeat, at least on the phone anyway. She had worried that Bella would regress after Daniel and Michelle married, but Ginny was more optimistic. She thought the visits with the therapist were doing Bella a world of good.

Alicia had halved the distance to the paddock when Noah broke away from the fence and ran to hug her. As Alicia hugged him back, she marveled at how tall he had grown in the past year. "I can't believe that you are almost as tall as I am."

His eyes beamed. "I think I'm going to be as tall as my dad. I'm trying out for basketball next year."

Alicia lifted her chin at the paddock. "Your mom looks good."

He turned his head. "Yeah, she's all healed up and feeling better."

Alicia decided to change the subject. "Are you going to take a ride around the paddock?"

Noah's smile dimmed. "Nah, my dad still won't let me ride after my accident last year."

Alicia cringed. "Right, I forgot."

John walked over and kissed her on the cheek. "How's my favorite personal trainer?"

"Good."

"And Cameron?"

"Healthy as a horse."

John turned to his grandson. "Hey, buddy, can you keep your Nana company until I get back over there…I need to talk to Alicia for a minute."

Noah shot his grandfather a curious look but then walked away obediently.

Alicia kept her voice light. "What's up?"

He sighed. "Don't get me wrong, Bella's doing a lot better than she was, but she's not…" Alicia could tell that John was struggling to come up with the right words. "She's not interested in…*living*…if that makes sense. She doesn't want to *do* anything. Ginny can't get her to go shopping, or have her hair done…or the numerous other outings she used to enjoy. We dragged her to a restaurant a couple of days ago, but I could tell she was uncomfortable. I think anywhere she goes reminds her of Daniel."

John took in a breath. "I'm telling you all this because Ginny and I think Bella needs to get out of the area and go somewhere that she isn't reminded of her ex-husband. Somewhere she's never been, and he's never been. Somewhere that, hopefully, she could start to let him go."

"So…" There was a mischievous twinkle in John's blue eyes. "I've purchased three tickets for a six-day cruise around the Greek islands."

Alicia smiled. "You and Ginny definitely deserve a vacation."

"Oh, it's not for me and Ginny. It's for you, Charley, and Bella."

Shocked rendered Alicia incapable of speech.

"You have about seven weeks to make arrangements. You fly out of Norfolk the twenty-first of June."

Alicia's brain began to function again. "Oh, my... John...no, I couldn't possibly..."

"It's already done. Everything is paid for...plane... boat...excursions on the islands." His eyes pleaded. "My daughter means everything to me. She needs to get away from here, and she needs you and Charley to watch over her." His tone turned mock stern. "Besides, you and Charley owe me for all the meals and board I provided during your years in college and for..."

Alicia burst out laughing. "Your idea of us paying off our debt is to send Charley and me on a cruise to Greece. How in my right mind could I turn down a deal like that!"

John breathed a sigh of relief. "Do you think you can get the time off from work?"

"I do believe that's a done deal."

"Don't say anything to Bella. We haven't told her yet."

Alicia shook her head. "I'd tell her sooner rather than later. You don't want the same fiasco as the temporary custody."

John nodded in agreement. On impulse, Alicia threw her arms around John and hugged him. "Thank you, John, for this generous gift."

John pulled back, wiping at his wet eyes. "No, thank you, for being one of my daughter's best friends and guardian angels." He put an arm around Alicia's waist. "Come on, I want to tell Ginny you said yes."

Alicia smiled at her surrogate father as they strolled to the paddock.

+ + +

Bella's violet eyes looked out from under the lip of her black riding helmet at the normalcy outside of the paddock. Her mother had an arm around Noah as he chatted with his grandmother. Her dad and Alicia had huge grins on their faces as they strode towards the paddock. Her hand tightened on the reins, and Lady Grey bobbed her head down in protest. Bella loosened her hold and continued to trot around the enclosure.

A stone settled in her gut as she looked at her friend and family. They looked happy...an emotion that hovered a mile outside of her reach. For the past month, she had tried to follow every suggestion and exercise that the therapist had asked her to do...as long as she didn't have to go anywhere. She relived happy memories with Noah, her parents, and her friends. If a memory of Daniel crept into her mind, she tried to push it away immediately–but rarely succeeded. She did deep breathing exercises and had tried a couple of yoga positions.

The therapist had told her to get back to the gym as soon as she healed and exert herself until she was exhausted. *No...too humiliating.* She didn't want to see the looks of pity from her female acquaintances. She exercised her father's horses instead. Her parents had insisted she go with them to a new restaurant in town a couple of days ago. The minute she walked through the door, despair had permeated her like a heavy shroud as she glanced around at all the happy couples and families.

Alicia waved from the fence, and Bella pulled her mind back to the present. She forced the corners of her mouth upward. Exhaustion suddenly overcame her, and she slumped lower in the saddle. Exhaustion was really nothing new, for she felt lethargic most of the time. The apathy had started the morning after Daniel remarried. Unable to sleep for the last seven months, suddenly that's all she wanted to do. She slept ten hours at night and took two naps a day and would find more opportunities to sleep if she could get away with it.

Her gaze settled on her son as she trotted Lady Grey close to where Noah leaned against the fence. Alicia was wrong. She did want her son to come home. But in the last two weeks, it had become increasingly difficult to sum up the energy to do what needed to be done to make that happen.

"Bella."

Jerked out of her reverie, Bella pulled sharply on the reins, causing Lady Grey to prance sideways.

"Get down off that horse and come visit with me and your son."

Bella mustered up a brighter smile for her friend as she halted her mare. "Sure." She pulled her black boot out of the stirrup and dismounted.

John swung open the gate, and Bella passed through, undoing the strap under her chin and removing her riding helmet.

"Before I take care of Lady Grey, your mom and I have a surprise for you." John shut the gate.

Bella's smile wavered. "A surprise?"

"Your mom and I know you're still struggling with…" John cleared his throat. "…everything that's happened. We thought that maybe a trip…a vacation away from constant reminders of…" he faltered.

Alicia took Bella's hand, grinning like a fool. "You, me, and Charley are going on a cruise of the Greek islands! Can you believe it?"

Her dulled brain made it hard to think. "A cruise?"

Noah's excited eyes looked at his mom. "A cruise… cool!"

A genuine smile touched her lips, and her fingertips caressed her son's cheek. "Cool, huh?"

"Way cool."

Bella turned to her dad. "I don't know…what about my therapist?"

"I called and asked…she thought it was a great idea."

Alicia's eyes implored. "Please, Bella. I think it will give you a whole new outlook on your life."

Bella looked around at all their beloved faces and didn't have the heart to disappoint them. "How could I say no to such a generous gift?"

Noah whooped. Alicia and her parents hugged her, but she could summon up no joy to match theirs. All she wanted to do was crawl back into bed.

Later, as they all sat around the table for dinner, John raised his iced tea glass high. "A toast…may Bella, Alicia, and Charley have the adventure of a lifetime on their cruise and…" His eyes moistened. "…to new beginnings."

Bella tapped the lip of her glass to her mother's glass as her eyes darted down the hallway to her bedroom. Daniel would pick up Noah in an hour, and then she could finally close her eyes and drift off into oblivion.

The large cruise ship knifed through the dark waters of the Aegean Sea, creating a steady breeze that blew back Bella's soft curls as she stood on the promenade deck of *The Poseidon* staring towards the bow. Her fingers gripped the railing, her heart pounding and her hands clammy. She had awoke an hour ago, sweating and trembling from a nightmare and emerged from her dream into a full blown panic attack. She could still taste the blood where she bit down on her lip so she wouldn't scream and wake up Alicia and Charley.

Her nostrils flared with the distinctive smell of the ocean mixed with diesel fuel. The deck was deserted at this hour in the morning. Even the merriest of revelers had retreated drunkenly to their cabins. She tilted her head back. The black sky overhead was speckled with pinpoints of light. Soon the gray light of dawn would push aside the darkness.

The smooth wood beneath her fingers felt velvety, and the sound of the water rushing along the side of the hull filled her ears. The panic triggered by the nightmare lingered at the edges of her mind. She shook her head tying to dispel it as she turned her thoughts back three days.

The Delta flight had touched down in Venice as the sun was setting over the canals. Despite sleeping on the plane, Bella had no energy–none. Charley and Alicia had been the opposite–two energizer bunnies, jabbering non-stop on the shuttle ride to their hotel. She had refused to join them for a drink in the hotel lounge, making excuses about jet lag. She had turned on her side in the bed, facing away from their whispers, as they entered the room, changing into sleepwear and brushing teeth.

The trip included two days in Venice on the front and back end of the cruise. Bella hadn't wanted to go out and explore Venice the next day, but her friends would not go without her–and she couldn't ruin this once in a lifetime experience for them.

In the last two months, she had become quite good at faking what she couldn't feel. She would widen her eyes to show wonder and amazement, laugh out loud for hilarity and silliness, use hand gestures to show interest in a multitude of subjects, and smile until the muscle around her mouth began to ache–so with a light-hearted laugh, she had grabbed sunglasses and a hat and headed out to explore the canal city.

Bella and her friends took a water taxi to a glass blowing factory, stopped for lunch at a quaint café beside the canal, and spent hours in the Piazza San Marco exploring St Mark's Basilica, Doge's Palace, and the Bell Tower. But all of her emotions on display were an illusion…inside she was dead.

Bella turned her head and looked towards the stern, a stray couple of hairs plastering themselves to her lips. She brushed them away as she thought about the visit to the island of Corfu yesterday. They had taken an hour boat ride tour around the island, the water a clear pristine aqua. She had begged off snorkeling, preferring to sit in a beach chair and watch her friends explore the shallow waters, fins flapping. Besides having no desire to look at fish underwater, she refused to put on a bathing suit. She had lost twenty pounds, and because she hadn't been to the gym in the last ten months her muscle tone was gone, her skin loose and flabby.

She had breathed a sigh of relief when Alicia and Charley had asked if she minded if they spent the whole day at the beach instead of touring the Achillion Palace and the Angelokastro Castle.

Bella jerked when the slight movement beneath her sandals changed...the ship was slowing. Her eyes drifted shut. *Lord, I can't do this anymore.* Sudden clarity pushed all other thoughts aside, and her eyes slowly opened. *No, I don't want to do this anymore...not without Daniel.* No tears threaten. As her thoughts turned briefly to her parents and Noah–her violet eyes stayed clear and dry–the ducts had dried up long ago. She was bone dry, a desert.

She leaned over the railing, staring...mesmerized by the inky black water. She raised a sandaled foot to the horizontal rail closest to the deck. She pushed up, placing the other sandal on the rail. She leaned over further, locks of blond hair whipping back and forth around her head. The gentle arms of gravity tugged at her upper body.

"Mind if I join you?"

Startled from her hypnotic state, Bella struggled to maintain her balance as she whipped her head to the right. A dark shadow pushed off from the steel wall of the promenade deck and moved towards her. As the shadow moved closer, it grew in substance. Bella removed first one and then the other foot from the railing back onto the deck. By the voice, she knew it was a man. He stopped a few feet away, his features hidden in the darkness. All that Bella could discern was that he was tall and thin.

"We could count to three and then jump together."

Bella's eyebrows drew together in confusion. "What?"

He moved a few steps closer, and alcohol fumes engulfed her. "I'm suggesting that we leave this miserable, unbearable, earthly realm together."

Bella shook her head and backed up two steps. "I don't know what you're talking about."

"I'm talking about not being able to live any longer without my wife and two daughters."

The word 'divorce' hung in the air. Heat infused Bella's cheeks when she realized she had said the word out loud.

"No, not a divorce, they were killed in a car crash by a drunk driver."

Shock rendered her speechless.

The featureless face tilted to the left slightly. "Well, are you game? It's going to be light soon."

Thrown into a confusing daze by the appearance of the stranger on the deck, comprehension suddenly slammed into her brain, and she gasped. *He wants to commit suicide…and he wants me to join him. Why would he think I want to…*Bella pushed the thought away.

After a moment of silence that stretched between them, he spoke again. "I realize I shouldn't have interrupted your own date with destiny. You had almost taken the plunge to your eternal rest when I spoke."

"I don't know what you saw, but...I wasn't...I need to...get back to...my room, I..."

"I saw you climb up onto the rail and lean over." His voice became soft and full of empathy. "Don't be embarrassed. I'm not judging you...I am you."

"No...no...you're..."

Feet pounded on the deck. "Bella is that you?"

Bella watched as the stranger melted back into the shadows.

"It is you!" Strong arms grabbed her and pulled her tight. "Thank you, Jesus...I'm glad it's you...it's so dark I was afraid it might not be you."

She could tell by the leanness of the body that it was Alicia. Her whole body was trembling. Labored breathing reached her ears, and more arms encased her. Both women started to weep. And there on the deck, as the ship approached land—stirrings of a long slumbering emotion—love for her friends. She lifted her hands to their heads and made soothing noises in her throat.

Charley and Alicia pulled away, Alicia speaking first, as she drew an arm across her face. "Thank God, you're okay. When I woke up to use the bathroom and you weren't in your bed, I was afraid..."

"Alicia," Charley warned.

"No." Alicia's voice was fierce. "I won't tip-toe around the subject any longer. Bella, I was afraid you were going to jump overboard and kill yourself."

"Alicia!"

"It's okay, Charley. She's right."

Charley and Alicia gasped at the same time. Bella clung to the railing as she faced the first hint of dawn and the silhouette of buildings in the near distance. "I didn't come up here intending on killing myself, but..." Bella's voice lowered to an anguished whisper. "...I almost did."

Charley choked out a sob. "Oh, Bella...no."

Alicia breathed out. "Why?"

"The simplest answer...I'd lost my will to care about anything and anybody."

"Even Noah?"

Bella's voice cracked. "Even Noah."

Alicia pulled gently on her arm, leading her to one of the deck chairs and lowered her to a seated position. She sat down next to her with Charley on the other side. Both wrapped their arms around Bella, leaning their heads against hers. Nobody spoke for the next few minutes, as the sky lightened around them.

Bella cleared her throat, and her friends straightened up. "If it hadn't been for the strange man... I wouldn't be sitting here talking to you."

Charley removed her arm and turned to better see Bella's face. "What man?"

Bella pointed at the railing with a finger that trembled. "I was standing on the lower bar of the railing, leaning over when I heard a man's voice."

"Thank goodness, he stopped you from jumping," Alicia expelled a long breath.

Bella shook her head. "He asked if he could join me."

"But he still stopped you from jumping by asking to join you at the rail."

Bella shook her head again. "No, he wanted to jump overboard with me."

Both Alicia and Charley gave horrified gasps.

Bella rose up from the deck chair and faced her friends, her voice quivering. "He said we could count to three and jump together."

Both women stared at Bella their faces masks of stunned disbelief.

Bella's eyes welled up. "He said his wife and two daughters were killed by a drunk driver." She pulled in a shuttering breath.

Charley's voice shook. "He encouraged you to jump? Why would anybody in their right mind encourage someone…"

"He wasn't in his right mind…and neither was I."

"Was?" Hope laced Alicia's words.

"When the meaning of his words sunk in…I was terrified…horrified that I had almost killed myself." Bella reached out hands that shook to each of her friends. Alicia and Charley stood up and entwined their fingers with hers. "For the first time in a very long time, I feel…something." Bella's laugh was shaky. "Ironic that it took almost dying to realize I want to live."

Tears streamed down Alicia's cheeks. "Really?"

"Really." Bella dropped her friend's hands. "We have a lot to talk about, but right now I need to go back to the cabin and get some sleep before breakfast."

Charley's smile trembled on her lips. "Yes, a nap is just what...never mind."

Alicia headed for the stairwell. Bella linked her arm through Charley's, pulling her close as they followed in Alicia's footsteps.

Bella opened her eyes three hours later to an odd sight. Alicia and Charley sat together on the pullout bed holding hands and staring at her. She rose up on her elbows. "Did either one of you sleep?"

Both shook their heads in unison.

Touched to the core, Bella's eyes welled. "Come here, both of you."

Her friends sat on the edge of the bed.

Bella smiled at both of them. "I have just had my first restful sleep since I saw Daniel with Melissa at Rudee's."

Charley's eyes full of hope stared into hers; Alicia's eyes showed wariness as she spoke one word, "Daniel."

Bella repeated her ex-husband's name, tasting the word on her lips, and waited for the pain to consume her. But instead of the heart wrenching agony that had been her constant companion for close to a year whenever she thought of Daniel, peace flooded her mind and swelled her heart. The corners of her lips lifted into a wide smile. "Nothing."

Alicia's eyes narrowed. "Nothing…are you sure?"

Bella closed her eyes, breathed in deeply, and then let the air out slowly and opened her eyes. "Yes."

A flicker of hope lit up Alicia's eyes for a brief moment and then died. "But for months...Daniel was all..." Alicia's words faltered.

Bella pulled her knees up to her chest and wrapped her arms around them. "I don't blame you for doubting me. I've lied to you for the last couple of months...tried to convince you that I was getting better. But coming within a hair's breadth of dying seems to have obliterated my obsession for my ex-husband. I don't know why, I can't explain..." Bella's eyes widened. "God...God did this!" Her voice rose in excitement. "The strange man that stopped me from making the worst mistake of my life...that wasn't a coincidence...it was God."

"Well, he didn't exactly stop you," Alicia said.

Charley darted narrowed eyes at Alicia and then turned to Bella. "We're going to ignore Miss Debbie Downer. If I may quote part of scripture—'With God all things are possible.'"

Alicia cringed and then sighed. "You're right. I do need to change my attitude. I'm just scared this optimism won't last and you'll start thinking about Dan and..."

"No, I won't." Bella scooted off the bed. "God intervened, and I have to be worthy of the faith he's put in me to make my life count." Her stomache rumbled. "Now, for the first time in a very long time, I'm starving. Let's go to breakfast."

✦ ✦ ✦

The formal dining room was nearly full with passengers indulging in a sumptuous breakfast ordered from an elaborate menu, which included European, Mediterranean, and American morning fare. Alicia led the way to their assigned table. Her eyebrows rose. Their table of ten, covered with a snowy white table cloth, stood empty. "Well this is a first."

Charley pulled out an upholstered chair. "Either our dining companions already ate or those not going on the excursion will be in later."

Bella swiveled her neck toward Charley. "I'm afraid I haven't been paying any attention to the schedule. What's the excursion today?"

"We're going into Athens to the Acropolis…to see the Parthenon."

"Good morning, ladies." Their assigned waiter, Dimitri, smiled down at them with two rows of dazzling white teeth.

Alicia rolled her eyes. All the waiters were, young, male, and handsome. Being of a suspicious nature, she had speculated that it had something to do with the fact that a large number of the passengers were women.

"What can I bring you ladies to drink?"

"Three mimosas."

Alicia jerked her head towards Bella as Dimitri walked off. "What?"

Bella winked at Alicia as she turned to Charley. "I want you to do a portrait of Noah and me when we get back to Williamsburg."

Charley's eyes sparkled. "I'd love to!"

"And I will need input from both of you. Right now, I'm leaning toward using Lady Grey with the pasture in the background."

"You don't need our input at all. That would be perfect. I'm thinking an evening setting when the sky has that hint of violet to match your eyes."

"Match my eyes? Seriously."

"Here you go, ladies." Dimitri said down a narrow goblet of champagne and orange juice in front of each of the women. "Do you know what you want to order?"

"Smoked salmon, scrambled eggs, and croissants with butter and jam," Charley said.

"Sounds yummy, I'll have the same," Bella said.

"Make that three." Alicia handed over her menu.

After Dimitri exited their table, Bella lifted her glass of mimosa and gazed with tear-filled eyes at Charley and Alicia. "I would like to repeat a toast I made back in April a year ago. 'To my very best friends...I love you both.'"

Alicia raised her glass, her own eyes becoming moist. "Love you back."

Charley's raised glass trembled slightly. "Love you more."

Alicia clinked glasses with her friends and took a sip. She lowered the glass and said, "You're right, Bella. I definitely see God's hand in this, and my heart tells me you are sincere." She cleared a throat clogged with tears. "I'm thankful, happy, so full of joy I could burst." She gripped Bella's fingers and stared deeply into her eyes. "It's you,

Bella…for the first time in fourteen months…you… my beloved friend, are back. There's pink in your cheeks and a sparkle in your eyes and…" Alicia's hand started to shake. "Oh God, Bella, I was terrified."

Bella squeezed her fingers. "I'm sorry." She took Charley's hand. "Daniel was my sun, my moon, my reason to exist. I did it all to myself. I brainwashed myself into thinking I had no life without him." Bella pulled her hands back. "And when I think about how I neglected Noah all those months." Tears glistened on her lashes.

Alicia shook her head, her voice soft. "Oh, no, you don't…no self-condemnation." Alicia raised her glass again. "Here's to family, friends, and new beginnings."

Bella smiled. "I will definitely drink to that."

Charley raised her glass. "Me, too."

Alicia took a drink and sent a silent prayer of thanks heavenward as their waiter returned with the food.

The loudspeaker blared into the dining room. "Attention cruise guests, the buses have arrived at the dock for the excursion to the Acropolis and will be leaving in twenty minutes."

"Time to go." Charley pushed back from the table, tossed her snowy napkin on the tablecloth and stood.

"Oh, no. I forgot my hat. I'll meet you at the bus."

"We can go with you, Bella."

"Don't be ridiculous…it will take me ten minutes, if that…go on."

Bella hurried out of the room and headed for the main elevators. She fast walked down the passageway to her cabin. As she took the card out of the pocket of her black capris to swipe the lock, footsteps halted beside her.

"Excuse me."

She turned her head and barely avoided an outright gasp at the specter beside her. She had to look up. He was very tall. His face was haggard—pale and drawn beneath his rumpled ebony hair streaked with gray. Black stubble covered his hollow cheeks and chin. His blue eyes were pools of infinite sadness. A polo shirt and khakis hung on his emaciated frame.

"I wanted to apologize for what I said to you."

Bella took a step closer to the cabin door. "I don't know what…"

"I was the one on the deck last night." He rubbed fingers across his forehead. "I had too much to drink…and mixed with the grief…it was inexcusable." He swallowed heavily. "I saw you leave the dining room…I just wanted you to know how sorry I am."

Before Bella could react, the man abruptly turned and walked down the passageway. She stared after him, one thought occupying her mind. *How did you recognize me? The deck was dark.* Shaking her head to clear the surreal moment from her mind, Bella swiped her card and entered the cabin. She grabbed the straw hat with the pink bow and shut the cabin door behind her.

She picked up her pace when the loudspeaker barked that the buses would be leaving in ten minutes. She arrived at the elevated ramp slightly out of breath. Not seeing her companions, she hurried down the ramp toward the three tour buses. She saw Alicia waving through the window from the second bus in line. She climbed on board and spotted Charley and Alicia halfway down the aisle. There was an empty beige cushioned seat beside Charley.

"What took you so long?" Alicia leaned into the aisle from her seat across from Bella.

"The weirdest thing…you won't believe it. The man that was on the deck last night…the one who asked me… that wanted me to…"

…Jump overboard together." Alicia finished.

"Yes. He followed me down from the dining…"

Charley gasped. "He followed you."

Bella shook her head. "Nothing bad. He wanted to apologize."

"Apology unaccepted. The nerve…if he had convinced you…" Alicia hissed.

"But he didn't. You should have seen him. He looked like the walking dead."

"Then you both could be extras on the television show with the same name." She quipped as she pulled herself back from the aisle to let two passengers walk to the rear of the bus.

"Alicia…Really?" Charley shot a disgusted look at her friend.

Alicia rolled her eyes. "I was joking."

Bella allowed a giggle to escape. "But she is right. And you never saw me first thing in the morning without makeup. I woke up every morning looking like death warmed over. Very scary." She giggled again.

"Oh, Bella, you giggled." Alicia rose out of her seat and gave Bella a hug. As she resumed her seat, the bus rumbled to life and the driver pulled the door shut.

Bella turned to the front as the bus pulled away from the dock. She literally vibrated with life. She closed her eyes. *Thank you again, Lord for the chance to get this right. I am forever grateful.* A pair of sad blue eyes materialized in her mind. *And, please Lord, help the man from the deck with his grief.*

✦ ✦ ✦

The pink ribbons trailing down from the back of Bella's straw hat rippled in the warm breeze as she stared at the ancient structure in front of her.

"I don't see it, Charley, do you?"

Charley shook her head. "No idea."

"Bella…what are you staring at?"

"What?" She pulled her mind back into the present.

"You've been staring at the Parthenon for the last fifteen minutes without blinking."

Bella focused on the damaged white temple with the soaring marble columns. It was magnificent. She looked around at large chunks of chalky marble strewn around the base of the temple. She recalled that the tour guide said it had been finished in 438 BC.

"Well?"

"Well, what…oh, you wanted to know what I was staring at. Actually, I wasn't staring…I was thinking."

"Okay, what were you thinking about?"

"The man from last night."

Charley's mouth turned downward. "Bella, I don't know if it's a good idea to dwell on something so…" She groped for the right word. "…negative right now. I mean you were depressed for months, I really don't…"

A young boy with curly hair, being chased by another boy, bumped into Charley. "Sorry, ma'am."

"Rick…Jack…get over here right now!" shouted a male voice from a few yards away.

Bella smiled as they ran off dodging small groups of people milling around the historical site. "He looks a little like Noah with that curly hair."

Charley cleared her throat. "About…"

Bella squeezed Charley's arm. "Don't worry. Thinking about him wasn't depressing me. His eyes were grief-stricken. I know how he's feeling. I want to help him somehow."

"Yep, she's back, definitely back." Alicia turned to Charley a twinkle in her eye. "Remember the kitten she found at William and Mary…"

"And the turtle…" Charley said.

"Oh, and the baby sparrow…" Alicia grinned. "Remember Bella found it in the middle of the road. It didn't even have feathers yet. She brought it to the dorm and put it in a shoe box and fed it Alpo after consulting with a game warden…"

"…and after a few weeks it started flying around the room." Charley started laughing.

And remember…"

"All right you two, very funny. I have no plans to stuff the man into a shoe box and feed him Alpo."

Charley and Alicia erupted in gales of laughter causing tourists around them to turn and stare.

Their laughter was contagious. It was five minutes before Bella could control her own fit of mirth. She swiped at her streaming eyes. "I can't remember the last time I laughed like that." Her heart swelled with sweet affection for her friends.

"I feel like a hundred-pound weight just dropped off my shoulders," Alicia said.

Charley nodded in agreement.

Bella looked around. "People are heading back down."

"Yeah, we better go."

Bella glanced once more at the majestic ruin and then followed her friends down the walkway to the bus, a pair of despairing blue eyes again at the forefront of her mind.

2 6

Every seat at their assigned table was occupied except for hers, Charley's, and Bella's as they pulled out their upholstered chairs and sat down that evening. Alicia scanned around the room. The first seating of the evening was packed. Alicia turned to her table companion, a high school teacher from Kentucky. Seated next to her was her husband, a supervisor at a bourbon distillery. The rest of their table companions represented England, Scotland, and Norway. "Celia, what did you think of the excursion?"

Celia's warm brown eyes lit up. "I loved it! I took lots of pictures and notes for my students. We're studying ancient civilizations in the fall term."

Alicia leaned forward. "How about you, Jeff?"

"Couldn't be happier if they pickled me in vinegar and served me on a bun," was Jeff's droll reply.

"Sensing a little sarcasm....Just saying."

Celia leaned into Alicia and whispered, "He'd much rather be home tinkering on his motorcycle."

"Good evening, ladies and gentlemen."

Alicia joined the rest of the table in greeting Dimitri. "Allow me to take your drink orders."

Alicia looked over at Bella on her left. Her eyes were darting around the room as if she were searching for something. "What are you looking for?"

Bella jerked in her seat. "What?…Oh, nothing."

"Ma'am, what would you like to drink?" Dimitri's black eyes seemed to bore into Alicia's.

"A white wine."

The smile he gave her before moving on to Bella's drink order was more than a bit suggestive. After Dimitri turned his attention to Charley, Bella leaned over and whispered, "He has a definitive crush on you."

"Crush? What are we, preteens? No, he's a hound dog on the scent. You'd think he'd get the hint. I've been ignoring his not so subtle signals for three days."

"Still it is kind of flattering. He can't be more than twenty-four and you're…"

Laughter bubbled up from Alicia's belly. "What?…an older woman, a cougar…wait, I know; we're in Greece, I must be a siren."

"No, if you were a siren, you'd be using your charms to attract *him*."

Charley and Celia turned from their separate conversations. "Who's a siren?" they chorused together.

"Alicia said Charley was." Bella wisecracked.

Charley's jaw dropped.

"Kidding…Dimitri's got *a thing* for Alicia.

Heat infused Alicia's cheeks, as Charley, Celia, Jeff, and the woman from Norway on Charley's left, stared at her. She glared at Bella.

Bella squeezed Alicia's fingers. "Sorry, didn't intend to tell half the table."

Dimitri arrived, balancing a large tray of drinks, and Alicia's embarrassment melted away. She didn't care if Bella embarrassed her ten times a day as long as she stayed the happy, care-free, fun-loving friend she had adored for the past sixteen years.

Bella stood at the porthole, looking out at the dark night. Water ran in the bathroom as Charley brushed her teeth. Alicia sidled up beside her and peered out the window. "Can't see a thing."

"I know. It was this dark last night up on deck. There were some stars, but no moon." She turned to look at Alicia. "I was standing here thinking about last night...and it was like it happened to someone else. I can't relate or connect myself to what happened. Isn't that weird?"

"Don't dwell on it, Bella. Consider it a blessing."

"I do. But there is something that I can't figure out from last night. It was so dark I could barely make out the railing much less the man who approached me. How did he recognize me in the dining room?"

Alicia pursed her lips and shook her head. "No idea."

"I haven't spotted him once all day. Not on the excursion or the ship. And we've been all over the ship today. We looked in the shops, sat by the pool, went to the fitness center and the spa."

"It's a large ship…he could have been anywhere." Her eyebrows pulled together. "Wait a minute…were you purposely looking for him?"

Bella hedged. "Well…um…"

"Bella, I know you empathize with him, but you need to let this…" Alicia gasped.

Bella turned and giggled.

Charley had emerged from the bath in pajamas covered in Disney's princesses. She sighed. "The girls bought these pajamas special for my trip." She picked up an iPhone encased in a glittering cover and handed it to Alicia. "Quick, take a picture to show the girls, and then I can bury these pajamas at the bottom of my suitcase."

Alicia reached out with her right hand. Her left hand covered her mouth, laughter bubbling between her fingers. She took the picture, and Charley marched back into the bathroom to change.

"Now that was hilar…" Her eyes widened.

"Bella, what's wrong? You're white as a sheet."

Bella walked unsteadily to the queen-size bed and sat down. She drew in a deep breath. "All of a sudden this image came into my mind of the man from last night climbing up on the…" Her stomach churned. "What if he goes back up on deck tonight and jumps? I need to try and find him."

Alicia's eyebrows shot up. "Bella, no!"

"I have to! He saved my life. I need…"

The bathroom door opened, and Charley emerged, a frown on her face. "What's with the raised voices?"

"Bella wants to go look for the man from last night."

"No!"

"That's exactly what I said."

Charley turned terrified eyes in Bella direction. "Bella, he's not in his right mind. He could be dangerous."

Bella scoffed. "He's skin and bones. I probably weigh more than he does. If you had seen his eyes you'd understand. He needs someone to talk to…to help him through the pain."

"Right, because it worked so well with you."

Bella's face fell.

Alicia's eyes reflected her regret. "I'm sorry…I shouldn't have said that."

"No, it's true. I know…I didn't listen to any of your good advice. I felt like you couldn't relate to what I was going through. I was alone on my own island of misery." She looked back up. "But I can relate to that man. I can help him. I know I can."

Charley squared her shoulders. "Okay, Bella, if you insist, we're going with you."

Bella shook her head. "No way. He won't open up with you around me."

Alicia crossed her arms. "Okay, what's your plan?"

"Go search the ship."

"And what if he's holed up in his cabin with a fifth of bourbon?"

"Well…I…I could take a blanket up on the promenade deck and sit in one of the deck chairs and see if he shows up to jump overboard."

"And when you fall asleep."

Bella huffed. She hated it when Alicia blasted sensible holes in her plans.

Alicia's tone was gentle. "The best we can all do is pray for him, Bella."

Charley nodded. "It's not safe to be wandering around in the dark on any of the decks."

Bella sighed. "Fine."

Charley grabbed Bella's and Alicia's hands and closed her eyes, as she voiced a prayer of protection for the man who had lost his wife and two daughters.

CHAPTER

2 7

Bella awoke with a start. The cabin was pitch-black. Charley breathed steadily beside her. *What woke me up?* She turned onto her side and picked up her cell phone from the night stand and pressed the button. *Three thirty.* She put her phone down and started to lay back when icy fingers travelled up her spine. She sat up. *Something's wrong... Alicia?*

Bella tossed back the comforter and placed her feet on the carpet. She slid her hands along the edge of the bed and then walked blindly in the direction of the pull-out sofa. Her shin connected with the edge of the bed, and she bit down hard on her lip. She moved her hands atop the comforter until she found Alicia's shoulder. She leaned down. *Breathing.* She heaved a relieved sigh as she stood up. *Then what...*Her heartbeats ratcheted up...*the man!*

Hands outstretched, Bella stepped cautiously to the table by the cabin door where she had tossed her key card. She picked it off the table and placed it in the pants pocket of her dove-gray pajamas. She slipped her feet into the sandals she had kicked off by the door earlier. Trying to be as quiet as possible, she unlocked the door and pulled it towards her. Subdued lighting entered the cabin. She glanced back at the sleeping forms on the two beds and then gently shut the door.

She stood frozen, uncertain, in the passageway, until a loud voice inside her head shouted...*MOVE...GO!* With heartbeats thudding in her ears, she ran for the elevators. She arrived on the promenade deck breathing hard. Her eyes widened. Lights were softly illuminating the deck. *Why hadn't there been lights last night?* Pushing the thought to the back of her mind she walked quickly to the other end of the deck. No one was there. She looked back in the other direction...no one.

Placing a hand over her racing heart, Bella stepped over to the closest red and white striped deck chair. Her foot hit something that clinked and rolled away. She looked down. It was an empty bottle. She reached down and picked it up, reading the label. *Whiskey.* Ice water shot through her veins. Her eyes were drawn like a magnet to the railing. She stifled a sob. *I'm too late.*

She walked on leaden feet to the railing. She bowed her head and closed her eyes. "Oh, God, no."

She raised her head, anger filling her. "No!" She drew back her arm and then brought it forward as hard as she could. The bottle flew into the inky blackness. A single tear trailed down her cheek. A thud and a curse above her had Bella whipping around and looking up. It was hard to see anything. The observation deck was parallel to this deck. She leaned back hooking her arm around the rail. She definitely didn't want to finish what she started last night. Bella could see a hand grasping the rail above her. A head came into view and her breath caught in her throat. *It was him.* Her eyes widened in horror.

She sprinted for the stairs to the upper deck heart beating wildly. She prayed as her feet pounded up the stairs. She emerged on deck and spotted him just ahead. He had one foot on the railing and was raising the other. "No! Stop!" Time seemed to move in slow motion as she raced to the bow of the cruise liner. Head down, the man started to lean over. *God, please.* A yard to go…Bella stretched out her fingers on both hands. He leaned over further. She halted inches from his back wrapped both arms around his middle, and aware of the danger of both of them falling jerked her body back with all of her strength.

One second she was upright; the next she was flat on her back with dead weight crushing her into the wooden deck—and she couldn't have been happier. She started to weep silently.

The body on top of her moved. She abruptly stopped crying. The voice was slurred and indignant. "What the hell!" He was waving his arms and trying to sit up. Bella raised arms that trembled and pushed hard on his back. She wiggled out from under him. Alcohol fumes… again…and sweat engulfed her as she wiped her eyes.

Grunting and swearing the man managed to turn onto his knees weaving slightly. "What do you think you're doing?" He squinted at Bella in the dim lighting. "A woman?" He leaned in closer, and Bella held her breath to avoid breathing in the disgusting fumes. "You look familiar."

She rose to her feet grimacing in pain. "What's your name? I can't keep calling you 'the man.'"

He looked taken aback. "My name?"

"Please."

"Alec." He struggled to gain his feet. Bella reached down to help, but he pushed her hand away. "You had no right to stop me," he hissed between clenched teeth as he rose up. He stood swaying, his face suddenly infused with blood. "I could be with my wife and daughters now!"

Bella stood her ground. "You saved my life. I had to stop you from jumping."

"No, you didn't!" He turned and staggered back to the railing.

"What's all this yelling?" Bella whipped her head around, as a steward appeared on deck.

Her heart racing again, she pointed at Alec. "He's going to jump."

Alec's hand gripped the railing as the steward dashed forward. He raised his foot, but it slid sideways off the bottom rail. As he tried to raise it again the steward reached him. He grabbed him around the middle as Bella had, but being twice Bella's size, when he jerked back with Alec in his arms he didn't fall. Alec put up a furious fight, cussing a blue streak.

The steward let go dropping Alec on to the wooden deck with a thud. He looked down and said in a strong Australian accent, "Stay put, mate." He pulled a two-way radio off of his belt and depressed a button. "It's Finn. I need security to the observation deck." He shoved the radio back into the holster on his belt. Breathing hard, Alec looked up at the steward, his eyes shooting daggers. "Go away. Leave me alone."

"I'm sorry, mate, but I can't do that. You're a danger to yourself."

Bella pulled in a deep breath, trying to slow down her heartbeats. She turned to the steward. "Sir, wherever you take him...you should restrain him. I pulled him off the railing right before you came."

"Do you know him?"

"No...I... ah...ran into him on the promenade deck last night. He was talking about killing himself."

Alec's eyes narrowed as he looked up at Bella. "Now I know why you look familiar." He gave a drunken laugh. "Oh, the irony."

Bella turned as two burly men emerged on deck. They strode over to Finn. "What's the problem," said a man with a blond beard.

"The gentleman is intoxicated. He tried to jump over-board..." Finn glanced at Bella. "...twice."

Alec gave a lopsided grin, raised three fingers, and waggled them. "Three times." He pointed a finger at Bella and slurred. "But she wouldn't let me join her."

Bella's gut clinched as Finn's puzzled gaze turned in her direction. She nonchalantly shrugged her shoulders.

"Well, obviously, third time wasn't the charm." The other security guard with a trimmed black goatee and Brooklyn accent reached down and pulled Alec to his feet. "How about we get you sobered up and find some-thing else to occupy your time on the ship."

The other guard grabbed Alec's free arm, and both men started to walk him to the stairs. "Wait...what about her?" He twisted his head around. "Slap some cuffs on her...she tried to jump last night."

Ignoring the outburst, the two men fast-walked Alec to the stairwell and disappeared. Finn turned to Bella and sighed. "I'll have to report this…spend most the day in paperwork. Will you be going on the excursion to Ephesus tomorrow?"

Bella nodded.

"Can you come to the security office about an hour before you leave and tell me what you witnessed?"

Bella swallowed heavily. "Is it necessary?"

"Yes, miss."

She nodded. "Ah…Mr…?"

"Just call me Finn, miss."

Bella chewed her bottom lip. "Where will they take him?"

"Sick bay. They'll put him on a bed, cuff him to the bed rail, and let him sober up. Later this morning he'll get a visit from the psychiatrist."

"Would it be okay if…I visited him?"

"I can check with the doc."

"I appreciate it. I would like to try and help…" Suddenly aware she was talking too much, she held out her hand. "Thank you for your help."

Finn gave her hand a light shake and held out his other hand. "After you, miss. I'll be escorting you to your cabin."

"No…no…that's not necessary."

"I insist. You shouldn't be wandering the ship alone at this hour in the morning."

Knowing she couldn't win the argument, Bella set off for the stairs. At the door to her cabin, she turned. "Thank you, Finn."

"I'll wait until you're safely inside."

Bella slipped the card in the slot and opened the door when it clicked.

"Have a good one, miss."

"Who…what?" Alicia's sleepy voice came from the direction of the pullout.

Bella quickly shut the door. A light snapped on. Alicia was staring in her direction. "I heard a man's voice…and the door close."

Bella slipped off her sandals. "It's nothing go back to sleep."

"What's going on?" Charley sat up in bed.

Bella groaned. "Nothing."

"Oh, it's something alright. I heard a man's voice and the door close. *And* Bella just took off her shoes."

Charley sent a horrified look in Bella's direction. "Did you go looking for that man?"

"Look, why don't we all go back to sleep, and I'll tell you about in a few…"

Alicia crossed her arms atop the gray and white striped comforter. "Now."

Bella sighed heavily and went to sit on the bed next to Charley. She spoke in detail about the last hour's adventure. Silence fell over the room. She crossed an arm over her chest to massage her painful shoulder blade.

Charley's voice was sympathetic. "Is that where you hurt yourself landing on the deck?"

"Yeah, one of many." She was staring at Alicia who had a mutinous look on her face. "What?"

"You should have woken us. We could have gone with you."

"There wasn't time. The voice in my head said 'Go... now!' Alicia, I'm not exaggerating when I say if I had been one second later, he would have gone over."

"Definitely a God thing." Charley beamed.

Alicia glared at her. "She could have died."

Charley shook her head. "God wouldn't let her."

"Alicia, I'm sorry I scared you, but you would have done the same thing."

"No, I wou...well maybe I would have." She sighed. "Bella, promise me you won't leave our cabin in the wee hours of the morning again...my heart can't take the stress."

Bella pursed her lips.

Alicia's eyes narrowed. "Okay, I'm sleeping on the carpet in front of the door."

Bella huffed. "Fine, but I can take care of myself."

"We can debate that in the morning. I'm going back to sleep." She flipped off the light.

Bella lifted her feet off the floor and slid them under the covers. Charley squeezed her shoulder, then turned on to her side. Within two minutes she was snoring softly.

Bella lay on her back, her arms crossed under her head. The image of Alec's enraged face pushed to the forefront of her mind. She closed her eyes as despair gripped her. How could she help a man who was laser-focused on killing himself?

CHAPTER

2 8

At the sound of her knock, the door was pulled inward by a man with swarthy skin and serious brown eyes. "Ma'am."

He stepped aside. Bella entered the small office. She looked around as the fingers of her left hand rubbed nervously at the knuckles of her right hand.

"I'll leave it to you then, Finn." The man stepped around Bella and out the door.

"That was Mr. Kappas, head of security for the cruise. Have a sit."

Bella pulled out a chair from under a square wooden table. She placed her hands on the table and then changed her mind and placed them in her lap.

"No need to be nervous, miss."

Finn smiled. He was a good-looking man in a weather-beaten kind of way...with skin the color of tanned leather and crinkles around his eyes. "Sorry, I've never been questioned before about..." She swallowed.

"No worries, I'll have you out of here in two shakes. I need your name and where you are from first."

"Bella Stanford. Williamsburg, Virginia."

"I'm assuming Virginia is in the USA because of your American accent. I don't know the different states."

Bella gave a brief smile. "That's okay. I would guess by your accent that you are from Australia." Finn nodded. "And I don't know the names of your...they're called territories, right?"

He smiled back. "That's correct...territories."

Bella's anxiety ratcheted down a notch.

"Can you tell me what happened last night?"

Unsure how Finn would react to 'God sent me to save Alec's life,' Bella decided to go with waking up restless and going for a walk on the promenade deck. "I heard a thud and looked up and saw this man trying to climb the railing. I rushed up to the observation deck and just managed to pull him back before he went over."

Finn was bent over a notepad writing down the information. "Go on."

"I fell back on the deck with Alec on top of me."

"Is that the gentleman's name?"

"That's what he told me last night."

Finn looked up and quirked an eyebrow. "After you prevented him from jumping, he introduced himself?"

"Not exactly. I asked him his name."

Finn opened his mouth as if to make a comment and then shut it again. "Okay, what happened next."

He yelled at me for preventing him from jumping and turned to try again. And then you showed up."

"Okay, is that it then? Anything else you want to add?"

Bella froze and then shook her head. *Please don't ask me about what happened two nights ago.*

"Then we're done." He pushed back his chair.

Bella gave an inward sigh of relief as she stood up. "Can I visit him?"

"Doc Cavannah hasn't seen him yet. You can check back with me after the excursion."

Bella nodded, took a step, and winced.

"Are you okay?" Finn's eyes had lit with concern.

"Just sore from the fall."

"Maybe you should see the doctor on duty."

"No, nothing's broken, and I have plenty of ibuprofen." *Because sometimes I get a headache from my last fall.* But she wasn't about to mention that to Finn.

Finn opened the door. "Thank you for being cooperative."

Bella nodded and stepped through the door.

Bella knocked timidly on the door to the sick bay. Dr. Cavannah had given permission to visit, if the patient was agreeable. Alicia and Charley protested vehemently against the visit, but Bella told them that she had to try to reach him and that she would see them at dinner.

A woman in her forties in a nurse's uniform opened the door. She glared suspiciously at Bella. "May I help you?"

"Dr. Cavannah said…"

"Ah, yes, he told me a woman would be stopping by to visit with Dr. Kaselberg."

Bella's eyebrows drew together. "Doctor? Are you sure we are talking…"

The nurse cut her off. "Dr. Cavannah only has one patient in sick bay."

"Oh. So, can I…"

"He doesn't want any visitors."

A telephone behind her rang shrilly. "I need to answer that. You can check back tomorrow."

Bella's shoulders slumped in disappointment. She watched the nurse step across the bay and through a door. She heard a 'hello', and then her voice rose. "Jason, darling." A pause and then. "No, perfect timing, I can talk. Only one patient and he's sleeping."

He's sleeping.

The door to the other room closed, and the conversation became muffled. Bella looked around the large bay. There were about two dozen beds with privacy curtains hooked to the walls—except for a bed at the far end of the room. The curtain was pulled around the bed. She chewed on her lower lip and then glanced again at the door across the room. Darting a quick glance over her shoulder, she stepped through the door and hurried to the closed curtain.

Pulling the curtain aside, Bella glanced at the sleeping man. Compassion welled within her as her eyes roamed over a grief-ravaged face. She slipped into the chair next to the bed. She placed her right hand over his pale hand cuffed to the bedrail. Eyes closed and voice barely a whisper, she prayed. "Lord I…" Tears choked her throat. "Oh, Lord I know the pain, the despair, and heartbreak this man is going through. Please take away the desire he has to take his life so that he can allow you, the great physician, to help him to heal as you are helping me to…"

The hand beneath her hand suddenly yanked free of hers, the metal cuff rattling. Bella jumped, her eyes flaring open.

His eyes were furious blue pools. "Who let you in? I said no visitors."

"I…know…I just wanted.…"

"You just wanted what? To pray over me…play the savior of the poor, pitiable, pathetic, suicidal drunk!"

Bella glanced anxiously over her shoulder. The nurse was sure to hear him. "I'm sorry…I'll go. I just wanted to help. I know what you're going…"

"You have no idea what…" He pulled in a ragged breath. "Get out now before I…"

She jumped out of the chair and strode as quickly as possible to the sick bay door. The other door was still closed; the nurse's voice barely audible. Bella darted into the passageway. She mentally kicked herself. *What was I thinking? I never should have…*Her eyes widened. She would get a severe dressing down by Finn tomorrow when Alec complained to the nurse.

Bella hurried into the dining room and pulled out a chair at the table relieved to see only Charley and Alicia in attendance.

Alicia cocked an eyebrow. "Well."

"You were right...big mistake. The nurse said no visitors, but I sneaked past her and into Alec's cubicle."

Charley's hand rose to her mouth.

"He was sleeping. I just wanted to say a prayer and leave, but he woke up."

"And?" Alicia cocked her eyebrow higher."

Bella winced. "He was not happy to see me."

"I take that as an understatement?" Alicia said.

"Oh, yeah...he told me to get out." Bella's face screwed into a mask of worry. "When he tells the nurse, I'm in for it."

Alicia gave a sage nod. "You'll be cleaning bedpans for the rest of the cruise."

"Ladies, what would you like to drink?"

Charley and Bella gave their orders, and Dimitri turned to Alicia. "I have a very special Pinot Noir I saved back just for you this evening." He winked.

Alicia pulled in a deep breath and let it out slowly. "Dimitri, I have been ignoring your overtures, hoping you would take the hint, but since that doesn't seem to be working, I will be blunt. I am sure you have many ladies on this cruise succumbing to your abundant charms, but I am not one of them. Our relationship is strictly waiter and guest. Capiche?"

Dimitri's eyes widened with shock and pink-bloomed on his olive toned cheeks. Bella guessed he had never been dressed down before. He quickly recovered–his professional mask in place again.

"I'll have sweet iced tea with lemon," Alicia said with a smile.

He gave a quick bow and retreated.

"Oh, Alicia, good for you." Charley giggled. "Did you see his face?"

"Whose face?" Celia said as she pulled out a chair.

A s Bella, Charley, and Alicia approached the gangway
the next morning, Finn approached.

"G'day, Ms. Stanford. Might I have a word?"

Bella turned to her friends. "I'll be right there. Save me
a seat on the bus."

Finn turned and walked a few feet away from the
guests bustling down the ramp. "Ms. Stanford, I wanted
to talk to you about Dr. Kaselberg."

Bella's heartbeats sped up. "I know I should have listened to the nurse. I'm sorry...I won't..." She pulled in
a breath. "I promise not to sneak into the sick bay again.
It's just that..."

The small creases around Finn's mouth crinkled around
a grin. "Crikey, miss. You got one over on Nurse Ironb..."
He abruptly cleared his throat. "No worries, your secret's
safe with me."

"But didn't Alec complain to the nurse?"

"Haven't heard a word."

Bella frowned. "But...then why did you what to talk
to me?"

"I wanted to let you know Dr Kaselberg was moved to his cabin last night and locked in. If you want to talk to him, you would have to call security first. And they will call Dr Kaselberg for permission."

Bella's heart sank. "My chances of visiting him there are nil to none."

"None of my business, and you can say so, but why are you interested in helping this man?"

Bella bit her lower lip. *Should she share what Alec told her?* She took in a breath and squared her shoulders. Yes…desperate times called for desperate measures. His life was more important than his privacy, and if Finn could help her to get in to see Alec…"He told me two nights ago that his wife and two daughters were killed in a car accident. I recently had a loss and understand a bit about…what he is going through."

Finn shook his head, his face reflecting sorrow. "That poor bloke."

"If you could think of a way, I could get permission from Alec to talk to him I would appreciate it." Bella hastily added. "I mean I know you must be very busy, but…"

Finn smiled. "You are a very caring woman, Ms. Stanford. I will see what I can do."

Finn's relaxed visage suddenly morphed into shock. Bella spun around. Clean shaven and hair combed, Alec walked to the gangway between two security guards. The guards stopped at the edge and Alec continued on down the ramp toward the buses.

Eyes wide, Bella watched Alec enter a bus. "What… but I thought…"

"I think I know what's going on."

Bella turned back. "What?"

"The cruise line...for insurance reasons...and to prevent themselves from being sued... can secure a person while on board ship if they are a danger to themselves. But they cannot prevent that person from leaving or returning to the ship."

"And they aren't liable if he kills himself on an excursion," Bella said in a cynical tone.

Finn nodded.

Bella blew out a breath and looked over her shoulder at the buses. "I better go." She turned back to Finn and held out her hand. "Thank you."

Finn shook it. "No worries, G'day."

Alicia stood in the cave on the island of Patmos and gazed around in reverent awe. This was the cave where John, 'the disciple whom Jesus loved,' was given the visions for the book of Revelation. It was quite roomy, carved out of gray stone, with a low ceiling. Depictions of Saint John graced the walls and lanterns hung on bars bolted to the ceiling. Wooden chairs were lined up against the cave wall and wooden benches sat in the middle of the room.

A monk with a long white beard and dressed in a black robe was talking quietly to an adolescent boy. In the right-hand corner was a railing that enclosed a silver crown embedded in the rock wall. This was where Saint John lay when he received the visions. Goosebumps rose on Alicia's arms, and her heart swelled with...*wonderment.*

"This is amazing," Charley whispered, "my favorite excursion by far." She stepped over to a twelfth century painting depicting John lying down with eyes closed. Above was God in heaven.

Alicia looked over at Bella sitting still on one of the benches. Her eyes were glistening with tears as she gazed at the paintings. She walked over and sat down beside her. "Something wrong?"

Bella shook her head and wiped her eyes with a fore-finger. "I'm grateful. I was thanking God for saving my life and for… all my blessings…you, Charley, Noah, my parents." She reached over and gripped Alicia's hand. "I almost destroyed a wonderful life."

Laughter bubbled up. "You just made me think of that Christmas movie, 'It's a Wonderful Life.' We could do our own version. I could play your sister. Charley could be your guardian angel. She is definitely the guardian angel type and…"

"Bella what is it?" Her eyes had welled up again.

"In the movie, Clarence stopped George from commit-ting suicide by jumping off a bridge…he was his guardian angel. Alec stopped me from falling into the sea…that makes him…in a way… my guardian angel."

Alicia suppressed the sudden rush of anger. "Bella, that man is no angel. Remember he encouraged you to jump, he didn't prevent you."

"He's flawed…he's tortured… but God has used many of his flawed creation to do his bidding." She gave Alicia a wan smile. "Jesus took Saul, a murderer…changed his name to Paul and made him a preacher of the gospel."

Alicia opened her mouth to retort, but instead smiled. "I hate to admit it, but you do have a point."

"He's here."

"Who's here?"

"Alec."

"The suicidal man is here?" Charley had stepped over to their bench.

Bella glared. "Please don't call him that…and yes he's here. I saw him get on a bus."

"But I thought he was locked up in sick bay."

"Apparently the cruise line could care less if he kills himself on land."

Alicia's lips thinned. "Well that's pretty cynical."

"Exactly what I thought." Bella pulled out her phone and looked at the time. "We should start heading back to the bus."

As Alicia stood up, Charley said. "Why haven't you gone looking for him?"

Bella hooked an arm through Charley's. "Two reasons. I'm fairly confident he isn't going to kill himself on the excursion, and I wanted this three-hour trip to be all about us."

Alicia felt tears threaten as Bella threw an arm around her shoulders and hugged her and Charley close.

Bella stepped off the bus and started when a hand touched her arm. Alec returned the hand to his side and stepped back. "May I speak to you?"

Alicia's eyes started to narrow.

"Alicia, Charley can you wait for me at…"

"At the top of the ramp. No problem."

"No, I meant…" But she was talking to Alicia's back. She was marching up the ramp with Charley in tow.

"Very protective, your friends."

"Very."

Alec rubbed the side of his cheek and heaved a sigh. "I owe you another apology. I was rude and insensitive when you came to the sick bay. And I can't even excuse it on alcohol. You have no reason to believe me, but normally I am neither rude nor insensitive. It's just that…"

The sudden grief radiating off of Alec like heat on asphalt had Bella backing up a step, her heart clenching in her chest.

"…the loss of my family has…" He pulled in a breath and used an arm to scrub roughly at his suddenly wet eyes. "…has made me…"

"Would you like to meet me on the promenade deck around seven?" Bella wiped moisture from her own eyes. "Maybe we can help each other."

"I can't. I'm not allowed to leave my cabin except for meals and the excursions."

"I think I can arrange it if you're willing."

Bella glimpsed wariness in Alec's blue eyes. Instinct told her not to push him. She stayed silent, sensing the inner turmoil. Could he trust her? Did he want to trust her?

He sighed deeply. "Okay."

Bella turned and walked up the ramp Alec behind her. At the top stood two couples–Alicia and Charley on the left and the two security guards on the right.

The two guards and Alicia had crossed their arms over their chests. Charley smiled.

3 0

"She has to go." Charley said.

"No, she doesn't." said Alicia curtly.

"Would you two stop arguing, already…I'm going." Bella picked up a pink shawl and laid it across her arm.

Alicia turned her back to her friends and stared out the porthole, arms crossed. "I don't trust him. He could hurt you."

"Finn will be right there keeping an eye out."

"That's not want I mean." Alicia turned back, her cheeks wet.

"Bella hurried over and took Alicia's hand. "What's wrong?"

"I mean emotionally. What if he says something that makes you think of the loss of your husband, and you become depressed again? Bella, I couldn't stand it."

Bella squeezed her hand. "I told you I'm fine. It won't happen."

Alicia's lips trembled. "Pinkie swear?"

Bella would have laughed at the kindergarten expression, but Alicia's countenance was serious. She held out her right hand, little finger crooked. Alicia crooked her little finger and slid it into Bella's. She looked into Alicia's green eyes. "I swear."

Alicia wrapped her arms around her friend. Bella hugged her back.

Charley cleared her throat. "Ten minutes until seven."

Bella pulled out of the embrace and walked to the cabin door. She turned slightly. "I'll meet you for dinner in an hour."

Charley smiled. "Good luck."

She shut the door and hurried to the elevator.

Stepping onto the promenade deck, Bella spotted Alec immediately. He sat in a chair halfway down the deck, his countenance stiff. Finn stood at the rail in the standard white uniform of a steward. Her heart beat a nervous tattoo against her chest as she strolled towards the doctor.

Dark clouds scuttled across the sky, and the wind whipped whitecaps across the water. Shivering slightly, she draped the shawl across her shoulders. As she drew near, Alec darted a glance in her direction.

"Hello." Bella smiled.

He acknowledged her greeting with a nod.

Bella turned to Finn. "I want to thank you for arranging our meeting."

"No worries…nice to be up on deck. I've been inside the ship all day addressing guests' complaints." Finn looked at Alec. "I'll move along the rail a bit and give you both some privacy if you promise not to try and jump overboard, Dr. Kaselberg."

Alec responded without looking up. "I won't."

Bella took a seat in the deck chair next to Alec, stretching out her legs. She followed Alec's lead and stared out at the turbulent water. "Looks like a storm is moving in."

Silence.

"Can I call…"

He stirred on the chair. "I'm afraid I'm not going to be very good company."

Bella pulled in a breath and decided to rip out a page from Alicia's book. "Did you love your wife and daughters?"

She continued to stare at the water as the chair next to her rattled. "What kind of insulting question is that?"

"Just wondering…because you don't act like you love them."

"What!"

Bella turned her head. Alec's face was beet red with rage. She spoke calmly, "would they want you to kill yourself over their deaths?"

The flush remained as Alec grappled with the right retort. "What about your loved ones? Would they have wanted you to do the same?"

Shame washed through her, and she dropped her eyes. "No, they wouldn't. But then I wasn't thinking about them. I was focused on my own self-centered needs." She lifted her eyes and looked dead on into Alec's accusatory eyes. "But I'm not anymore. Not since you stopped me from jumping."

Alec grunted. "I didn't try to stop you."

"But you did stop me, and that's all that matters." She looked back at the water through the railing, the strong breeze ruffling her loose blond curls.

The silence stretched between them as Bella tried to think of the right thing to say.

Alec spoke, and Bella jerked. "Have you really stopped wanting to kill yourself?"

"I never wanted to kill myself."

"Could have fooled me."

Bella's tone became reflective. "I woke up from a nightmare and needed to get out of the cabin. I came up here. I welcomed the dark as I made my way to the railing. I remember feeling empty, like a hollowed-out log...a vessel emptied of all emotion. I had convinced myself that if I didn't have Daniel, I had nothing. Even the love I have for my son couldn't fill that void. I remember looking down at the water. It was...*hypnotizing*. I felt serene. I wanted to get closer to that source...I put a foot on the rail and then the other. I wasn't aware of anything around me until you spoke...it was like being jerked from a deep sleep."

Bella turned her eyes back to Alec. "Your words that night slapped me awake. Almost dying, helped me to realize everything I had to live for...my friends, my parents, my son..."

Alec stirred again on his chair and cleared his throat. "I'm glad. But you still have your son. I will never see my daughters again."

Bella started to open her mouth and say 'yes you will... in heaven' but a very clear voice in her mind said *this is not the time, my child.*

Instead she said, "I cannot begin to understand that type of loss. But I do understand suffocating with heart-wrenching pain–literally unable to breathe and willing to do anything to escape it."

Alec didn't comment, and Bella let her eyes drift back to the water as the silence stretched longer than before.

Bella sighed deeply and glanced over at the cadaverous form on the chair next to her. Tears dampened Alec's cheeks. A sorrow so deep had her hand clutching her chest over her heart. "Why did you agree to meet me?"

He used the loose sleeve of his shirt to wipe his face. "I came on this cruise to get away from all the well-meaning, but meaningless, expressions of sympathy from my friends and family. I wanted to be alone. But being alone meant I could think about my wife and girls 24/7. By the second day, the pain associated with the memories became intolerable. That night, I started to drink to numb the pain…it didn't work. And that's when I decided, in my drunken stupor, that the only way to get rid of the pain was to kill myself…then I could be with them."

"I've tried to kill myself two nights in a row, and you interfered both times–once intentionally and once unintentionally." He turned and looked at Bella a wry expression on his face. "I thought I'd ask if you're psychic."

Bella shook her head. "If I was psychic I would have stopped my husband's infatuation with Melissa before it began."

She glimpsed a ghost of a smile on Alec's lips. "I suppose that's true. But how could you possibly be in the right place at the right time twice?"

Bella took in a fortifying breath. "Do you believe in God?"

Alec frowned and moved slightly in his chair. "I'm not comfortable talking about religion."

Bella looked up. Finn was heading back in their direction. The hour must be up. "Would it be all right if we talked again?"

"I don't think…"

"Please."

Finn stopped by Alec's chair. "I need to escort you to the dining room."

Alec rose and turned to Bella. "Why do you want to help me? You don't even know me."

"I can tell you tomorrow."

Alec looked out over the water. The wind pushed strands of his dark hair back and forth. He shook his head. "You're wasting your time, but I'll meet with you again."

Bella looked up at Finn. "Do you think you could arrange…"

"No worries. I'll let you know what time works for me tomorrow."

"Thank you, Finn. Goodnight, Alec."

He gave a slight nod and followed Finn. Bella turned back to the windswept waves, a ghost of a smile on her lips.

✛ ✛ ✛

Bella, Charley, and Alicia settled into the burgundy colored leather chairs at a round table in one of the ship's lounges. It was the smallest and therefore more private. Alicia looked around. The room was decorated in a nautical theme. Paintings of mast ships at sea on the paneled walls, two large world globes on stands, and a teak ship's wheel attached to a pedestal were tastefully arranged throughout the room. She smiled, when a waiter paused beside their table. She ordered a white wine along with her friends.

Charley leaned into the table. "Okay, Bella, I can't wait any longer. What happened with Alec?"

Bella shook her head. "Not much. It seems he only agreed to see me because he wanted to know if I was psychic."

Charley screwed up her face. "A psychic?"

Alicia stared at her friend. "Why would he ask you that?"

"Because I prevented him from killing himself two nights in a row."

The waiter arrived with the drinks, and each took a sip.

Alicia set down her wine. "You were with him for an hour. You had to talk about other things."

"He didn't say much. I tried to draw him out, but the only information he volunteered was about taking this cruise. He was ducking out on all his well-meaning family and friends."

"Sounds like someone else we know." Alicia quirk a brow at Bella.

"And that's the whole point. I know exactly how he feels." She blew out a breath. "I just don't know how to reach him."

Charley's eyes twinkled with mirth. "Bella the Psychic. We could take you on the road."

"Ha-ha." She smiled.

"Anything else?" Alicia took another sip of wine.

"I asked if he believed in God. And he said he's wasn't comfortable talking about religion."

"Well, that answer could be taken a few different ways."

"I know. But I didn't get a chance to ask, because Finn walked over and said our hour was up. I've arranged to meet with him again tomorrow."

"I know I'm the naysayer of our little group, but Bella, have you thought about the fact that Alec is in a very bad way, and you're not a therapist?"

"I know, but right now I really believe that God wants me to try to help in any small way I can."

"Can't argue with God, Alicia," Charley said.

Alicia started to reply, but instead picked up her glass and took another sip. After placing it carefully on the table, she took Bella's hand in her hand. "What about you? Did you feel any depression? Any type of negative feelings?"

Bella smiled. "No, Doctor Alicia, just a deep sadness for what Alec is going through."

Alicia relaxed her shoulders and sighed with relief. "I was…"

"…worried that I might regress. I know…and I love you…but you do realize that you've become a worse worry wart than I am. We both need to take a page out of Charley's book and Zen out."

"Zen out?"

Bella put her thumb and forefingers together, closed her eyes and started to hum. Alicia joined Charley in a fit of giggles.

Bella cracked open an eye. "It's working. I can feel the center of the universe in my navel."

Alicia and Charley's fits of mirth drew frowns from the other patrons in the lounge. Alicia covered her mouth and stifled the hilarity as the last remnants of her year-long burden evaporated into the deepest crevices of her mind.

CHAPTER

3 1

Charley stared with peculiar interest at the donkey. "This is a joke, right?" She looked back at the sign which read, "Lindos Taxi."

Bella knew it would be a battle trying to get Charley to mount the donkey. "Nope…this is the only transportation up to the acropolis. You could walk. It would only take you a couple of hours with all the rest stops."

Charley bent back her head and looked up and then swiveled her head back to the sign. "But it says 'taxi.' Everyone knows a taxi is a *vehicle.*" She glared around in a circle as if daring anyone to refute her. The other tourists within earshot just shrugged.

"Come on, Charley. Where's your sense of adventure." Bella prodded her forward.

"You know I have never been on the back of an animal in my life, because I *know* I'll fall off." Anxiety laced her words.

Alicia squeezed her arm. "You'll be fine."

"No, you guys go. I'll be fine right here." Her body had started to tremble.

Bella, noticing the tremors, squeezed her hand. "Okay.

There's an outdoor café a couple of buildings back. We'll come get you when we're done."

Bella mounted her donkey with the skill of a natural horsewoman. She looked over her shoulder at Alicia who was staring at Charley. She turned her gaze to Charley as well. Still trembling, Charley looked like she was about to burst into tears. Alicia hurried over, talking to Charley in a low voice. Charley pointed at a tourist sitting on the ground crying and then started talking. It looked to Bella as if she were pleading with Alicia.

Alicia walked up to Bella's donkey. "I'm going to stay with Charley."

Bella's eyebrows pulled together. "Why?"

"Do you see the tourist on the ground crying? Charley overheard her saying the ride was terrifying–that the donkey path going up is on the edge of the hill and there is no railing. Charley doesn't want us to go. She's afraid we're going to fall off the side of the hill. I don't want her stressing the whole time were gone. I'll stay with her and convince her you'll be fine since you ride all the time."

"But you'll miss seeing the ancient fortifications."

Alicia smiled. "I think I'll live if I miss one out of the twenty or so ancient ruins we visit on this trip."

Bella's left hand rubbed at the back of her neck. "This is really unlike Charley. She isn't prone to freaking out. Maybe I should stay, too."

"No, you go on. I'll take good care of her. You're the history major. You love this stuff."

"Okay, if you're sure."

As Bella took off, Alicia waved and walked back to Charley. A young man mounted the donkey behind her, and she turned her gaze forward. Five minutes later, the guide set off, holding the halter of the lead donkey. Bella was second in line. Disappointed though she was in not sharing this part of the excursion with her friends, Bella still enjoyed the ride up the hill.

She knew immediately when she arrived at the spot that scared the tourist. The path narrowed quite a bit and if the donkey stumbled, they both would fall a couple dozen feet onto the scrub bushes and scattered rocks below. Trusting the agility and surefootedness of her little steed, Bella pushed any thought of falling to the back of her mind.

Dismounting on the pinnacle of the island of Rhodes, Bella looked around in wonder. The ancient fortifications sat at one end of the flat plateau. The center was strewn with the ruins of a temple. To her left, construction had started on a new temple to Athena. A crane stood next to a foundation and four stone pillars. She walked across the pebble strewn dirt to where the construction site sat on the edge of the plateau overlooking the Mediterranean Sea. Her eyes widened in amazement.

A gentle breeze blew through her hair as she gazed out over the water. It was a breathtaking brilliant blue. Tiny white boats bobbed here and there on the gentle waves. She took in a deep breath, threw her arms out to her sides and closed her eyes. Her heart swelled with a joy she had not felt in…well…forever. Bella slowly lowered her arms and opened her violet eyes as she continued to take in the beauty of the scene before her.

She wasn't sure how long she had been standing there when rocks scraped behind her. Someone else had come to enjoy the view. The person stopped beside her, and she turned her head to the left.

"Beautiful isn't it?"

Alec had his hands thrust into the pockets of a pair of loose-fitting jeans. His black beard stubble was back, but his hair was combed. The breeze tossed a few strands over his forehead giving him a slightly younger, boyish look.

Bella turned back to the view of the sea. "Yes, it is."

Several minutes passed as Bella stared out over the water unwilling to interrupt Alec's contemplation of the tranquil scene.

"Where are your two companions?"

Bella's gaze turned back to Alec. "Charley was afraid to ride the donkey—and then became convinced that we were all going to die after overhearing another tourist say the ride was terrifying. Alicia decided to stay with her."

"I know the spot she's talking about. I considered throwing myself over the edge, but that wouldn't be fair to the donkey."

Bella's eyes widened. "No, you didn't!"

The right side of Alec's mouth lifted the tiniest bit. "I'm kidding…a little gallows humor."

Bella's eyes narrowed. "Well, it's not funny in the least."

"I think you'll be happy to know that I've decided there's no point in trying to commit suicide again. You'll just find a way to stop me." The left side of Alec's mouth curved up to match the right side. "I guess that makes you my guardian angel."

Bella's eyes widened with surprise. "Would you believe I told my friends yesterday that you were my guardian angel?"

Alec turned and stared at Bella as his voice rose. "What! That is the most ridiculous thing I have ever heard. I wanted to join you, not stop you."

Bella smiled. "But you did stop me, and I will be forever grateful." She brushed hair out of her eye. "Speaking of angels, I thought you didn't like to talk about religion."

"I...well...saying you're my guardian angel...well... were not strictly having a discussion about..." He paused.

"That explains it."

"Explains what?"

"Why you are 'uncomfortable' talking about religion. It would be hard to have a conversation on the subject when you can't complete the first sentence." She nodded sympathetically.

Alec laughed, and his face underwent a transformation. The haunted, haggard countenance disappeared, and Bella glimpsed for a moment the handsome man he used to be. She was determined to make him laugh again.

Alec's eyes suddenly lit up with surprise. "That's the first time I've laughed since..." He swallowed and looked back out to sea. "Why am I able to drop my defenses so easily around you?"

Bella pursed her lips. "Maybe it's because I'm a stranger—and I'm probably the only person you've come across that understands a devastating loss. Even though my ex-husband's not dead...I mourned him for months like he was dead."

"I guess there's no point comparing one loss to another." He sighed heavily. "It really is beautiful. Bethany and my girls would have loved this trip."

Bella chewed on her lip as she looked out over the calm waters stretching to the horizon. "I'd love to hear about them...if it's not too painful."

"It is, but maybe it will help ease the pain a little." Alec walked around a young woman taking a picture with her smartphone and strode over to the foundation steps of the new construction. Bella followed. They both eased down onto a step. Two tourists passed in front of them talking excitedly.

Alec leaned over, clasping his hands together between his knees. He stared off into the near distance. "I met Bethany at Virginia Commonwealth University in Richmond."

Bella jerked with shock. "VCU? What a small world. I went to William and Mary."

It was Alec's turn to look stunned as he pivoted his head in her direction. "Really?"

"Yes...sorry to interrupt."

"Anyway, she was working towards her nursing degree, and I was doing my undergrad in biological science. We started dating our junior year, and we were engaged our senior year. We married the summer after we graduated and before I started at The Medical College of Virginia to become a surgeon." Alec's mouth curved up in a sweet smile of remembrance. "I just wanted to elope, but she insisted on the whole elaborate wedding thing."

"Of course...I started planning my wedding when I was five years-old."

Alec laughed. "That's exactly what Bethany said."

"She worked as a neonatal nurse at the Henrico Doctors' Hospital to support us while I went to med school. Gillian, my first daughter, was born right after I graduated med school. Evie was born four years later." His eyes suddenly became anguished. "Oh, God...yesterday would have been her birthday...how could I have forgotten her birthday?"

His shoulders started to heave. Bella didn't stop to think. She scooted over on the step and wrapped her arms around Alec. He froze and then jerked backwards. Bella instantly dropped her arms and moved away stammering, "I'm...I'm sorry. I shouldn't have assumed...I..." Her words died out when she saw two men and a woman a few feet away staring, mouths slightly agape.

Not noticing the attention they were getting Alec took in two heaving breaths trying to control his emotions. "Don't apologize. You didn't do anything wrong. I'm the one who should apologize." He wiped at his eyes.

"No, you shouldn't. It's a bad habit of mine–hugging. I hug anyone for any reason...happy, sad, laughing, crying...taking out the trash."

"Taking out the trash?" Her witticism had the desired effect–curiosity replaced the anguish in his eyes.

"Oh, yeah, those are my biggest hugs. Noah, my son, gets one every time."

Alec took in a breath. "Tell me about your son."

Bella smiled. "He's a great kid. He graduated from elementary school a couple of weeks ago. He's pumped about starting Berkley Middle School in the fall. A stone plummeted into her gut, and the enthusiasm dropped from her voice. "Correction…he'll get to attend Berkley if Daniel reverses the temporary custody."

Alec stayed silent, but a question lurked in his eyes.

Bella sighed. "I had custody until one night a few months ago when I took too many sleeping pills and fell down the stairs. Daniel was furious and filed for temporary custody."

"Did you try to…"

Bella interrupted. "No…but he didn't believe me. I couldn't sleep the night the divorce was granted and took some extra sleeping pills. I woke from a nightmare about my son…went to check on him and fell down the stairs."

Concern showed in the depths of Alec's eyes. "Are you okay?"

Bella arched an eyebrow, and Alec laughed. She turned her head slightly and then stood up. "Looks like people are heading back down the hill."

Alec rose beside her. He looked slightly to the left, his gaze focusing on the sparkling blue sea. Bella caught the words as he murmured to himself. "Yes, they would have loved it."

Bella spoke to distract his thoughts. "Finn said he could arrange for us to meet at eight…if that is okay with you. I know we've been talking up here… but if you wouldn't mind…"

"That's fine, but I'd rather not meet on the Promenade deck again. I found it hard to carry on a conversation last night while looking at the railing that I almost did a high dive off of."

Bella cleared her throat and started walking towards the donkeys. "Okay, where would you like to meet?"

"Do you know where the small nautical-theme lounge is?"

Bella bit her lower lip. "I do…but don't you think it's a bad idea for you to be around alcohol?"

"Oh…right…but no…that's not why I chose that location. I wanted privacy…and I'll be fine. I'll let you do the ordering for both of us."

"Okay, then we can belly up to bar and get a Shirley Temple for me and a Roy Rogers for you."

Alec let loose with an honest to goodness belly laugh as they reached the donkeys and Bella grinned. "I'll see you in the lounge tonight." She walked to one of the free donkeys in line and mounted.

"Okay, spill. I can't believe you made us wait this long to tell us about what you saw on the acropolis. Did you get lots of pictures?" Alicia plopped down on the canary yellow towel she had spread across the padded pool lounger. The sun overhead beat down through a cloudless sky. "You could have told us on the walk to the bus, on the bus, or in the cabin."

"I know, but I didn't want to be rushed." Bella slipped on her sunglasses and stretched out on the lounger crossing her ankles. She checked her phone for the current temperature.

"Rushed? We didn't need every little detail."

"Leave her alone, and let her tell it her way. I love having stories to look forward to," Charley piped in as she lay down on her own chaise lounge.

"And you have my donkey to thank for that. He was very steady on the path up and down the hill."

Charley's cheeks flushed a rosy pink. "Okay, maybe I went a little overboard about your imminent demise by donkey."

Alicia's eyes widened. "A little. You were hysterical... sobbing into your tea that we might not ever see Bella again."

Charley shook her head. "Honestly, I don't know what came over me." She paused, and then her eyebrows shot to her hairline. "Panic attack! I've never had one, but that must have been what it was."

Bella nodded. "Possible. I know all about them having had a few during the separation." She shivered. "They're horrible."

"I've never had one. What do they feel like?" Alicia said.

"Death," Bella and Charley said together. They looked at each other mouths open.

Charley shut her mouth and ran nervous fingers through her gray hair. "I was positive that if I got on the donkey, I was going to die. *Pos...i...tive.* And then my heart started pounding really fast. I couldn't stop the anxiety. It just kept building and building."

Bella took a breath. "One day last year, I was convinced if I put one foot outside the house I would die. Just like Charley...the panic built and built until I was sobbing hysterically."

Alicia talked through the fingers covering her mouth. "That sounds horrible. I hope it never happens again to either of you."

"Me, too." Charley and Bella said together.

Bella cleared her throat. "I didn't visit any of the sites on the acropolis...well, except the partial reconstruction of the temple."

Charley's eyebrows dipped downward. "What?"

"I was too busy talking the whole time I was up there."

Charley and Alicia both rose up on their navy-blue loungers and stared at Bella.

Charley's eyes showed confusion. "Talking to whom?"

Alicia's lips thinned. "Dr. Kaselberg, I presume?"

"Alicia, please don't say anything negative. It was a good conversation. He said he wouldn't try to jump off the ship again...and he opened up to me about his wife and two girls. I made him laugh twice."

Alicia plastered a neutral look on her face. "And why has he changed his mind about committing suicide?"

"That's not important. What is impor..."

"Bella, that's really important. Why did he change his mind?" Charley twisted her heavy mane of hair and clipped it to the top of her head with a barrette.

"He said there was no point...I would just stop him." Bella mumbled.

"I didn't hear you. What did you say?"

Bella heaved a sigh. "He said there was no point. He believes I'm his guardian angel, and I'll just stop him again."

Shock rendered Alicia speechless.

Charley beamed. "That is so sweet."

Alicia turned to face Charley. Charley shrugged. "Well, it is."

"Anyway, I'm making progress. We're meeting again tonight at eight."

Alicia's heart started to thud dully in her chest. "I'm having a bad feeling about this man. What if meeting you on the Acropolis wasn't a coincidence...what if he followed you. There was no Finn to protect you up there today. He's not...in his right mind, Bella. Are you forgetting that the security team has to lock him in his cabin? What if he is becoming obsessed with you?"

Bella glared at her friend. "They lock him up for his own protection not mine. And you don't know him like I do."

"Like you do! Bella, he's a stranger. I'm just trying..."

She whipped off her sunglasses and stood up abruptly. "I know...you're just trying to protect me. Well, give it a rest." She stalked off to the refreshment stand.

Charley reached over and rubbed Alicia's arm. "I know how worried you are, but God's got this. He'll protect her."

Alicia sighed. "I know...'trust the Lord with all your heart and lean not on your own understanding.'" She looked over at Bella ordering a beverage over ice." "But sometimes it's just hard."

Charley echoed Alicia's sigh. "I know."

32

A lec waved as Bella entered the nautical lounge for the second night in a row. He was sitting at a table that offered the most privacy. Finn was leaning casually against a polished dark cherry wood bar in conversation with the bartender. As she drew near, Alec rose and pulled out a chair at the table. "Thank you." She settled in her chair and smiled across the table.

"I decided to brush up on my manners in my cabin. I'm afraid they have been sadly neglected."

"I understand. I haven't used them myself in the last year. But that wasn't the only thing that went by the wayside. I neglected my child. Half the time he had to get his own breakfast …and lunch…because I couldn't drag myself out of bed. And sometimes I didn't leave my bed until dinner."

Alec nodded in sympathy and then looked up as a cocktail waitress with wispy blond hair and fair skin approached. "Good evening. Can I get you a drink?"

Alec raised a finger. "I've got this…one Roy Rodgers and one Shirley Temple."

A split second of surprise passed over the waitress' face and was gone. "Yes, sir."

Bella giggled. "Did you see her face?"

"Worth the price of admission."

Bella rubbed at the knuckles of her hands that lay atop the table. "Did you drink a lot before this trip?"

"No. As a surgeon, I had to be sharp at all times…day or night…I rarely ever drank. If I wasn't on call, I might have a drink occasionally. But there are times when you have to go in when you aren't on call. A couple of years ago they had a major pile-up on I-95 outside of Richmond and the hospitals needed every surgeon they could get a hold of." Alec cleared his throat. "What about you?"

"Occasionally, I have a glass of wine." She stared down at her knuckles. "But I did get drunk once…the day Daniel moved out. He finished packing and came into the living room to tell me he was leaving, saw the condition I was in, and took Noah with him. When he brought Noah back the next day, he said if he ever saw me in that condition again, he would file for custody." She sighed. "There were many times I was tempted to drown my sorrows, but then I would remember the look of contempt and disgust on Daniel's face the day he moved out…and I couldn't bear for him to look at me that way again."

The waitress placed their drinks on the table. "That will be ten dollars."

Bella reached for her purse. "I'll pay for mine."

"No, you don't. Remember I brushed up on my manners, and a gentleman pays when inviting a woman for drinks."

"In the last century, maybe."

Alec laughed as he handed the waitress a ten-dollar bill and two ones as a tip. "You have the best sense of humor."

"I have a confession. I have been trying extra hard to get you to laugh."

Alec's grin transformed his face. It was the first smile she had seen, and it was contagious. She grinned back as she picked up her Shirley Temple and took a sip. "Yum… exactly as I remember it tasting when I was eight."

Alec picked up his own version of Seven-up and cherry juice and took a sip. His face screwed up into a grimace. "Ugh. That is horrible." He raised a finger and caught the waitress's eye. She sidled over to their table.

"Sir."

"Could I have a bottle of water?"

"Yes, sir." She started to move away.

"Make that two."

"Yes, Ma'am."

Alec raised an eyebrow. "I thought you liked yours."

"Way too sweet, but wasn't going to complain because you paid for it."

Alec looked around the lounge area.

"What are you looking for?"

"Two eight-year-olds."

Bella guffawed as the waitress set two water bottles and two glasses on the table. Alec reached for his wallet again.

"No charge." The waitress smiled. "The look on your faces when you took a sip…too funny." She swept up the two drinks onto her tray and departed.

"Glad we made her day." Alec twisted the lid off his water and took a long drink.

Bella poured half the contents of her bottle into her glass and took a drink to wash away the sweet aftertaste of the Shirley Temple.

Alec's countenance turned mock serious. "Speaking of manners…"

"I don't think we were."

The laugh lines around Alec's lips became more pronounced. "Ignoring that remark…don't you think it's about time we formally introduced ourselves."

"Absolutely. It's high time we brought back twentieth century etiquette."

"My name is Alec Kaselberg." He held out his hand. "Nice to meet you."

"Arabella Stanford. How do you do?" Bella gave his hand a firm shake and then withdrew it into her lap. She picked up her glass and spoke before taking a sip, "Is Kaselberg German?"

"Yes. Originally our name was Kasselberger. I think a great-great grandfather shortened it to Kaselberg when he immigrated from the Fatherland because it sounded more American." He took another drink from the bottle of water. "I won't ask about Stanford. I assume that is your husband's name. What about Arabella? I believe you are the first Arabella I've met."

"It's Latin…very old name. My mom chose it out of a baby book. She liked that the name meant 'yielding to prayer.'"

"Do I call you Arabella?"

Bella smiled. "Heavens, no. It will take you a full minute just to get out the syllables. Everyone calls me Bella."

Alec took a drink and heaved a sigh, his mood becoming somber. "Bella, last night I asked you why you wanted to help me, and you said you would tell me today." He looked into her eyes. "Why are you taking time out from your friends and the pleasures of this cruise to basically *babysit* me…a stranger."

"At the risk of making you uncomfortable…it's because that is what Jesus would do."

Bella took a sip of water as Alec shifted his position in his chair. His lips started to part, and then he pressed them firmly together.

"I did make you uncomfortable."

Alec blew out a breath. "I was raised Catholic. But… and I'm being honest here…Mass was boring. My attention was constantly drifting from the rituals and chanting of the service. When I left home for college, I never attended another Mass. All my attention was focused on the sciences. Even if I had been so inclined there was no room for church. Eating…sleeping…attending class… and studying is about all I had time for."

Sadness weighed heavy on Bella's heart, and time pressed in on all sides. How do I convince him, in the one day left to the cruise, of Jesus' love for him? She was jerked from her thoughts when Alec spoke.

"Am I some type of charity case?" A hint of anger underscored his cynical words.

Bella's tone was indignant. "Of course not!"

"What then?"

"I have done a lot of charity work through my church. I visit members in the hospitals, take them to doctor's appointments, bring food to their homes, help financially, and send cards. I *sympathize* with their trials. This is totally different. I *empathize* with you and what you are going through." Tears threatened and her voice quivered. "I actually feel your pain, and it *hurts*." She dropped her gaze to her lap, rubbing at her knuckles.

A few seconds of silence passed and then Alec cleared his throat. "I'm sorry for being cynical."

Bella looked back up, eyes glistening. "Alec, every human life is precious. I can't stand by and allow you to throw that life away without doing everything in my power to convince you that Jesus loves you and he does not want you to do this." The corners of her lips quivered upwards. "As miserable and truculent as I was, Charley and Alicia never gave up on me."

A hint of amusement laced Alec's words. "And you refuse to give up on me."

Bella nodded.

Alec sat in silence, staring at his water bottle as he rubbed a nervous finger over the label. Bella quickly dabbed at her eyes with a white cocktail napkin while he wasn't looking at her.

After a few seconds he cleared his throat and looked up at Bella. "Thank you."

Her gaze met Alec's, and she smiled. "You're welcome."

As Alec brought the bottle back up for a drink, Bella cleared her throat. "Would it be out of line to ask how the rest of your afternoon went? I mean…"

Alec took in a deep breath. "I know what you mean. It was much better than yesterday. If a depressing thought tried to push its way to the surface, I would push it back down with a good memory. Do you remember when I talked about my wedding earlier?" Bella nodded. "Back in the cabin, I went over the whole ceremony in my mind, and it helped to keep the dark thoughts at bay."

Bella smiled. "What was your favorite part of the ceremony?"

"That very first glimpse of Bethany in the wedding dress. My breath literally caught in my throat. She walked towards me. I saw her trying to hold back tears, and suddenly I was too…and I remember thinking that it was the most amazing thing in the world that this woman loved me and I would never *ever* give her cause to regret…"

A vision filled Bella's mind and Alec's voice faded away.

The pounding of her heart loud in her ears, Bella glided slowly down the aisle to the man she loved more than life itself. She could feel wetness on her cheeks as she sucked in a breath. She picked up her pace to shorten the distance as quickly as possible. Her father released her, and Daniel took her hand. A small sob escaped her lips and…Daniel frowned. He bent down and whispered in her ear, "Bella, pull yourself together." He turned to the Pastor, his frown quickly replaced with a smile.

The vision faded, and Bella's cheeks flushed with heat. *How could I have been so blind?*

"Bella?"

Bella's eyes refocused on Alec. "I'm sorry?"

Alec's eyes showed concern. "Is there something wrong? This look came over your face…"

Bella's fingers lightly touched her flushed cheek. "It's nothing."

The corners of Alec's mouth turned down. "No…it was definitely something. I've been sharing my painful thoughts with you…please let me help."

Bella shifted her hand to her lap and stared at the burgundy tablecloth. "It's too humiliating to discuss."

"And it wasn't humiliating when you pulled me off the railing and I collapsed on top of you?"

A smile trembled at the corner of Bella's mouth. "You're right." She took a fortifying drink of water and refused to look Alec in the eye. "My husband told me last August that he was in love with another woman when he married me…that he was forced to marry me—or someone like me—by his father."

Alec's eyebrows shot to his hairline. "What!"

"He was in love with an Asian woman attending William and Mary on a student visa. His father said if Daniel didn't marry a *proper Caucasian girl,* he would have her visa revoked."

"Daniel's father blackmailed him into making an arranged marriage…and your ex went along with it."

Bella nodded.

Alec's eyes narrowed, and his lips thinned. "That apple didn't fall too far from the tree."

Bella's stomach gave a sudden nauseating flip. She couldn't sit here another second reliving the most humiliating moment of her life. She pushed her chair back and stood. "I'm sorry...I have to go."

Concern stared out of Alec's eyes. "I'm sorry...I shouldn't have insisted..."

"No...it's not you. I'll see you tomorrow." Her heart was thumping. "I...goodbye."

Sheer willpower alone prevented her from rushing from the room. She maintained measured steps until she was clear of the lounge and then rushed for the nearest elevator clutching at her stomach. She paused outside of the elevator doors on the observation deck and swallowed hard against the bile rising up in her esophagus. Once it had retreated, she glanced around sighing with relief–only two people occupied the deck. Most of the passengers would prefer the promenade deck to sip drinks and talk with companions or enjoy the sea air. She quickly crossed to the railing gripping it tightly and taking in deep breaths. Her stomach finally began to ease up. She took one last deep breath and looked up at a canopy of stars.

"Oh, my God, Bella!"

Bella turned around. Charley and Alicia were racing towards her. Alicia reached her first throwing her arms around her back and pulling her away from the rail.

Alicia started weeping. "No, Bella, you promised. You said you wouldn't…"

"I'm not."

Alicia dropped her arms and stepped back, face wet and body trembling.

Bella wiped a tear from Alicia's cheek. "I'm not up here to jump. Why did you think I was?"

Alicia's cheeks tinged pink beneath the tears. "You were leaning…" She looked over at Charley. "Charley and I went to the lounge at nine to join you for a drink, but Alec said you had just left, and that you looked upset. I had a bad feeling and rushed up here and saw you leaning against the railing…" Alicia swiped at her wet face. "I'm glad I was wrong."

Charley's voice was laced with concern as she looked steadily at Bella. "Why are you upset?"

Bella led her friends over to the deck chairs. She perched on the edge of one chair, and Charley and Alicia sat across from her on another. She repeated the conversation about Alec's wedding and then told her friends about the vision. "Alec saw the look on my face and insisted on me sharing what I was upset about. Repeating the story of the most humiliating day of my life made me sick to my stomach. I told him I had to go, and then I came up here."

Charley took Bella's hand. "I know Daniel's betrayal must still hurt."

Bella shook her head. "No…it's actually self-incrimination." She looked down at her hand lying in Charley's. "How could I have been so blind? You both saw through him. Neither one of you liked Daniel. I…"

Charley jerked up straighter on her chair. "But how did you know I didn't like him? I never said a word."

She squeezed Charley's hand and looked at Alicia. "And you warned me not to marry him…you were afraid he might hurt me one day. I remember how furious I was that you dared to suggest that the man I adored could hurt me." She sighed. "But you were right."

Alicia stood up, stepped to Bella's deck chair, and eased down beside her. "Believe me when I say I wish I hadn't been right."

Charley smiled brightly. "Changing the subject…seems like you're making headway with Alec, Bella." Charley said.

"I agree." Alicia admitted grudgingly. She rose from the deck chair and leaned back against the railing her blond highlights glinting in the deck lighting. "I'm really sorry, Bella for reacting the way I did when I saw you at the rail. I guess I haven't been able to completely let go of my fears where you are concerned…and…I still may have a ways to go."

Bella looked up. "I know. And I feel horrible about putting you through all of this anxiety."

"No apologies…but speaking of anxiety…can we leave? I don't like it up here at night."

"Sure." Bella rose, pulling Charley up with her. "Would you think me ungrateful if I said I was glad the cruise is almost over? I want to go home and hug my son. I need to hold him close. When I think about how I almost threw away my future with Noah…"

Alicia nodded. "I can't wait to hug my boys…"

Charley smiled. "…and kissing my girls sounds really good right now."

Bella walked to the elevator Charley and Alicia at her side. "Do you two mind skipping the lounge? I'm suddenly exhausted."

Charley laughed. "You read my mind."

Bella woke with a start, heart hammering. She leaned over and checked the time on her phone–eight a.m. Bright light winked between the slit in the blackout curtain covering the window. She had been dreaming... about Alec...

They had both been on the Acropolis of Rhodes looking out over the water. He had turned to her and said in a calm manner, "I can't live without them." He took a purposeful stride and jumped off the edge of the cliff. She tried to stop him, her fingers reaching, but they grabbed only air.

The scream in her mind had awakened her. Bella rolled onto her back nestling her head into the pillow and gazed up at the dark ceiling. She breathed deeply, trying to slow down her jumping heart as Charley gently snored beside her. Only one day left...one more conversation with Alec. What could she possibly say that would make a difference? She groaned in her despair.

"Bella...something wrong?" Charley's groggy voice spoke beside her.

Bella heard the words, but they didn't register....*Jesus I need your help. Give me the words that will convince this man not to try and end his life once he is off this ship.*

"Bella?"

She continued to gaze into the darkness. A responsibility that was not hers was weighing heavy on her heart.

"Bella."

"Arabella…answer Charley. If I have to get out of this comfy bed and come and find out what's wrong…" Alicia's words promised dire consequences.

"Sorry. Nothing's wrong…bad dream."

Charley was sitting up next to her. "What was it about?"

"Alec was jumping off a cliff, and I tried to stop him, but couldn't."

Alicia grumbled as she left her bed, and then bright sunshine blinded her as she drew back the curtains. Bella sat up as Alicia turned around and faced her. "I don't know Alec at all, but from your description of him, I am pretty sure he would not want you to spend the last day of a wonderful cruise depressed about him."

Bella rubbed at a crick in the back of her neck. "No, he wouldn't."

"Bella, it was a horrible dream, but it was just a dream."

Charley's logic pushed away the aura of gloom surrounding her. She looked from Charley to Alicia and smiled. "Okay, my bon companions, what do you want to do today?"

Charley raised her hand.

Alicia pounded the air with an invisible gavel. "The cabin recognizes Miss Charley."

"I vote we skip the excursion and laze around the ship. We could get massages, look for souvenirs in the ship boutiques, lay out by the pool, go to a couple of shows, and eat lobster."

Alicia's face fell. Charley's eyes widened. "Oh, Alicia, I forgot you missed the Acropolis yesterday because of me. We can go on the excursion."

Alicia turned to Charley. "I don't care about that. Why don't you want to go on the excursion to Olympia?"

"I…well…" Charley fidgeted on the bed.

"Charley?"

"I didn't want to say anything, but my legs and feet are still sore from yesterday's excursion." She sighed. "To be honest I've never endured this much pain in my life with all the climbing and walking we've been doing."

Alicia frowned. "Charley, you should have said something."

Charley scooted off the bed and shoved her feet in slippers. "Alicia, you'll be glad to know as soon as I get home I'm going to start going to the gym and get rid of these extra pounds. I had no idea how out of shape I was until this trip."

Bella grinned. "Charley, you definitely need a massage."

"But I don't want to stop either of you from going on the excursion."

Alicia tapped her chin. "It's a hard decision…a walking tour to see more busted up marble statues or a day of pure relaxation. Bella, what's your take?"

Her gaze softened. "Whatever my two generous, loving friends want to do."

+ + +

Bella watched from the observation deck as the passengers filed off the ship to the tour buses. She was looking for one passenger in particular. She leaned into the rail as a familiar head of dark hair came into view. Alec walked down the gangway behind three women. He reached one of the buses and paused before boarding. He slowly turned his head and looked up. She waved, and he saluted her back.

She continued to watch until the bus pulled away. Pulling her turquoise beach wrap a little closer around her, she hurried back to the pool. Alicia and Charley were standing in the shallow end talking. She threw her wrap on her deck chair and stepped down the steps into the tepid water.

Alicia's eyebrows shot up. "You're wearing your bathing suit!"

"It's our last day. I'll never see any of these people again. I decided I don't care if the suit's big on me. I want to enjoy the pool."

"What took you so long? We've been here fifteen minutes." Alicia leaned her elbows on the edge of the pool and lifted her legs until they were floating on top of the water.

"Well…um…it took me awhile to come to the decision to wear my suit."

"It's actually not that loose on you."

"My appetite has returned with a vengeance. If I'm not careful it will soon be too tight…not too loose."

Charley sat down on the top step, the pool water lapping over her legs. "This time next year, I plan to be in a suit two sizes smaller than this one."

Alicia nodded her head. "Good for you, Charley." She turned to Bella. "What time are you meeting Alec?"

"Eight again."

"Where?"

"Same lounge as last night."

"Okay, Charley and I will join you at nine."

Bella looked through the railing at the island where athletes had trained for the first Olympics in 776 B.C. "Did you know the men trained for the Olympics naked?"

Charley's eyebrows shot up. "What?"

"I knew that. I read it somewhere," Alicia said as she looked at Bella. "How did you find out?"

"I researched a few of the islands two years ago because…" She sighed. "…I was planning to surprise Daniel with a family trip to Greece this summer."

Charley's eyes widened. "Why didn't you tell us? We could have gone somewhere else."

"My dad had already bought the tickets remember."

Alicia nodded. "To surprise you."

Bella brightened. "But you know what? I am glad he did…because it was this trip that laid the ghost of Daniel to rest."

Alicia let her feet fall back to the bottom of the pool. "I'm going back to my chair…the water's too warm."

Bella dipped lower in the water and then stood up. "I'm going to do laps until I'm exhausted and then I'm going back to the cabin and take a nap."

Charley leaned back on the step. "When you're ready I'll go back with you for that nap."

"Not me. I want to lay here in the sun for at least an hour and enjoy the view." Alicia grabbed the chrome rail and pulled herself out of the pool. She waved over her shoulder as she walked to the deck chair and eased onto her stomach.

Bella dove under the water, then emerged stroking and kicking to the other end of the pool, enjoying the sensation of her muscles moving through the water. At the other end of the pool, she paused before starting another lap. After a few laps, she lifted her dripping arms out of the water and crossed them over the edge of the pool as she gazed at the aquamarine sea. Bella sighed and smiled–peace draping her like a gossamer shroud.

3 4

A hand gripped her elbow, and Bella nearly screamed. "Sorry, Ms. Stanford, I didn't mean to startle you." Finn removed his hand. "Dr. Kaselberg went to the restroom." He cleared his throat. "I wanted to tell you before he gets back that I admire what you've done for him. I knocked on his cabin door earlier today and had a cuppa with him."

"Cuppa?"

"Cup of tea. I was direct. I asked him if he had plans to try to off himself when he gets home."

Bella's eyes widened. "What did he say?"

Finn's face crinkled into a smile. "He laughed. Said he liked my...ah...bluntness. I don't know what you two have been talking about, but it seems to have worked. I don't think he'll try to kill himself again."

Bella sagged against the wall of the lounge in relief. "That is...the best news."

Finn smiled. "He was singing your praises, miss. He said you'd helped him through a very rough patch and that he had decided to live for his wife and girls–not die for them."

She quickly straightened as Alec emerged from around the corner of the short hallway to the restrooms.

"I'll be at the bar if you need me." Finn walked off.

A mix of emotions brought on by Finn's revelations had Bella reverting to the old habit of rubbing her knuckles.

"Hi, Bella."

"Hi, Alec." Suddenly aware of what her hands were doing, she dropped them to the sides of her lavender sundress and said the first thing that came to mind. "Looks like someone got too much sun today." Alec's forehead, cheeks and nose were pink.

"I forgot my hat...again. Shall we sit at the same table?"

"Sure." Bella led the way, and Alec pulled out a chair for her to sit.

Alec folded his hands together on the tablecloth and looked at Bella his eyes quizzical. "Why didn't you go on the excursion?"

"Charley wasn't up to it, and we didn't want to leave her behind."

"You are a very caring person, Ms. Stanford."

Bella squirmed a little before changing the subject. "How was the excursion?"

Before Alec could answer, the waitress from the night before sidled up to the table. "How about a round of chocolate milk tonight?"

The bubble of laughter that burst forth between Bella's lips relaxed her. "You should replace the comedian at the ten o'clock show."

"Then how would I get paid alimony?"

It was a few seconds before Alec controlled his laughter to the point of asking Bella what she would like to drink. As he placed the orders, Bella couldn't help compare this Alec with the one she had met in the hallway outside her cabin. His face was no longer a ghostly hue, but a healthy pink, albeit partially due to the sunburn. The deeply entrenched lines around his mouth and across his forehead had started to smooth out. With his hair groomed and cleanly shaven…

Alec turned back with a spark of laughter still lingering in his eyes, and her assessment was forgotten. "She is really funny."

"I agree."

"But so are you. You two should consider an act together."

"Me?" She gave a slight chuckle. "I'm not a comedian."

"Maybe not. But I've laughed more in the last two days then in the last six months."

Bella smiled. "Me, too. And it has been wonderful."

The waitress returned with two sparkling waters. Alec paid amid Bella's protests. After the waitress left, Alec lifted his glass. "To Bella…my guardian angel." He took a sip.

"Really, I'm not your…"

Alec stared into Bella's eyes. "To me you always will be."

"Fine." Bella lifted her glass. "To Alec, my guardian angel." She sipped her drink.

He laughed out loud, showing nice, even white teeth. "I would have to be the sorriest excuse for an angel ever."

"Speaking of which…"

"What…me being the sorriest excuse for…"

"No, speaking of angels…" Bella lifted her glass a slight quiver to her voice. "To my savior, Jesus Christ, for bestowing grace and protecting two miserable suicidal sinners from making an irreversible mistake."

Alec hesitated for three very long seconds then lifted his glass and drank with Bella. He carefully placed his glass back on the cardboard coaster. "I'm not certain that he intervened, but you believe he did, and I respect that."

Bella breathed in and exhaled slowly. "On the night of your second attempt on the observation deck, I woke out of a deep sleep with a horrible feeling of dread. Something was *wrong*. I could hear Charley breathing. I got out of bed to check on Alicia. I was standing by her bed when your image literally seared my brain. I knew in that instant what you were going to do. I rushed out into the hallway, but paused, unsure where to start looking. And then a voice in my head, *God's voice*, said, "Move…Go!"

"I ran as fast as I could to the elevators. I got out on the promenade deck. You weren't there. I heard a noise and looked up and saw you." Bella's eyes implored. "Alec, none of that was happenstance."

Alec's gaze was a little less skeptical. "Well, I admit that it does shoot holes in my belief that it was a coincidence that you were up on that deck. I thought you were wandering around again because you couldn't sleep."

"I was sleeping just fine until God woke me up." She looked down at her bubbly drink, rubbing her fingers across the condensation on the glass. "I would like you to consider that God and his Son are real and do watch over their creation. You can believe in science and also have a relationship with our savior."

Alec rubbed the back of his neck. "Bella, you need to look at it from my point of view. I live my life based on concrete facts…proven theories." He held up his hands. "These hands have gone into the human body countless times. I trust in what I can touch and see–bones, tendons… arteries…tissue."

Bella glanced up at the clock on the wall encased in a ship's wheel and back to Alec. "I don't have enough time to try to convince you otherwise, but would you promise me two things?"

His eyes became wary. "What?"

"Keep your mind open…God saved you, and I believe he has a special plan for your life. And read a book called *A Case for Christ.*

Alec sighed. "I can't promise…"

"Let me ask you a question. Do your patients ever do anything special for you to say thank you?"

"All the time…why?"

"If you are as grateful to me as you say you are for saving your life on the observation deck…then this is how you can thank me."

"Sounds more like you're demanding payment for an IOU." Alec grumbled, but his eyes showed amusement.

"Whatever works."

Alec laughed. "Okay, I will seriously take it under advisement."

Bella's eyes never wavered from Alec's as she sat in silence tapping her glass.

Alec blew out a breath. "Fine, you win. And I thought no one would ever match my wife with her dogged determination. I could never win with her either."

Bella's heart swelled with hope for Alec's future. Happy, she lifted her glass, took a sip.

"Do you still want to hear about the excursion?"

Bella nodded.

As Alec launched into a detailed account of his trip around Olympia, Bella sighed with pleasure at the sparkle in his eyes and the enthusiasm heightening his words. He was definitely on the mend. She couldn't have wiped the smile off her face even if she tried to as she listened to Alec talk for the next twenty minutes.

Alec's words came to a halt and an easy silence engulfed them. After a minute, Alec spoke in a conspiratorial whisper. Bella had to lean in to hear. "I took something."

Bella's eyebrows drew together. "What do you mean?"

He reached into his blazer pocket and pulled out a small smooth white stone. "A souvenir." He handed it to Bella.

She looked at what her fingers held and knew immediately what it was…a piece of marble off one of the statues. Her lips parted in an 'O' of shock. "Alec, you can't take this as a souvenir."

"Actually, it's more like a talisman. I wanted…no I needed something to tie me to this trip when dark thoughts try to take me down that long dark tunnel again. This is to remind me of our talks and my promise to myself to live for my wife and daughters."

Bella started to open her mouth and then shut it. She chewed on her lip and then grinned. "Well, I've never been an accessory to a crime. But then Alicia is always harping about trying new things. I guess your theft of a national treasure is safe with me."

"I hoped you'd see it my way." He slipped the stone into his pocket as Finn walked over.

"Sorry to interrupt, mate, but I've got rounds to make."

"Can you give us five minutes?"

"I'll wait by the doorway."

As soon as he was out of earshot, Alec turned to Bella and laid his hand over her hand where it rested by her glass. She was not prepared for the shiver his touch sent through her body. She hoped that the shock didn't show on her face.

"I can't ever thank you enough for saving my life. And I will never forget how you've gone out of your way to lift my spirits these last few days." Alec's eyes glistened with unshed tears. "You go back to that boy of yours and show him how much you love him every minute of every day." He wiped at his eyes. "Promise me."

Bella's eyes welled up. "I will, I promise."

"Good." He withdrew his hand.

Her hand missed the warmth of his fingers. A sudden truth slammed the breath from her lungs, and she almost gasped. She didn't want to say goodbye. She didn't want their talks to end. She had benefited from these talks as much, maybe more than he had. Alec had made her feel needed in a way Daniel never had. They had bonded in a way she couldn't explain to herself much less anyone else, and she suddenly felt bereft at the thought of losing that bond.

She took in a fortifying breath. "Alec, this doesn't have to be the end to our meeting now and then to encourage each other. We only live about an hour apart." A corner of Bella's mouth quirked up. "Instead of AA, we could be SBJA...Ship Board Jumpers Anonymous."

Alec's eyes reflected regret. "I'm leaving."

Bella sat back in her seat. "What do you mean...you're leaving?"

"I can't stay in Richmond with the memories of my wife and girls everywhere. If I'm going to live for them, I have to start a whole new life...completely different from the old one."

"But where would you go?"

"I've been thinking about it a lot today...maybe join *Doctors without Borders* and go to Africa or Asia."

"But that's so far away." She whispered.

"What?"

She cleared her throat. "Nothing." Sadness lay heavy on her heart–she would never see Alec again. Straight ahead, within her line of sight, Finn was looking at his watch. "I think Finn wants to go." Alicia and Charley appeared in the doorway. Bella forced the corners of her mouth up. "You will be a blessing to many wherever you go. I will pray for you." Her voice became mock stern. "And don't you dare renege on your promise to me."

Alec stood. "I won't. Make your life count for something...for me."

Bella was desperate for time to slow down, but her friends were crossing the room at what seemed like lightning speed.

"Goodbye, Bella."

Bella's mouth quivered slightly as she smiled. "Goodbye, Alec."

Her friends reached the table, and Alec nodded a greeting as he left to join Finn. Charley and Alicia each pulled out chairs and sat.

Alicia picked up Alec's glass. "What have you two been drinking?"

"Sparkling water."

"No...no...no, that won't do. Our last night on the ship needs to be celebrated with a different type of bubbly."

"I don't like champagne," Charley said.

"You drink mimosas."

"That's different."

Alicia rolled her eyes and looked at Bella. "How about you?"

"It doesn't matter to me." Her voice was listless.

Alicia's eyebrows pulled together as she leaned toward Bella. "Is something wrong?"

"Hi, ladies. What will it be?" The waitress smiled at their group.

"Three white wines?" Alicia looked to her companions and they both nodded.

"Coming right up." The waitress walked off to the bar.

"Bella?"

Bella sighed. "I'm going to miss Al…um…the talks I had with Alec."

Charley commiserated. "That's right. This was your last time together."

"I thought we could meet occasionally in Richmond, but he's moving."

Alicia face reflected shock. "He lives in Richmond?"

Bella nodded.

"Where is he going?"

"Africa or Asia."

"That seems a bit extreme."

The waitress returned with the wines.

"I've got this…no arguing." Charley pulled a credit card out of her canvas bag.

"Thank you, Charley." Bella sipped her wine. "He said he picked those places so that he won't be reminded of his family all the time. I guess wherever he moved in the states he could still be reminded of his family if he passed by a chain restaurant they frequented. But working in… say…Nigeria, he shouldn't come across a lot of Olive Gardens."

Charley lifted her wine glass to her lips. "Do you think they have American restaurants anywhere in Africa?"

"McDonald's." Alicia deadpanned.

Bella laughed. "Absolutely. Everywhere I've traveled overseas there was a McDonald's."

A few moments of silence reigned as they sipped their wine. Alicia broke it with a question. "Where should we go in Venice tomorrow? We went to all the major tourist sites when we arrived."

Bella set down her glass. "I have a request, but if you don't want to do it, I understand."

"What, Bella...what would you like to do?"

"When we explored Venice, I was physically there at the sites with you, but I only pretended to appreciate them. I don't remember anything about that day. I have no idea where we went. Could we go to those places again so I can truly experience them?"

Charley and Alicia each grasped one of Bella's hands and squeezed.

Alicia released her hand. "I could go to a couple of those sites five days in a row and still not see it all." She lifted her glass. "A toast to Bella's father for giving us the most amazing trip of our lives."

Bella clinked her glass with her friend's and sipped. She set the glass down on the red table cloth, her heart swelling with emotion. "I have the most thoughtful, generous parents in the world."

Charley leaned forward her wine glass gripped lightly in her right hand. "You should call your parents and let them know that you're okay."

Bella cringed with guilt. "You're right. With my worries about Alec I forgot how worried my parents have been. What time is it in the states?"

Alicia looked up at the clock. "I think they are about five hours behind us…should be about four-thirty back home."

Bella pulled her cell phone out of her clutch. "I'll go into the hallway and give them a quick call."

"Take your time."

Bella pushed her chair back and walked out of the lounge. Two upholstered chairs and a table with a flower arrangement were grouped halfway down the passageway. She took a seat and pressed favorites on her phone. She pressed a finger on her parent's name.

"Bella?" Her mom's shocked tone came through loud and clear.

"Hi, Mom."

"Is anything wrong? I didn't expect to hear from you."

"You should have expected to hear from me. I should have been calling every day. I just want you and Dad to know…"

"Hold on honey, I'm putting you on speaker. Your dad's here with me."

Bella's throat suddenly clogged with tears. "Hi, Dad."

"Hi, honey." Her dad's tone seemed overly cautious, and it broke her heart.

Bella ran a hand under her runny nose. "I wanted you both to know that a miracle happened on this ship. I'm free, as I told Charley and Alicia, of Daniel's hold over me."

"Oh, Bella, that is great news." Bella heard the tears in her mother's voice.

"How, honey?" Her father's voice revealed a sense of relief.

"I don't have time to go into the details. I'll tell you everything when I get home. But I will tell you that God intervened in a very unique way."

Bella's could hear her mother crying.

Her father cleared his throat. "Okay, honey, we'll be at the airport with Noah to pick you up."

Bella breathed out her son's name. "I can't wait to kiss and hug him. I'll see you in two days. I love you both."

"Love you, too."

Bella disconnected the call and leaned back in the chair. Talking to her parents had erased the last of her melancholy over Alec. Excitement coursed through her body as she contemplated the prospect of starting over. With Jesus on her side all things were possible. Suddenly as giddy as a six year-old, Bella rose to join her friends.

The captain's voice issued from the intercom. "Ladies and gentlemen, we are beginning our descent into Norfolk International Airport."

Bella straightened in her seat and rotated her shoulders.

"How was your nap?" Charley turned to her right as she closed her Francine Rivers' novel.

"Wonderful."

"It should have been. You slept for four hours. Wish I could sleep like that on a plane." She heaved a sigh. "I've been awake the entire flight."

Alicia, seated to Charley's left, flipped through a magazine she had bought at the airport in Venice. "I think I got about two hours...too excited about seeing my boys."

"And my girls."

"And Noah." Bella hastily added. "And my mom and dad."

Alicia and Charley looked at each other as Alicia said, "I think we're leaving a couple of someones out."

Charley cocked her head. "Leaving someone out…let me think…no, can't think of anyone."

Alicia laughed. "Your husband, you goof."

Charley grinned. "I would never leave him out. My long-suffering angel of a husband who changed dirty diapers for a week, settled the princess wars, soothed tears, tantrums and…well, I could go on and on. I have never met a man with so much patience."

Bella smiled. "You both have been truly blessed with your husbands."

"Absolutely." Alicia cleared her throat and changed the subject. "Bella, what is the first thing you plan to do when you get home?"

"Sell the house."

Charley's eyes widened. "But you love that house."

"No, it was always Daniel's house. I thought it was too big for the three of us, but he insisted. He wanted to live on a golf course. I wanted a backyard for Noah, but never mentioned it because I knew I wouldn't win. But I did make it into a home…I was content there the last couple of years."

"Any idea what neighborhood you want to live in?" Alicia closed her magazine.

"No. But I have a couple of months before school starts again to look at what's listed. I'd really like to be moved in somewhere before Noah starts school."

"Do you think Daniel will fight you on getting custody back?"

Bella quirked an eyebrow and laughed humorlessly. "No, Alicia, he'll be relieved. After he moved out, he never asked if Noah could stay for the whole weekend. He'd pick him up on Saturday and drop him off on Saturday. Why? Because he wanted Sunday set aside for Melissa. And he hasn't had any alone time with Melissa since he obtained temporary custody." Bella grinned. "The minute he's convinced I'm back to normal, Noah will be dropped at my doorstep along with all his belongings."

Charley squeezed her hand. "I'll be praying that that's true."

"It is. I can't..." Bella abruptly stopped talking when Charley tightened her grip on her fingers and shut her eyes. The plane had hit turbulence inside the clouds, jerking the plane slightly up and down. After a few long minutes, Bella glanced through the small round window. The clouds disappeared above them, and the airplane ride smoothed out. Charley opened her eyes and let go of Bella's hand. Bella closed and opened her left hand to get the circulation flowing again in her fingers.

Charley gave a sheepish grin. "Sorry about that."

"Not a problem. I always bring along a spare." She waggled the fingers on her right hand.

"Honestly, I don't know why I tense up in turbulence." She leaned past Bella and looked out the window. "Almost there. I can see the airport."

Butterflies awoke and fluttered inside Bella's stomach as the stewardess gave instructions for the landing.

The excitement was palatable as Bella and her friends picked up their pace past the screening stations. Their seats had been towards the back of the plane, and, looking ahead, Bella could see crowds of people embracing loved ones. Where were Noah and her parents? Her eyes scanned right and left, and suddenly there they were to the left of a group of six people greeting each other. Noah saw her and started running. Bella let go of the handle of her carryon and opened her arms, tears coursing down her cheeks. They wrapped arms around each other, and Bella's heart soared. "Noah, I missed you so much." She whispered in his ear.

"Me, too, mom." He pulled back from her hug. "Did you have a good time?"

Bella wiped her face. "I did. I'll tell you all about it on the way home."

Noah's eyes were large pools of happiness. "Mom, you look so much better."

Bella threw an arm around her son's shoulders as her parents moved towards them. "I am better…a lot better."

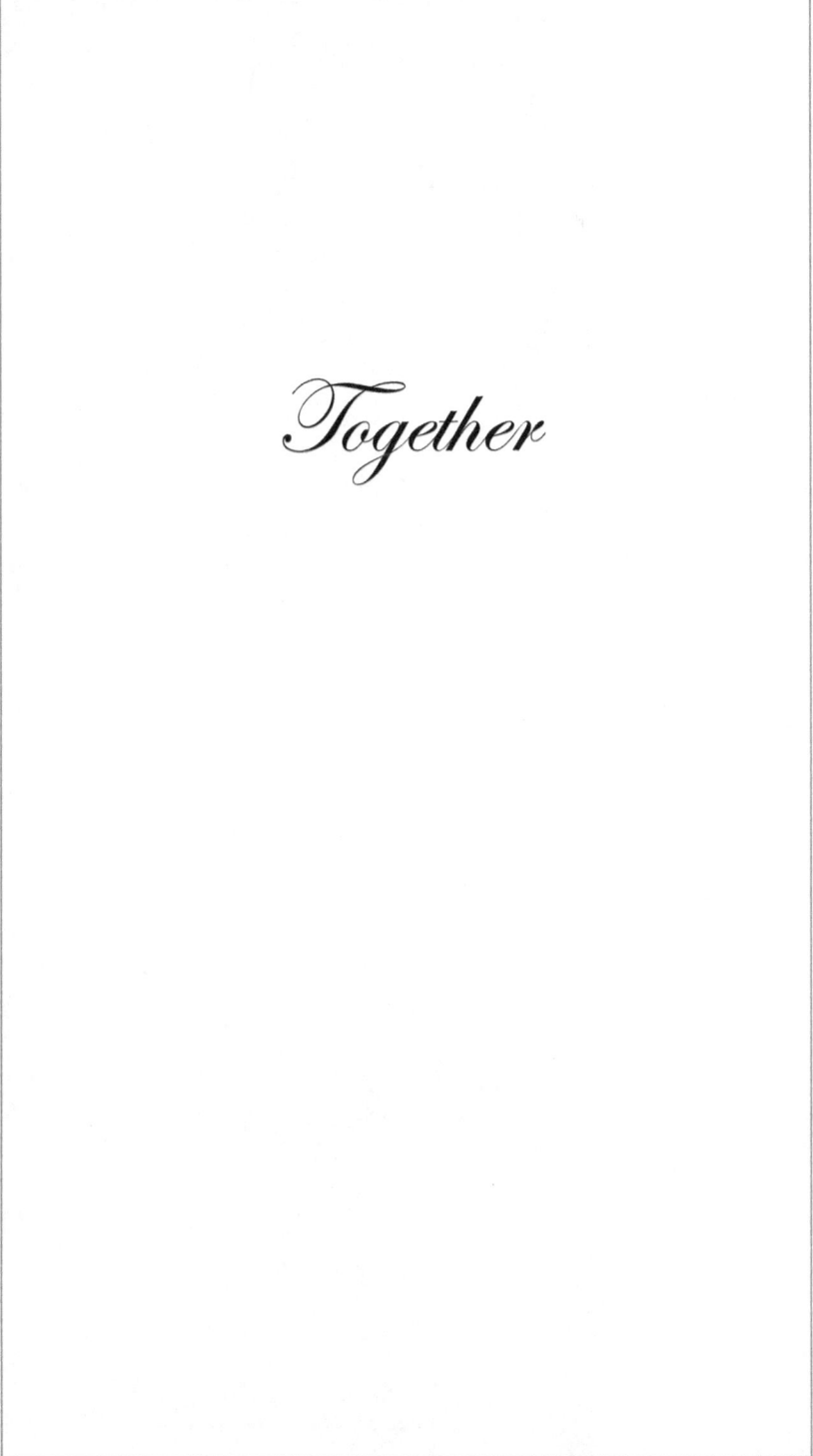

Together

CHAPTER

36

The house was a beehive of activity, and Bella could not stop grinning. The three boys had finished their lunch and retreated to Noah's room. Charley's oldest was protesting loudly that the boys wouldn't let her in to play video games. Charley scooped up the kids' paper plates and dumped them in the trash can, while Alicia and Bella laid out plates of sandwiches and fruit for the adults on the kitchen table. The seven adults sat down at the table with water or iced tea in hand.

"Mom, didn't you hear me? Noah won't let us in his room." Hannah whined.

Charley set down her glass. "And he doesn't have to. You have three choices…you can either go in the guest room and finish watching your movie, play quietly with your sisters, or go into time out."

Hannah huffed as she marched off to the living room rug, plopping down next to Madison and Addie. Charley turned back to the table and eyed Alicia. "Didn't you mention something about trading kids for a few days last year?"

Jarod choked on the bite of sandwich he was swallowing. He took a drink and cleared his throat. "What?"

Alicia turned to her husband. "She's kidding."

Charley's big bear of a husband, Dex, laughed. "No, she's not."

"I'll take them for a week." Everyone stared at Ginny, mouths agape.

"Oh, come on, you all know how much I adore children. I would have had six of my own if I'd been able."

Bella looked over at her mom. Ginny had been rushed into emergency surgery hours after Bella had been born. Doctors couldn't stop the sudden bleeding and had performed a hysterectomy.

"That is sweet of you Ginny, but…"

"No buts, Charley. I'm going to check my calendar and give you a date after we get back from this trip."

Bella laughed. Charley's face had lit up like Christmas had come early. "Sold, mom."

"The roads are clear from here to Timberline." John tapped his smartphone and took a bite of his sandwich.

Jarod swallowed a bite of apple. "Great. I was a worried after that winter storm blew through West Virginia two days ago."

"The powder should be great in the mountains," Alicia said.

Bella took a bite out of her banana. "Can't wait."

"You two can tell me all about each day of skiing when you get back to the lodge. Madison, Addie and I are going to spend most of the week in the craft and arts room."

Charley was not a skier. Bella and Alicia had encouraged her to learn how to ski on a trip to Massanutten during a college break, but Charley refused. Bella started as three pairs of feet pounded down the short hallway.

"Are you done yet? Can we go now?" Kelen's chin rested on his folded hands, his eyes imploring.

Bella grinned. "Almost, buddy. Give us ten minutes to clean up."

Groans escaped the mouths of all three boys. They turned and trudged back to Noah's room.

"I really like your new home, Bella...very cozy." Charley popped a couple of grapes in her mouth. "And I'm not surprised it's only one floor."

"I hated those stairs in the other house even before I fell down them. I'd hoped to find a place by the end of August, not mid-November, but nothing I looked at suited me." She looked around the open space encompassing the living, dining and kitchen areas. "It's perfect. I knew it the moment I walked in the door. I signed the papers the next day."

Alicia's eyes narrowed. "And you were sneaky about it, too."

Charley laughed. "Bella told me the story. She called and told you she had bought a house, and you were ticked that she hadn't *consulted with you* before buying it."

"And she was still mad when I picked her up to go see it."

Charley finished the tale. "You picked Alicia up at her house drove two blocks and pulled over to the curb. You opened the door, and Alicia wanted to know what you were doing. And you said, 'Don't you want to see my new home?'"

Bella laughed as she glanced at Alicia. "The look on your face. That was the first time I have ever been able to surprise you."

Alicia gave a begrudging smile. "You got me good. Best surprise ever…you moving in two blocks from us."

A loud wail had the adults' heads swiveling towards the living room. Hannah's voice was indignant. "Madison took Addie's baby doll."

Dex hopped up to soothe the tears.

Charley glanced at Ginny. "You sure you want to deal with this for a week?"

Ginny laughed as Bella pushed back her chair. "We'd better clean up and hit the road before the smaller male population starts a riot."

Alicia walked down Bella's front steps, automatically looking for her Chevy Equinox, forgetting for a moment that, two weeks ago, she and Jarod had traded her car for a van with more room for carting around their son's friends.

The corners of her lips turned up as she gazed at her new 'used' van. They had obtained an unbelievable deal on the four-year-old Honda Odyssey. A real blessing, it had turned out to be the perfect vehicle for this trip. It seated eight, which meant John, Ginny, Bella, and Noah didn't have to travel in a separate vehicle.

From the sidewalk, Alicia's boots crunched through an inch of frozen snow to the curb. She pressed a button on her car remote, and the side passenger door slowly slid open. Cameron, Noah, and Kelen climbed into the back. Jarod started the engine as John sat down in the front passenger seat. Alicia watched Charley and Dex strap their girls into car seats as she waited for Bella. Bella appeared on her porch, locked the door, and hurried over. Alicia slid onto the middle seat of the second row, next to Ginny. Bella sat down on her other side.

Bella laughed. "Well, this isn't going to work."

With their ski jackets on, there was no wiggle room. "Jarod…can you put the heat on full blast for a few minutes? We have to take off our jackets." Alicia gathered the three jackets and turned in her seat. "Cameron, lay these across the suitcases." She turned back, hastily strapping on her seat belt as Jarod pulled away from the curb, following behind Charley's van.

"How many hours until we get there?" said a voice from the third row of seats.

Ginny turned her head. "About four and a half hours, Noah." She turned back around. "Are those video games the boys are playing going to keep them occupied for the whole trip?"

Bella and Alicia grinned and said together. "Yes."

As Jarod turned right out of the neighborhood Bella sighed with contentment. Alicia turned her head slightly. "What is it, Bella?"

"I have an anniversary today."

Alicia was sure that Ginny's mask of puzzlement matched her own. "An anniversary?"

Bella lowered her voice. "Six months since God saved me and set me on a new path."

Alicia counted backwards in her head. "You're right it's the 23rd of December."

Ginny gave her daughter's hand a squeeze. "You have never looked happier."

"I have never felt happier." Bella continued to keep her voice low. "I never realized the scope and depth of the self-esteem issues I suffered because of Daniel until they evaporated six months ago."

Alicia suddenly laughed out loud. "I just thought of something completely random."

"Care to share?" Bella said.

"Remember on the airplane, when we were talking about when you might get…" She glanced over her shoulder to make sure Noah wasn't listening and then lowered her voice. "…custody of your son back? And you said, 'the minute Daniel thinks I'm back to normal.' You hit that nail smack on the head. Noah was back with you ten days later."

"And the day after dropping Noah off, he and Melissa were on a plane to Europe." Bella affirmed with a certain "I told you so" air.

Bella then took in a deep breath. "I have an announcement…I've decided I'm going back to school."

Alicia squeezed her friend's hand. "That's a great idea."

"I've already signed up for classes at William and Mary."

"Honey, that's wonderful. What will your masters be in?"

"Clinical Mental Health Counseling."

Ginny's eyebrows pulled together. "I haven't heard of that one."

"I'd like to try to help people who are going through what I went through. Pay it forward."

Alicia nodded. "Like you did with Alec."

"Yes."

Kelen's voice interrupted their conversation. "How much longer?"

As her laughter melded with Bella's and Ginny's, Alicia couldn't help comparing this Christmas holiday to last year's dismal, depressing holiday season. Sudden gratitude flowed through her, and in a fair voice she started singing the first refrain to 'Joy to the World.'

A loud, "mom" was groaned from the back of the van as Bella, Ginny, John, and Jarod joined in. Tears of joy streamed down her cheeks while Alicia continued to sing over the protests of the boys.

CHAPTER

37

The Valley Resort was a large structure of wood and stone. Bella admired it through the window of the van as Jarod, Dex, and John walked into the lobby to register. Switching her line of sight, she calculated that there was at least two feet of snow on the ground. Groups of skiers, dressed in colorful garb, passed by, skis and poles in hand, some going toward the lifts in the near distance, others returning to the resort.

Bella pulled on the door handle as their men exited the lobby pulling luggage carts. She stepped out and pulled in a lungful of the crisp, cold air. She arched her neck and watched a couple of wispy clouds laze across the baby blue sky. Shivering, she turned back to the van for her jacket. Ginny passed it to her, and she quickly zippered herself into it.

Charley walked over as John and Jarod started loading luggage onto one of the carts. "How was the trip?"

"Great. Boys did real well."

Charley looked over at her van where her three girls were insisting, in loud voices, that they wanted out of the van. "Unfortunately, I can't say the same. The DVDs' kept them quiet the first couple of hours, and then they

287

got bored. Addie fell asleep, but Madison and Hannah managed to fight back and forth from different car rows." The two oldest girl's voices grew even louder. "I better go set them free."

John, Ginny, and Alicia pulled the carts into the resort lobby, while Jarod and Dex drove their vans to parking spots. Bella grasped Madison's hand as she followed Charley into the warmth of the lobby. Christmas music played from hidden speakers. She gasped in delight as the automatic doors swooshed shut. She stepped to the left out of the doorway and looked up. Thick wooden beams crossed the ceiling. To her left a whole row of floor to ceiling windows looked out over the valley and mountain. Straight ahead, flames danced in a huge stone fireplace, their reflection dancing on the polished wooden floors. The lobby desk was to her right, and between the desk and windows, groupings of chairs and sofas in earth tones invited cozy chats.

Alicia and Charley walked over, each clutching a little girl's hand.

"Are you envisioning what I am?" Bella said.

"Dex insisting that he put the girls to bed so I can sit on that comfortable sofa facing the fire, a glass of wine in hand?"

Bella laughed. "Close. I was thinking about the three of us on the sofa in front of that fire with hot chocolate and marshmallows."

Alicia sighed. "Both sound great."

Cameron and the other two boys bounded over from the tall windows, excitement plastered all over their faces.

"Mom, can we go snowboarding now?" Cameron pleaded.

Alicia shook her head. "It's too late. We'll be going down to dinner in an hour."

"Aw, mom, can't we eat later."

"I know how excited you are, but it takes a while to decide which ski packages we want... and then we have to get fitted with equipment—besides everyone's hungry."

"I'm not." Kelen insisted.

"It's getting dark out."

"But they have lights for night skiing." Noah looked at Bella.

Alicia blew out a breath, and Charley giggled.

Alicia turned to Charley. "You just wait...Hannah will be a preteen soon."

"Mom." Cameron brought her attention back to the situation at hand.

"Go ask your dad."

Cameron's face deflated. "He already said no."

"Thought so. Tomorrow will be here before you know it."

Shoulders slumping, all three boys walked over to the carts where the three men stood patiently waiting. Ginny emerged from the restroom and walked over to John.

Madison tugged on Bella's fingers. "Can we watch cartoons?" Bella gazed down at Charley's mini-me. "Sure, Maddy, let's go."

✦   ✦   ✦

Three hours later, Bella, Charley, Alicia, Ginny, and John sat in one of the groupings close to the stone-frame fireplace. The heat of the flickering flames gave off pleasant warmth as Bella sipped her wine. She had given in to the majority who opted to hold off on the hot chocolate until tomorrow, after skiing most of the day in the frigid temperatures.

John sat forward in his upholstered arm chair. "I feel guilty sitting here while Jarod is watching the boys."

Alicia smiled at John. "He's coming down. Bella and I agree that they're old enough to be by themselves for an hour or so in the room." She looked up. "Speak of the devil."

"I think you mean angel." The right corner of Charley's lips quirked up

Jarod walked over and sat on the loveseat next to Alicia. She glanced over. "How are the boys?"

"Great...tearing up the empire."

"Jarod, do you want something from the bar?"

"No, thanks, John...time to start watching my girlish figure." Jarod patted his stomach "Beer can really pack on the pounds." He turned to Bella. "Noah wants to join Kelen tomorrow and learn how to snowboard. I don't mind teaching him."

Bella shook her head. "I asked Daniel, and he said no. He said it was a lot more dangerous than skiing."

"And no point arguing...what Daniel says goes." John's tone was bitter.

Ginny touched John's hand with her fingers. He looked over. "You need to look on the bright side. This is our first vacation with our grandson. And we've seen more of Noah in the last year than in the last ten years combined."

Time to change the subject. Bella turned to Charley. "Dex is going to teach Hannah how to ski?"

"Yeah, she wants to try. Dex skied for a few years with friend's families when he was a teen—his parents weren't skiers. He doesn't have any interest in skiing himself on this trip. He'll spend the whole time helping Hannah."

"He is wonderful with the girls," Ginny said, "it's too bad he can't join us tonight."

"Won't join us." Charley sighed. "They have a babysitting service here in the resort. I tried to get him to come down." Her smile was rueful. "I love Dex to pieces, but sometimes it's hard living with an introvert. He hates social gatherings. He'd much rather be upstairs with the girls playing and reading to them than down here with us. Remember when the Tidewater Art Gallery showcased my paintings last month and I couldn't find him? The owner of the gallery found him hiding in the men's bathroom."

"Oh, that's where he went. I wondered." Ginny took a sip of her wine.

Bella smothered a yawn. "I think I'm going to call it a night. I've been up since five this morning, and Noah will probably be waking me up early to get to the slopes."

Alicia set her empty wine glass on the coffee table. "I'll go with you. The boys aren't going to let Jarod and I sleep in." She stood up.

Charley settled herself deeper into the sofa. "I'm staying right here. I haven't had a relaxing break like this from tantrums and crying since our cruise."

"John and I will stay with you, Charley."

"I'll stay a bit longer, too." Jarod pushed up from the loveseat. "I think I'll go get a bottled water." He kissed Alicia on the cheek and headed for the lounge.

Bella blew a kiss to her parents before following Alicia to the elevators.

38

Skiers traversed down the intermediate slope under an impossibly blue sky. Patches of snow that had yet to be flattened by skis sparkled like diamond dust. Bella widened her skis looking through them to the slope below. She watched a couple of teenagers on snowboards whiz past a skier bent double adjusting her boot. Her hand tightened slightly on the safety bar as the ski lift passed over a tower.

Ginny swiveled her shoulders and waved from the lift in front of them. Noah lifted a gloved hand and waved back. John sat next to Ginny, and Alicia and Cameron rode together in the lift behind them. Bella glanced at the sign on the tower they were approaching. It warned that skiers should lift up the points of their skis before disembarking. She and Noah did as instructed and skied off the lift a minute later.

She followed Noah, sliding up smoothly beside her parents. Alicia and Cameron joined them, Cameron arriving with only one foot strapped to his snowboard.

John lowered his goggles over his eyes. "Remember, Cameron and Noah, if you get to the bottom before we do you wait for the rest of the group. No going off on your own. We ride the lift up together."

"That's not fair Papa, you'll take *forever*."

Alicia grinned. "Obviously, Noah's never skied with John."

Bella shook her head. "First time." She reached under Noah's chin to make the sure the helmet strap was secure.

Alicia turned to Cameron. "Remember your dad's rules. No going down the slope like a bat out of...Hades. And stay out of the skiers and other snowboarder's paths."

"I will, Mom."

Bella blinked. Cameron's voice startled her sometimes with its sudden change to the deep tones of puberty. She followed as the group moved to the lip of the slope. Cameron strapped his other foot to the board, turned sideways, hopped, and started his run down the slope. Noah pushed off with his poles and followed Cameron. The three women laughed as John caught up with Noah four seconds into his run and waved his pole at his grandson as he passed by.

Bella lowered her goggles, pulled in a breath, released it, and pushed off. She skied in a zigzag pattern...not comfortable tearing down the slope as she used to as a teenage and a twenty-something. Exhilaration pumped through her body as she kept an eagle eye on her son further down the slope. Cameron was nowhere in sight, but she wasn't worried. He was a responsible kid with a good head on his shoulders.

She and Ginny were the last to reach the bottom, skiing sideways to come to a stop. As the boys took off for the lifts, Bella hooked an arm through her mom's arm and sighed with contentment.

The sun was lowering in the sky when Bella skied off the lift for the last run of the day. She rotated her shoulders and bowed her back to help relieve her aching muscles. Ginny blew her husband a kiss before skiing off down the slope. Alicia stopped beside Bella as Cameron started his last run. "I'm glad this is the last one. I'm beat."

Bella's eyes widened as she smiled. "No way. Not the piloxing queen."

"Oh, yeah. Muscles I haven't used in a while are screaming."

"Mine too."

"Come on, mom, I'll race you down the slope." Noah's face was flush with excitement.

"Can't buddy. I'm really sore…and I don't want to risk a fall. Race your Papa again."

"Come on, Noah. I'll let you win this time." Grinning, John poled over to the top of the slope. He and Noah planted their poles, slid back and forth on their skies and pushed off.

Bella paused at the lip of the slope for a few seconds to watch her two loved ones race down the hill. She positioned her skis and poles, but before she could push off a snowboarder all in black jumped in front of her and tore down the slope.

Alicia fumed. "What an idiot."

As Bella and Alicia started their run, Bella watched the snowboarder dodging other skiers and snowboarders with only inches to spare as he picked up speed, barely avoiding a collision with a teenage girl. As he continued his reckless run down the slope, Bella's heart suddenly jumped in her throat. *Noah and her father were directly in his path!* Instinct had her turning her skis straight down the slope to chase after him and protect her son. He was closing the gap fast. *Why wasn't he swerving around them!* Bella, realizing she wasn't going to catch the out-of-control snowboarder started screaming, "Look out!"

Bella didn't know if her dad heard her yell or some instinct had him looking over his shoulder. All of a sudden, he maneuvered toward Noah to try and block the reckless snowboarder. The scene before Bella seemed to slow down in motion as she stared in horror. At the last possible second the snowboarder tried to slice to Noah's left to avoid the inevitable collision. Too little, too late. He clipped Noah's left ski and both went flying through the air.

A yell of anguish burst from Bella's throat as she tore down the slope to her son's screaming, crumpled form. John had released his bindings and stuck his skies in the snow in an 'X' formation to alert the ski patrol before kneeling beside his grandson. Bella whipped the points of her skis hard to the left to slow down and came to an abrupt stop. She unclipped her bindings and dropped to her knees, her heart thudding in her chest and her gloved hands trembling. Noah was sobbing in agony.

John spoke in calm measured tones. "Noah, your mom and I are right here. Tell me what hurts."

"My leg!" Noah sobbed out.

"Which one?

"Left…left!" Noah lay on his side, wailing.

Bella gripped Noah's gloved hand. "Okay, honey, help should be here any minute." She looked up the slope and sobbed with relief as she glimpsed the bright red jackets of the paramedics skiing down to them with a toboggan. She glanced to her right. Alicia had a gloved hand over her mouth and tears streaming down her face. "Alicia, can you go on down and tell Mom what happened."

Alicia nodded and took off as three members of the ski patrol arrived. Two stopped by Noa,h and one headed to the snowboarder.

"Move back, please, we need to make an assessment," said the taller of the two men. He knelt down next to Bella's sobbing child.

The other man turned to John. "Mister…?"

"John…just call me John, and this is Bella."

"John, Bella, I need you to put your skis back on and meet us at the bottom of the run."

"But I want…"

John turned Bella towards her skis. "We need to do as they say. Noah's in good hands. They handle accidents multiple times a day."

As she pushed her right boot into the binding her tear-filled eyes narrowed at the sight of the snowboarder who had crashed into her son. He was climbing to his feet assisted by the paramedic. Anger burned white hot. She shoved her other boot in its binding. Grabbing her poles, she skied down to the snowboarder ignoring her father's shout to wait.

The paramedic looked over as Bella came to an abrupt stop beside him. "Ma'am, you…"

Bella ignored him, her rage needing instant release. "What is wrong with you?! You could have killed my son!"

"Ma'am…" The paramedic tried to block her as she moved closer to the snowboarder.

John skied to a stop beside Bella. He put his hand on her arm. "Bella…"

Bella jerked her arm away, chest heaving and heat burning her cheeks. "You broke his leg!"

The snowboarder turned unfocused eyes in her direction. "I'm sorry, I didn't see him."

Bella leaned in and sniffed. Her eyes widened. "You've been drinking!"

John grabbed her arm. "We have to go. They have Noah strapped down."

The rage disappeared, as fear took over. She allowed John to steer her away and followed him down the mountain, tears streaming down her cheeks. She and her father beat the paramedics down the slope, as they had to go at a slower pace. Cameron, Alicia, and Ginny were huddled together.

Ginny broke away and rushed over. "How is he?"

John hugged her. "We think it's a broken leg."

Bella watched the paramedics until they reached the bottom of the hill and then rushed over. Her son wasn't moving. Fear had become a living, breathing monster– ready to consume her. "What's wrong? Why isn't he moving? Please…he isn't…"

"He's passed out from the pain, Ma'am." The paramedics tone was reassuring.

Without turning her head, Bella sensed the presence of the others. "Do you know how bad…his injury is?"

The taller member of the ski patrol spoke. "Most like-ly…a fractured tibia. We've called for a medical evac. We cut away the ski pants on the left leg. The break didn't puncture the skin. But we don't know how many pieces the tibia could be in or if the fibula is broken, too. We need to get him to the hospital as soon as possible."

"I'm coming with him."

"Yes, ma'am, you can follow us to the helipad."

Ginny removed a glove and wiped the tears from her daughter's face. "I'll bring you a change of clothes."

"I'll go with you to the helipad to take your skis and poles," John said.

Bella hugged her mom then turned to follow the to-boggan carrying her son.

Alicia, John, and Ginny approached the equipment shed, Cameron in tow. Alicia blew out a relieved breath when she glimpsed Jarod and Kelen second in line to turn in their snowboards. "Jarod!"

He whipped his head around.

"Can you turn in our equipment? We have to get to the hospital."

"Noah broke his leg," Cameron said.

"How?"

John's voice was grim. "An intoxicated snowboarder."

Jarod helped John gather everyone's skis and poles and lean them up against the large open window of the shed.

Alicia kissed her husband. "I have no idea when we'll be back."

"No worries."

She, John, and Ginny headed to the lodge at a brisk pace. Alicia pulled her gloves off, stuffing them in the jacket pockets. She pulled her cell phone from an inside pocket and texted Charley, letting her know what happened. Charley texted back saying she would meet her at her room.

The lobby doors slid open, and Alicia, John, and Ginny rushed to the elevators as fast as they could manage in their ski boots. As they exited the elevator, John said they would meet back in the lobby in twenty minutes. Alicia hurried down the hallway to her room. Charley enveloped her in a hug when she reached her door. She pulled away and swiped her card in the lock.

Twenty-one minutes later, Alicia was back in the lobby, she and Charley rushing to join John and Ginny by the glass doors. Ginny had a large bag slung over her shoulder.

John had his phone in his hand. "I've put the address to the hospital in the GPS."

Alicia walked through the doors and into rapidly-descending darkness. She hurried to her van. The four of them piled in, and Alicia backed out of the lot. "How far to the hospital?"

John looked down at the phone that was calmly instructing no one in particular to 'proceed to the route.' "It says thirty-five minutes."

Alicia put her blinker on as she approached the road.

"I wish it had been me."

Alicia glanced over at John seated next to her before turning right.

"It's his second break in a year and a half." He continued his tone grim. "And we're going to have to deal with a tirade from Daniel when he arrives."

Alicia darted her eyes to the right and back. "Did you call him?"

"No. But I'm sure Bella has. And she probably got an earful on the phone."

"But it wasn't her fault!" Charley was incensed.

"Doesn't matter. She was the one with Noah when it happened. She took the full force of his anger when Noah broke his arm. He blamed her," Ginny said.

The occupants of the van fell silent, and Alicia wondered if their thoughts were similar to hers. *Bella will be stressed enough dealing with Noah's broken leg. She shouldn't have to deal with Dan's wrath.* She was startled from her dour musings when the female voice on the GPS told her to turn right onto a main highway. Her hands turned the wheel. Twenty-five minutes to go.

The code alarm went off, and Bella froze mid-stride in her pacing of the emergency waiting room. *Noah!* She rushed over to the receptionist manning the desk. "Please, is there any way to find out if that alarm is for my son?"

The young woman nodded. "Yes Ma'am. What is his name?"

"Noah Stanford."

"I'll let you know as soon as I find out."

The woman picked up the phone, and Bella moved back a couple of steps, rubbing the knuckles on her right hand, and then the left hand as she waited.

"Bella!"

Bella turned toward the sound of her mother's voice. She was striding through the glass doors.

"Ms. Claremont."

Bella took a step towards her mother.

"Ms. Claremont."

Bella's head jerked slightly. *She means me.* She had switched back to her maiden name two weeks ago. She turned to the receptionist, conscious of holding her breath.

"The code wasn't your son."

Bella released the held breath as her mother dropped a bag to the floor and gave her a quick hug. "How is Noah?" she whispered.

Bella shook her head. "I haven't…" She suddenly turned towards the sound of the double doors opening next to the desk.

A doctor in a white coat walked out and addressed the room at large. "Ms. Claremont?" Bella's heart pounded in her ears. "Yes."

The doctor, a young man with jet black hair, held out his hand. Bella shook it. "I'm Dr. Murray."

The words erupted from her. "How is my son?"

"I'm afraid he has a tibia fracture that will require surgery. Since he is a minor, you'll need to sign a form giving us permission to perform the operation."

Bella let out a gasp and covered her mouth. John put his arm around her.

"He's had an x-ray and is getting a bone scan now. After that he will be prepped for surgery." The doctor smiled reassuringly. "You son is being operated on by one of the best orthopedic surgeons in the country. He is in very good hands."

John inhaled. "How bad is the break?"

"It's a displaced fracture. The tibia was broken into two pieces that don't line up. The good news is that it doesn't appear that the fibula was broken. The surgeon will go in, line the two pieces up and hold them in place with a plate and screws. He's viewing the x-rays now."

The doctor smiled reassuringly again. "I need to get back to the ER. A nurse will come and get you when the scan is done. Then you can come back and sit with your son before surgery."

Bella tried to smile and failed. Her heart was a panicked bird beating against her rib cage. *Surgery? He'll be given anesthesia...what if he...*

"Bella."

"What...huh?" She became aware of Alicia staring at her.

"What is it? You're white as a ghost."

Bella took in the worried looks on her family and friends faces. "Sorry...I...they're going to put Noah under..."

"He'll be fine. Remember...I had three C-sections with my girls." Charley squeezed Bella's hand. "Bella...God has this under control."

She pulled in a deep breath and nodded. The bird in her chest stopped panicking.

"Bella?"

She looked at her mom.

"Did you call Daniel?"

"Right after Noah went into the ER."

John's lips thinned. "What did he say?"

"He would throw an overnight bag together and drive up."

John's eyebrows drew up. "And?"

"That's all he said."

John frowned. "Really?"

Bella smiled. "Really. I had braced for a tirade. But he was actually calm and just said he would drive up."

"Well…" John cleared his throat "Well."

"Honey, would you like to change?" Ginny picked up the bag with Bella's clothes.

"Oh, Mom, thank you. My lower legs feel like they're about to detach with the weight of theses boots." Bella took the bag from her mom.

Bella left the restroom dressed in jeans, Uggs, and a black sweater, the clothes bag slung over her shoulder and ski boots snuggled in her arms.

John walked forward, relieving her of the bag and boots. He glanced at Alicia. "Can I have the keys to your van?"

Alicia handed the keys to John and turned to Bella, her eyes glistening. "Oh, Bella, I'm sorry that this happened to Noah. It's so unfair."

Bella squeezed Alicia's hand. "Thank you."

"Ms. Claremont?" Bella turned towards the receptionist. "I need you to sign a couple of forms for the surgery."

Bella walked over to the desk. As the woman explained each form and asked for Bella's signature or initials, her thoughts kept returning to the doctor's diagnosis.

"That's it." The receptionist smiled encouragingly.

Bella nodded and walked back to her family and friends.

Ginny handed Bella her purse and put an arm around her daughter's shoulder. "Come on. Let's go see if the cafeteria is open. It will probably be another thirty minutes at least until you can see your son."

"No, mom, I..."

"Honey, you have to eat to keep your strength up for Noah. You need a distraction. You can't sit here worrying yourself to death."

"Mom, I can't..."

Alicia sighed dramatically. "Well, I haven't eaten since eleven-thirty...I've burned off those calories on the slope...I'm starving...but you are my best friend and I refuse to leave your side."

Charley tried to hide a smile as she launched at Alicia with mock outrage. "Hey, I thought I was your best friend. Ungrateful...two timing..." She turned to Bella. "You are now my best friend, and I insist you let *me* sacrifice nourishment to stay at your side." She turned back to Alicia and stuck out her tongue.

Bella chortled. "Okay, you win. I'll come with you. Just let me tell the receptionist where I'll be and to page me when I can see Noah."

Bella took a bite of her fried chicken, and immediately the stress molecules coursing through her body eased up. She picked up her napkin and wiped a bit of grease that had dripped onto her chin.

"How is it?" Charley licked her lips as she stared at the chicken breast dangling from Bella's greasy left hand.

"Charley, if you want a piece of chicken go get it. It's okay to indulge once in a while." Alicia's voice was a mixture of exasperation and amusement.

Charley looked down at her baked pork chop. Her face morphed from longing to determination. "No, I've come too far. One piece will lead to two, and before you know it, I'll be a hundred and seventy pounds again." She sliced off a piece of pork chop and shoved it in her mouth.

Bella swallowed a bite of mashed potatoes. "Thanks for insisting I eat. I needed this."

"Noah will be fine, honey." John took a sip of his iced tea. "You probably don't remember me telling you, but when I was a teenager, I fell off the first horse I ever rode and broke my femur in three places. I was in traction for almost a month, a full leg cast for six months, and physical therapy for almost two years. And here I am good as new."

"John!" Ginny's shocked face had turned to face her husband. "That is not helping."

"What...what did I say?"

Ginny turned to Bella. "Honey, Noah's break is not that bad. He will not be in traction, I'm sure he won't be in a cast for six months or therapy for two years." She turned back to her husband and glared until he cleared his throat, and then he spoke, "Your mom's right...thoughtless of me...sorry."

The hand that held Bella's forkful of food had frozen halfway to her mouth at the word 'traction.' She breathed out the held breath and placed the fork in her mouth.

"I, for one, would sue that intoxicated snowboarder." Alicia's eyes flashed with anger.

John's eyes were narrow slits. "I'm calling the police department tomorrow and make sure he gets charged. If he's not punished, he'll do it again, and the next time someone might die."

Bella knew the multitude of emotions in her chest jockeying for the upper hand was showing on her face when she saw the look of alarm on Charley's face. She closed her eyes and breathed deep. *God is in control.*

The alarm had moved to Charley's voice. "Bella are you alright?"

Bella opened her eyes and nodded.

An overhead speaker came to life. "Would Ms. Claremont please come to the emergency room."

Bella wiped her hands with her napkin and pushed back her chair. Ginny started to stand up. "No, mom, you and everyone else stay and finish eating. I'll be the only one allowed in to see Noah. I'll let you know when he's being wheeled into surgery." She hurried out of the cafeteria, her heart thumping against her ribs.

A nurse in navy blue scrubs pushed aside the curtain and stepped aside. Noah's face was as pale as dishwater and his eyes squeezed tight, leaking tears. Bella rushed to her son's side.

"Noah," she whispered.

He opened his eyes and started crying harder.

"Oh, Noah, honey." Bella's eyes welled even more as she took her son's hand.

The nurse hovered at Bella's side. "I'm sorry, but you only have a couple of minutes. The surgeon's prepping, and the operating room nurse will be here soon to wheel him to surgery."

"Mom… it hurts so bad." Noah hiccoughed. "They said they can't give me pain pills because I'm going into surgery."

"Only a couple of minutes more and they'll give you something to make you sleep and take the pain away through the IV attached to your hand."

Sensing a presence, Bella turned to see Dr. Murray stop by her side. "Hanging in there, champ?"

Noah tried to put on a brave face and nodded.

Dr. Murray turned to Bella. "Normally, the surgeon would take a few minutes to explain the procedure he is going to perform on your son, but he wanted to start right away before swelling is an issue. He'll talk with you after the surgery."

"Is the caboose ready to leave the station?" A nurse in surgical gown and cap smiled brightly.

Even with the pain he was in, Noah managed to roll his eyes. Laughter bubbled up, but fear squashed it as Bella squeezed Noah's hand and moved away from his bed. "I'll be the first face you see when you wake up, honey. Oh, I almost forgot. Your dad's on the way." Noah's eyes lit up. Bella wiped at her eyes. "I love you."

"Me, too, mom.

The nurse disengaged the brake and wheeled the bed out of the curtained cubicle. Dr. Murray placed a hand on her arm and squeezed. "He'll be fine Ms. Claremont. Dr. Kaselberg is the best there is."

Frozen…adrenalin pumping through her body…Bella stared at Dr. Murray's back as he left the cubicle. *Alec?*

40

A hand gently tugged at her arm. "Ms. Claremont?" Bella blinked and swiveled her head to the right.

"I'll escort you back to the emergency room. The receptionist will give you directions to the waiting room for friends and family of surgery patients."

Bella knew she should respond, but she was still trying to grasp the impossible. *Alec...here?*

The nurse in the navy scrubs tugged again, and Bella followed like an obedient puppy. As the doors to the emergency room waiting area came in to view, she shook her head in denial. *No...it's just a coincidence. He can't be the only Kaselberg.*

The nurse stopped. "Right through those doors." She turned to go back the way she had come.

"Wait!" Bella emerged from her shock. "What is Dr. Kaselberg's first name?"

The nurse's eyes drew inward in thought, and then she smiled. "I believe it's Alec." She turned and walked away.

Bella stared after her...her heartbeats thrumming in her ears. *Alec...here? But he was going to...Africa.* A smile curved her lips at the thought of seeing Alec again. She took a step and froze. Her eyes widened, and her hand shot to her mouth. *He's operating on my son!* Six months ago, he was locked in his cabin so he wouldn't kill himself and now he's operating on my son? Her heartbeats increased, and suddenly it was hard to breathe.

A young woman in tights and a long sweater stopped beside her. "Ma'am are you okay?"

Bella mentally slapped herself and pulled in a deep breath. "Yes, thank you."

"Are you sure? You're white as a ghost."

Bella pulled in another breath. "Yes...my son just went into surgery."

"Oh...I understand. Can I get you a cup of water or something?"

"No...my family is waiting for me. Thank you again."

Bella managed to put one foot in front of the other and soon reached the doors to the emergency waiting area. Drawing in another breath to try to slow down her racing heart, she walked through the door. Ginny and Charley jumped to their feet in alarm. Alicia and John followed.

Ginny moved to her in a rush. "Oh, God, Bella what's wrong? Did something happen to..."

"No...no... Noah's fine. Well...he's not fine...in a lot of pain...but he's being wheeled into surgery." Bella was finding it hard to concentrate.

Ginny sagged with relief as the other three huddled around Bella. "The look on your face I thought..."

I need to be alone...now. Bella cleared her throat. "We're supposed to go to the surgical waiting room."

"I'll go find out where it's located." John walked off.

"Bella, you don't look good," Alicia said.

"I…" Bella could feel perspiration on her forehead. "I just need to be alone for a few minutes. I'll meet you in the waiting room."

Charley nodded with sympathy. "You're having a hard time dealing with the surgery. It's okay. Join us when you're ready."

Bella accepted the hugs and then moved to an empty row of vinyl chairs and sat down. She waved with a hand that trembled until her father, mother, Alicia and Charley disappeared through the doors that led to the main part of the hospital. She covered her face with her hands. *Noah…please…God, keep Noah safe. What if Alec isn't emotionally stable? What if he snaps? Please don't let him make a mistake with my son.* Bella lifted her head and wiped her eyes.

"Bella."

Bella froze eyes wide. It was the same voice that had been in her head when she was on the cruise…God's voice.

"I am in control."

Shame had Bella bowing her head and closing her eyes. *In the cafeteria, I put my total faith in God to take care of my son and now I've shown God how shallow that faith really is.*

Bella squared her shoulders and pulled in a shaky breath. She didn't understand why Alec was allowed to operate so soon after trying to commit suicide–she shook her head, forcing the image of Alec climbing the railing out of her head—but she would trust in God to take care of Noah.

She rose from the chair and left the emergency room.

✦　✦　✦

"How long has it been now, Dad?"

John looked at his watch. "Three and a half hours."

"Why is it taking so long?" Bella rubbed her fingers across her knuckles.

"I don't know honey." John sighed.

Bella rose from her chair and paced across the patterned gray carpet. *You are in control…but please, God.*

"Would you like me to get you another cup of coffee, Bella?"

She stopped and looked at Alicia. "No, I'm bouncing off the walls from the three cups I've already…" She paused at the thinning of Alicia's mouth and the narrowing of her eyes as they focused to the left of her. She whirled around as Daniel walked through the doorway holding the hand of his very pregnant wife. His eyes found Bella.

"They said at the desk that Noah's still in surgery."

Although she was working on forgiving Daniel, she wasn't quite there yet. But for Noah's sake, she managed to have a cordial relationship with him and Michelle. She nodded as she rubbed her knuckles. "It's making me anxious."

"Understandable."

Four jaws dropped. Bella would have found it funny any other time.

"One of the nurses filled me in on the type of break and surgical procedure. Can you fill me in on what happened on the ski slope?"

Bella sat back down in the padded chair of variegated Prussian blue and dark gray. "He was hit from behind by an intoxicated snowboarder."

The color in Daniel's face heightened and then faded when Michelle squeezed his hand. "Is he being charged?"

"You can take it to the bank. I'm calling the police station tomorrow," John said, his eyes flashing anger.

Bella's eyes flicked back to Daniel. None of the past antagonism usually reserved for her father was evident as he nodded. "Good."

Daniel gently pulled Michelle down beside him in a chair across from Charley. Bella almost smiled when Alicia crossed her arms and legs in an aggressive manner. It looked like Alicia was having just as hard a time forgiving Daniel as she was.

Silence rained until Charley—ever the diplomat—started a conversation with Michelle about the baby. Butterflies erupted in Bella's gut. She jumped out of her chair and walked to the window to stare out at the cold night sky.

"Ms. Claremont?"

Bella turned and gasped. It was Alec...but it wasn't. The man standing in the doorway exuded health and vigor. He was thirty pounds heavier. His face had gone from an invalid pallor to ruddy. His hair had been professionally clipped to a basic military style cut. The only thing familiar to Bella was the blue eyes and slight stubble probably due to a late night in the operating room. Emotions warred within her, and it wasn't a pretty mix. She wanted to hug him and slap him at the same time.

Bella's shock was reflected on Alec's face. He took a step forward then stopped as if he suddenly realized his purpose for being in the waiting the room was not to gape in shock at someone he hadn't seen in six months. Alec addressed the room at large. "Is there a Ms. Claremont?"

Bella walked towards Alec. Her heart started to pound in her chest. *Please, Lord Jesus, good news.* "That's me. How is my son?"

Confusion flitted across Alec's face and was gone. "Your son came through the surgery fine. It took longer than anticipated because we discovered a slight fracture to the fibula that wasn't visible in the x-ray. It had to be repaired along with the tibia. He has a plate and screws to hold the broken pieces of bone together, which will be removed once the bones knit back together. He's young and healthy...three or four months, and his leg will be good as new."

As the fear drained away, Bella's knees weakened, and she backed into a chair. She looked up. "Will he be able... to walk normally?"

Alec smiled. "Absolutely."

Same smile.

"Would you like to sit with him? He should be waking up soon?"

"Yes." Suddenly remembering Daniel, she looked over at him. His face showed his relief. Holding out her hand towards her ex-husband, she turned back to Alec. "This is Noah's father, Daniel. Can he come to?"

"Of course." Alec turned to the gray-haired female volunteer sitting at a small desk. "Can you page Jessica to escort Noah's parents to post-op?"

She nodded.

Alec turned back to Bella. "Noah will be out of it most of the night. I start my rounds at eight in the morning. I'll talk to you and Daniel then."

He turned and left the waiting room. Bella turned her gaze back to her friends and family and jerked back at the expressions on their faces. Alicia and Charley couldn't have looked more shocked if Daniel had announced he was leaving Michelle and coming back to her. Her parents' expressions were milder...puzzlement.

Alicia found her voice first. "What is Alec doing here?"

Bella tried to pull off a nonchalant shrug. "No idea."

"But I thought he was going...to Asia...or Africa." Charley's shocked expression had morphed to confusion.

"You know Noah's surgeon?"

Bella turned to Daniel. "Yes...we...uh...met on the cruise ship."

He shook his head. "That makes this a very small world."

"Is that the doctor that..."

Bella whipped around and glared at her mother, hoping her message was clear. Ginny swallowed, pressing her lips together.

Bella spoke in even tones. "Yes, mom, that's the doctor Charley, Alicia, and I met on the ship."

"Ms. Claremont?"

A nurse stood in the doorway. "I'm here to take you to your son."

Daniel squeezed Michelle's hand and rose to his feet. Bella heard Charley ask Michelle if she would like something out of the vending machine before following the nurse to a section of the hospital that held cubicles of post-op patients. The nurse pulled aside the gray-green curtain. Daniel drew in a breath.

Noah lay on the bed perfectly still. His dark lashes stood out against the porcelain paleness of his cheeks. Bella gazed at his chest and didn't release her own drawn-in breath until she watched it rise and fall twice. Daniel moved two chairs close to the bed, and they sat down. Bella placed her fingers on Noah's hand, and Daniel brushed a hand through their son's hair.

"He looks so…" Bella grappled for the right words. "… helpless."

"I was thinking…young…younger than his age."

A rotund nurse with freckles came through the curtain and walked to the other side of the bed. She leaned over. "Hey, Noah. Time to wake up. Your folks are here."

Bella watched her son's eyelashes flutter.

The nurse's voice rose an octave. "That's right, wake up, now."

Noah's chin rose, and then he moved his head on the pillow.

"Almost there, Noah. Wake up and say hello to your mom and dad."

Noah's lashes fluttered again, and his eyes opened.

"Good job, Noah." Noah turned his head towards the voice. The nurse flashed a brilliant smile. "Your folks are here."

Noah swallowed heavily and moved his head on the pillow. His barely-focused eyes fell on Bella. A small smile appeared. "Mom." Bella's eyes filled as she squeezed her son's hand. "Your dad's here." His eyes moved to the right. "Dad?"

Daniel squeezed Noah's shoulder. "How do you feel?"

Noah's tongue reached out and licked his lips. "My mouth's so dry."

The nurse picked up a cup with slightly melted ice chips. "Lift your head, Noah, and open your mouth." Noah complied, and the nurse spooned a few chips on his tongue. Noah sighed, laying his head back on the pillow. The nurse returned the cup to a bedside tray and turned to Bella and Daniel. "He'll be moved to a room within the next hour. Will you need cots in the room?"

Bella nodded. "I will."

Daniel shook his head.

"I'll be back when it's time to move him."

Bella turned back to Noah. She leaned over, smoothing back his hair. "Do you know how much I love you?"

Noah's smile swelled her heart. "A lot."

"You came through surgery like a champ, Noah."

Noah blinked at his dad. "Did they fix my leg?"

"They sure did. A few months and you'll be good as new."

Noah nodded. His eyes started to close. "I'm sleepy."

Bella ran her fingers gently across Noah's hand. "You go back to sleep, honey. I'll be here all night."

"And I'll see you in the morning." Daniel leaned over and kissed Noah's forehead.

"Can you sit with him until I come back? I'm going to tell everyone to go back to the resort."

Daniel nodded.

As Bella entered the waiting room, everyone but Michelle jumped to their feet.

"How is he?" Ginny's tone conveyed her concern.

Bella smiled. "He's fine." Four tense bodies visibly relaxed. Maybe, five, but Bella wasn't looking at Michelle. "Now, I want you all to go back to the resort and get some sleep. I'm sleeping on a cot in Noah's room."

"Oh, no, honey, we can…"

"No, mom, you go rest, and come back in the morning."

"Are you sure, Bella?"

The corner of Bella's mouth quirked up. "Well, Charley…unless you want to watch me sleep…then be my guest."

Charley laughed.

Alicia hugged Bella. "We'll be back bright and early."

Bella shook her head. "No, you won't. You are not spending your Christmas vacation sitting in Noah's room with me. You, Charley and your families will ski and enjoy all the other perks the resort has to offer. Come for a visit after dinner."

Alicia shook her head. "I'm not leaving you here all day tomorrow with just your parents for company."

"Hey." John said in mock outrage.

She cringed. "Sorry, John…I didn't…"

Ginny, put an arm around her waist. "How about a compromise? You and Charley spend the morning with your families, skiing or whatever and come to the hospital after lunch."

Alicia leaned into Ginny. "Okay."

Bella waved her arms in a shooing gesture. "Now go… all of you."

After two minutes of kisses and hugs, Bella's parents and friends left the waiting room. As she stepped forward to leave the waiting room, shame washed over her. Since Michelle had arrived, she had been purposely avoiding eye contact with her. She hadn't wanted her here–had assumed Daniel would come by himself. She closed her eyes. *I know, God.* She sighed heavily and turned to Michelle. "Thank you for coming…and thank you for caring about my son."

Michelle smiled. "You're welcome. He's a wonderful boy."

Guilt assuaged, Bella hurried from the room and back to her sleeping son.

41

A hospital orderly picked up the barely-touched break-fast tray off the rolling bed table and departed the room. When the day nurse had stepped into the room a few minutes ago, Noah told her that he felt sick to his stomach. She left to order some meds to take away the nausea. Bella thought it was probably due to the pain medication. She had felt the same her first day in the hospital. She looked down at her iPhone–nine o'clock. Where was Alec?

Last night had been fairly uneventful. Noah had stirred and moaned a couple of times as the pain meds started to wear off, but then a nurse would arrive and push a button on a monitor, and he would sink back to sleep.

Daniel sat in a chair next to Noah's bed, conversing with him in a quiet tone. Bella and her parents sat in a recliner and two chairs next to the window. She glanced out the window at the bright sunshine and then whipped her head around as footsteps approached.

Alec walked through the door a smile on his face. "Mr. Stanford, Ms. Claremont and…" He looked at John and Ginny.

"These are my parents, John and Ginny Claremont." Bella stood along with her parents.

He walked over and shook hands with her parents. "Nice to meet you."

Alec's eyes shifted to her eyes and he held out a hand. "Bella, it's good to see you again." She hesitated for a beat, shook his hand then quickly pulled her own hand back to her side.

Alec walked over to Daniel. He rose and shook Alec's hand. "We didn't formally meet last night. "I'm Dr Kaselberg." His gaze shifted to Noah. "How are you feeling young man?"

"Kind of sick to my stomach." Noah swallowed convulsively.

"I heard. We have some meds on the way. Do you mind if I examine your leg?"

Noah shook his head. Alec pulled back the white sheet and Bella had her first glimpse of her son's leg. She lifted a hand to her mouth. John grabbed her other hand, and Bella wondered if it was more to anchor himself or her. The swollen limb had a long incision on the outside of the leg starting below the knee and ending just above his ankle. The sliced tissue was being held together by staples. Though purple bruising stood out against the tight pale skin around the surgical site Bella, didn't noticing any angry red flesh.

Alec pulled the sheet back over the leg. He patted Noah's shoulder. "Looking good, buddy."

"Mom said I have a plate and screws holding the bones together." A sheen of perspiration covered Noah's forehead.

"That is correct. As soon as it heals, in a few of months, they'll be removed."

"How long do I have to stay in the hospital?"

"If we don't see any sign of infection…about five days."

Noah groaned.

Alec's eyes showed sympathy. "It won't be much fun. But we have to make sure your leg is healing properly so that you can get back on the ski slope next year."

Noah's eyes lit up. "I'll be able to ski again?"

"Absolutely."

He turned to the adults in the room. "I have a few minutes if you have questions."

Ginny stammered. "His leg is so swollen."

"Not infection. That's the body's normal reaction to the trauma of the injury. It's down from last night and will continue to go down each day.

Bella cleared her throat. "When will he be able to travel back to Williamsburg?"

"Once he's released, he can travel home…but I would advise a medical transport that will keep his leg stable."

"I'll take care of the medical transport." Daniel said as he smoothed back Noah's hair. "Will he be able to get around on crutches?"

"Yes…no weight-bearing on the leg for the first few weeks. After that he'll be fitted with a special brace to immobilize his leg, but still allow him to walk." He smiled at Noah. "It's a pretty cool brace. I think you'll like it. Now you rest up, and I'll be by again tomorrow."

Daniel held out his hand. "Thank you, Dr. Kaselberg."

"You're welcome." He shook Daniel's hand and turned to Bella. "Could I speak with you in private?"

Now I can find out why he was allowed to operate on my son. Bella followed Alec from the room. Once out of earshot he turned to her. "I can tell by the look in your eyes that you're angry that I was allowed to operate on your son so soon after…what happened on the cruise. Can you meet me for lunch in the cafeteria at eleven thirty so I can explain?"

Bella tried to tap down on the infuriation simmering in her chest as she answered, "Yes."

Her eyes followed his gaze to the nurse's station. Two nurses were staring…interest alight in their eyes.

Alec cleared his throat. "I need to get back to my rounds."

Bella gazed after him as he walked to a door a few feet away and enter. She pulled in a deep breath to try and calm her anger as she walked back to her son's room.

CHAPTER

42

Bella stepped into the elevator and rode it down to the first floor. As she walked toward the cafeteria her thoughts whirled. *Does the hospital staff here know what happened on the ship? Did he tell the medical board at the hospital in Richmond?* The butterflies from last night awoke in her stomach and collided with each other. She stopped mid-stride. *No, I can't have this conversation.*

She made an about face and froze. Alec was striding towards her. He smiled, and Bella's instinct was to return the smile…but her son's face rose to the forefront of her mind and wiped out the brief feeling of warmth generated by his smile. "I was just coming to tell you I can't meet for lunch…I need…"

Alec's smile disappeared. "Please, Bella, let me explain."

"I…"

"Please."

The sorrow in his eyes was so bottomless, if she fell into them, she would never surface. Compassion touched her heart. Not trusting herself to speak, she nodded. He led the way to the cafeteria and a table in the far-left corner. He pulled out a chair for her to sit.

Once he was settled in his seat, his pain-filled eyes bore into hers. "I don't know how else to put this...the look on your face is like a knife through my heart. You are the one person in the world I would never, ever hurt for any reason. What you did for me...for my very soul...on that ship can never be repaid."

Alec wiped at his moist eyes. "You gave me my life back...and a reason to live that life. He cleared tears from his throat. "I am so sorry. If I had known that was your son, I would have called in Dr. Pierce to perform the surgery."

The compassion found fertile ground in her heart and grew. Her violet eyes filled. "I'm sorry, Alec. I was wrong to rush to judgment." Her voice dropped to a whisper. "I was so scared for my son."

"You don't need to apologize. If I found out a doctor who operated on my daughter had tried to commit suicide six months before...I would have reacted the same way." Alec leaned forward over the table. "As soon as I returned to the states, I informed the medical board of my attempted suicide and was immediately put on medical leave. I was given a physiological eval and put under the care of an excellent therapist."

"Are you wondering why I turned myself in, instead of keeping it to myself...pretending it never happened?" He drew in a breath. "I needed to be *sure* I was mentally competent and capable of performing surgeries. One of the promises in the Hippocratic Oath is 'first, do no harm.' I take that promise very seriously."

Suddenly conscious of rubbing the knuckles hidden in her lap, Bella removed her hands from her lap and rested them on the table. "How long were you in therapy?"

"Five months. I was released from my therapist's care a month ago and taken off medical leave."

"Why did you come here?"

Alec leaned back. "It's not a long story, but why don't we grab a sandwich first. I have a surgery scheduled for one o'clock."

Bella rose. "Sure."

They walked back to the table with their trays and sat down. Alec took a huge bite of his roast beef on rye. He chased the bite with a chug from his water bottle and then spoke. "I told you I planned to go overseas…and I still do…but I wanted to begin my new lease on life where I could do the most good."

He took another bite of his sandwich then cleared his throat. "This area has one of the highest statistics for broken bones because of the skiing and snowboarding. The surgeries keep me busy and I have less time to think about…" He sighed and took another bite of his sandwich.

Bella's hands twisted her bottle of water back and forth on the table her sandwich untouched. "You were much braver and stronger than I was. Daniel still doesn't know that I almost killed myself." Bella's voice dropped to a whisper, "I was afraid I wouldn't get my son back."

Alec touched his fingertips to her hands, stilling her agitated twisting of the bottle. An electric shock shot up her arms. He dropped his fingers to the table. "Bella, there is a stark difference between our trips to the promenade deck. You did not step on the rail intending to kill yourself…I did. There is nothing you need to confess to Daniel."

A burden she wasn't aware she had been carrying lifted from her shoulders, and her mood lightened. She picked up her sandwich and took a bite. They finished their meal in a compatible silence. Feeling Alec's eyes on her, Bella looked up from her plate.

"I've thought about our time together more than a few times in the last six months."

Bella's cheeks heated with a guilty flush. Alec had come to her mind a couple of times in the first month she was back…but soon thoughts of him had faded away to the nether regions of her mind.

"I've missed the way I could let my guard down with you…" Alec's eyes drifted away from hers and gazed into the near distance, and the words he spoke next seemed to slip out as an afterthought. "…more than I thought I would."

A sudden warm tingling coursed through Bella. When his intense blue eyes focused back on her, she smothered an involuntary gasp. "I wish the circumstances had been different, but I am glad to see you again…Arabella." He smiled.

Bella's heartbeats picked up as she smiled back. "Me, too."

He glanced at his watch. "Well, it looks like our hour is about up." He looked around the room and gave a theatrical sigh. "I guess Finn couldn't make it…I'll have to escort myself to the operating room."

Bella barked out a true belly laugh and then covered her mouth in embarrassment. Alec grinned. "I'll see you tomorrow when I check on Noah."

Bella lowered her hand and smiled as he pushed back his chair and returned his tray. After Alec disappeared from the cafeteria, Bella arose from the table with conflicting emotions assaulting her again. She shook her head. She would deal with them later.

✦ ✦ ✦

"Easy listening" music emitted from the speakers of the crowded Italian restaurant as Bella and her parents, Charley and Alicia followed the hostess to a table. The hostess passed around menus and departed. Ginny, Alicia, and Charley's voices collided as they spoke simultaneously.

"How could the doctor…

"…believe Alec…"

"…doing in West Virginia…"

John's voice rose above the fray. "Ladies, one at a time."

The voices ceased. Alicia turned to Ginny. "You first."

Ginny opened her mouth and then shut it, as a tall African-American waiter stopped by their table. As soon as he departed with the drink orders, Ginny spoke, "How could that doctor be allowed to operate on my grandson so soon after trying to commit suicide?"

Bella knew John had suggested an early dinner at this restaurant two blocks from the hospital so they could discuss Alec in private. Daniel and Michelle were sitting with Noah and would go to dinner after they returned.

Bella gave her mom a reassuring smile. "We discussed it over lunch today."

Alicia quirked an eyebrow. "You had lunch with Alec?"

Charley beamed at her. "How nice."

John frowned at Charley as the waiter returned with drinks. "Are you ready to order?"

Five guilty pairs of hands picked up the menus. John smiled. "Give us about five minutes."

Ginny lowered her menu. "So why...?"

John touched her hand. "Let's order first."

Bella smiled inwardly. If Ginny had been a cartoon character, steam would be shooting from her ears.

After the orders had been placed, Ginny narrowed her eyes at Bella.

"Mom, I felt the same as you when I realized he had operated on Noah. He could tell I was upset this morning when he checked on Noah and invited me to lunch to explain. He told me that as soon as he got back to Richmond, he told the medical board what happened, and they put him on medical leave. He was under the care of a therapist for five months and was cleared last month to operate. He also told me if he had realized Noah was my son he would have called in another surgeon."

"I still don't think he should be operating on patients after all you told me about him."

"Mom, I'm sure he would not have been cleared by the medical board if they had the least little doubt that he was competent enough to perform surgeries."

Charley's eyebrows drew together as she sipped her iced tea. She looked up with a smile. "It's another God thing. One of the best orthopedic surgeons in the country just happens to be in this tiny ski resort town at the exact same time that Noah breaks his leg."

Bella squeezed Charley's hand. "I believe your right."

Alicia took a drink and then set down her ice water. "I didn't recognize him at first. He looks completely different. He must have put on twenty-five pounds at least. Alec has… an air of confidence, assurance that he didn't have before, and something else…can't think of the word…"

"Serenity," Bella said. "He's living for his family, and it's made him happy."

John gave Bella a quizzical look before clearing his throat. "All I know is that he has done a fine job on Noah's leg…and I'd like to give a toast." Glasses of iced tea and water were raised. "To Dr. Kaselberg, thank you for the fine surgery you preformed on Noah's leg."

"You're welcome."

Five gasps intermingled as Alec stared down at their table. "I see you're trying out my favorite Italian restaurant."

"I think it's the only Italian restaurant within fifty miles." Alicia deadpanned

Alec grinned. "You got me there."

"Are you on dinner break?"

Alec turned to Bella. "No, I'm done for the day."

"Please join us for dinner."

"No, I don't want to intrude."

"Please, on me…for Noah." Bella ignored Ginny's frown, as she smiled up at Alec.

"Really, you don't…" Alec stopped speaking as Bella narrowed her eyes.

Alec smiled. "I'd be delighted."

Their waiter appeared. "Ah, Dr. Kaselberg, a table for one?"

"I'll be joining these special guests."

"Absolutely." The waiter grabbed a chair and squeezed it in next to Bella.

"I'll have my usual, Demonte."

"Very good, sir."

Ginny opened her mouth, and John quickly interjected to ward off a possible awkward question. "Have you been skiing yet?"

"I don't ski."

Charley was nodding. "Because of the injuries."

Alec nodded in return. "Yes, because you have no control over the amateurs and reckless showoffs on the slopes."

Everyone held their breath as Ginny spoke. "I'm actually thinking about hanging up my skis after this vacation."

At least four people sighed in relief as Bella turned to Alec. "When do you expect to receive the go ahead for your trip?"

Alec sighed. "Not for sure, hopefully soon."

The waiter arrived with a large tray full of Italian dishes, and Charley drew in an appreciative breath. "Yum."

Small talk continued as everyone dug in to the delicious food. As the meal drew to a close, Alec turned to Bella. "Would you be free for lunch tomorrow?"

"Yes." Charley covered her mouth in horror. "Did I say that out loud?"

Everyone laughed, as Bella said she would love to.

The bill arrived, and the haggling and protests began. John won out and the rest of the table gave effusive thanks.

Alec rose and turned to Bella. "I'll get with you tomorrow about where and when. What is your cell number?"

Bella gave it to him, and Alec entered it into his phone. He said goodbye and left. As if on collective puppet strings, all heads turned to Ginny.

"What?" Ginny said as her cheeks pinkened a bit. "All right, I may revise my opinion. He did seem perfectly sane."

Bella laughed as she rose from the table.

Bella looked over the small brick façade and then up at the sign that said, 'The Ski Lift Diner,' while the lemon sun sat directly overhead in a brilliant blue sky. Bright blue curtains hung in the two windows facing the street. "Bet it took all of three minutes to come up with the name for the diner."

"I'll take that bet. Winner buys lunch."

Bella laughed, as Alec opened the door, causing an old-fashioned bell to tingle over their heads. The décor was what one would expect. Old wooden skis, poles, and snowshoes jostled for space on the walls amid at least fifty framed photographs. The photos were a mixture of landscape shots of the different seasons of the area and of people who had eaten at the diner.

The inside had room for only ten tables; each table had seating for four. A woman with graying hair poked her head around the door to the kitchen. "Sit anywhere, be out in a moment."

Bella hid her amusement. There was only one table open. Once settled at the table, Bella looked around. "Well it is a slight upgrade from the cafeteria, but they really should pay you doctors more."

Alec smiled. "I have missed your sense of humor."

"I like this place...very homey."

"Just wait until you taste Marjorie's chicken and dumplings and apple pie. You'll think you've died and gone to heaven."

"Speaking of which..."

Alec groaned. "Religion already."

Bella laughed, remembering their conversations on the ship. "Did you keep your promise?

Alec gazed at Bella with eyes full of innocence. "What promise?"

Bella drummed her fingers and narrowed her eyes.

Alec sighed as if heavily put upon. "Yes, mother...I did."

Bella smiled with the pleasure that infused her. "Well... what did you think of the book?"

In a neutral tone, Alec said, "An inspirational story about a man's conversion from an atheist to a Christian."

Bella swallowed her disappointment at his tone. "Thank you for keeping your promise."

Alec cleared his throat. "And for the record...I do believe Jesus is God's son."

The woman from the kitchen bustled over. "The usual, Doc?"

"And if I may..." Alec's eyebrows rose, and he looked at Bella. She nodded. "And the same for the lady."

A young woman with Marjorie's features bustled over with two waters as the door opened with a tinkle and a group of four skiers entered. Bella viewed the disappointment on their faces when they gazed around at the full tables. They retreated from the room. She turned back to Alec her eyes immediately locking on Alec's eyes. She sucked in a quick breath, her heart fluttering in her chest. Her mind was awhirl. Was it because she hadn't seen him in six months...or because he no longer looked like *her* Alec...or because he was no longer needy, desperate, suicidal, but instead exuded confidence, that had Bella shocked to her core at her sudden attraction to this man?

Bella shook her head. *No...I cannot have those types of feelings for Alec.*

"No? Did you change your mind? You want something else." Alec's eyes reflected his confusion.

"What?" It was Bella's turn to be confused.

"You shook your head. I thought you changed your mind about what I ordered.

Heat infused Bella's face. "No, not at all. I was thinking of something else."

Alec smiled and changed the subject. "Noah seemed in better spirits this morning."

Bella sighed with relief. As she talked about Noah, she pushed all thoughts of Alec to the back of her mind.

There was a soft knock on Noah's door, and it opened with a quiet swish. Bella set aside the book she had been reading her eyes opening wider as Alec came into view. He walked over to Noah's bed and gazed down at her sleeping son. He turned and walked over to Bella.

Bella's eyebrows drew together as she whispered, "I didn't know you made night rounds?" She looked at the clock on the wall. It was ten o'clock.

"I don't. I had a month of paperwork I've been putting off. I just finished it and decided to take a quick peek at Noah." He glanced at the chair next to Bella. "I'm still a bit wired. Would you like company?"

Bella's traitorous heart jumped in her chest. "Sure, but we need to keep our voices down."

Alec smiled. "I wasn't planning on talking. Just being around you is...calming. You help me to relax. Go ahead and read your book."

Bella's mouth gaped open. *Read my book?*

Laughter was evident in Alec's eyes as he reached over for the book and placed it in Bella's hands. He settled more comfortably in the chair and closed his eyes.

Bella closed her mouth as her heart filled with warmth. Her eyelids slowly closed. *Thank you, Lord, for this gift of compassion that has helped Alec.*

CHAPTER

44

Bella skied off the lift beside Alicia and joined her mom. Jarod, Cameron, and Kelen were snowboarding on a different part of the slope. Bella grimaced as she looked over at her mom. "I should be with Noah, Dad, and Daniel in the same room together…"

Alicia gave an exasperated sigh. "He's fine. Michelle is there. She can referee. You needed to get out and have some fun."

Bella shivered as she looked up at the leaden sky and a frigid breeze swept over her. "It's cold up here this afternoon."

Ginny looked up. "Forecast is for a couple of feet of snow tonight."

"Well let's get going then. I don't want to get trapped up here away from Noah." Bella skied to the edge of the slope and pushed herself over. Her mom and Alicia soon joined her. Even with the ski mask, the cold penetrated, and her face started to pin-prickle.

As she skied around a teenager her thoughts turned to the night before. After thirty minutes of silence–except for a turn of a page now and then–Alec made Bella jump when he suddenly rose out of his chair brushed her cheek with his lips and said goodnight. Shocked into speechlessness, she hadn't even said goodnight. Why had he kissed her check?

A tree loomed up suddenly on her right, and she nearly screamed. She swerved–her heart racing in her chest. The slopes were no place to reminisce. She turned her focus outward and raced down the slope to the bottom with no mishap.

When Ginny reached the bottom, she skied over to her daughter. "Are you alright? You scared the life out of me when you almost hit that tree."

Bella hugged her mom. "Sorry. My concentration wavered for a moment."

Alicia lifted her goggles, fear clearly evident in her eyes. "What were you thinking that was so important you almost killed yourself?"

"Nothing. Come on, I'm fine. We have to get back up there." Bella headed for the lift.

Ginny and Alicia followed twin frowns on their lips.

After two more runs the ladies agreed through frozen lips that they'd had enough. After changing clothes at the lodge, they met in front of the huge fireplace, hands reaching toward the warmth.

"Hey, what are you three doing here?" Charley walked over and joined her friends. "I thought you were skiing?"

Alicia reached over and grabbed Charley's hand. Charley jerked her hand away. "Oh, my word, your hand is frozen. I'll go and get hot chocolate."

Bella accepted the mug from Charley and sighed with relief. "I can feel my fingers again."

Ginny pressed a finger on her lip. "I thought it would never thaw."

Alicia sipped from her mug. "I believe that is the coldest I have ever been."

Bella drank the last of her hot chocolate and rose from the upholstered chair. "I need to get back to the hospital."

"Oh, Bella, just a little longer." Charley said.

"No, I'm taking no chances of getting snowed in away from Noah."

Ginny stood. "I'll go with you and come back with John."

Alicia handed over the keys to her van and hugged Bella. As Bella grabbed her jacket the front doors opened, and Jarod and the boys came in. Cameron and Kelen rushed to the fireplace.

Alicia looked at her husband with bemusement. "This has to be a first. Missing out on three more hours of snowboarding."

"What?" Jarod shouted. "Can't hear you, my ears have icicles embedded in them."

Bella laughed as she headed for the door.

Bella stood at the hospital lobby doors as Ginny and John pulled out in Alicia's van. It had started to snow, and Bella chewed her bottom lip, praying they had no problems getting back to the lodge.

"Hey there."

Bella whipped around at the sound of Alec's voice. "Hey, yourself."

"Watching the snow fall?"

"No, a little worried about my folks driving in this back to the lodge."

Alec smiled reassuringly. "They should be fine. I finished my last surgery. Do you want to go get a bite in the cafeteria?"

Bella smiled. "Love to, but I thought I'd bring my tray up to Noah's room and eat with him."

"Can I join you?"

"Sure, Noah would love it."

Bella and Alec settled into chairs with trays on their laps as Noah spoke. "How was the skiing today, Mom?"

Bella grimaced. "Cold, bitter cold."

"How many runs did you do?"

"Three."

Noah's eyebrows shot up. "Only three."

"And I bet that was three too many." Alec bit off a piece of fried chicken.

"Even Jarod and the boys got back three hours early."

Noah's mouth formed an 'O.' "No way."

"Way."

Bella glanced out the hospital window as she swallowed a bite of chicken. The snow was coming down harder and the wind had picked up. She looked over at

Alec, and he nodded. "This is shaping up to be a bad storm."

"Shouldn't you get back to your apartment?"

"When it's this bad I stay at the hospital for emergencies."

Noah grinned. "Cool, you can bunk with me."

"Love to buddy, but your mom has the only other bed in the room."

"We could kick her out."

"Noah!" Bella's eyes widened.

Laughter burst from between Alec's lips, which he quickly tried to cover up with a bite of broccoli.

"Kidding, Mom."

"You better…"

Their conversation was interrupted by a code call.

"That's me." He set his tray on the window ledge, most of his meal done. "Enjoyed sharing dinner with you—bye."

Alec hurried from the room.

Speaking to herself, Bella mumbled, "I wonder what that was about?"

"What, mom?"

"Nothing. Do you want to play a game?"

"Sure, Star Wars."

Bella rolled her eyes. "Again?"

Bella opened her eyes and quickly shut them against the blinding light coming through the window. An orderly must have opened the blinds. She turned her gaze and squinted over at Noah…still asleep. She stretched her arms above her head and yawned. Her eyes settled on the clock on the wall and then widened…almost time for rounds. She jumped out of bed, grabbed some clothes, and dove into the bathroom.

When she emerged from the bathroom, one of the nurses was taking Noah's vitals.

"Good morning, Jackie."

A nurse with pretty auburn hair turned and smiled. "How'd you sleep?"

"Great. How are the roads?"

The nurse grimaced. "Really bad…nothing's moving but the snowplows. Two feet of snow."

"I guess you had to stay last night, too."

"I volunteered…usually do when the weather's this bad." She looked at the vitals. "You are good to go buddy."

Alec walked in looking like he hadn't slept a wink.

"Bad night?"

"A pile-up on the road. Three patients with broken bones."

He walked over to Noah. "How you feeling, Noah?" He scrutinized his leg.

"Not too bad. When can I go home?"

"Day after tomorrow."

Noah didn't hide his disappointment. Alec squeezed his shoulder. "It will go by faster than you think." He turned to Bella. "See you later."

"Get some rest."

"Plan to. Going to finish my rounds and then go crash."

Bella watched him walk through the door as Noah's breakfast was brought in.

As day turned into night, Bella hid her disappointment from Noah. She hadn't seen Alec at all. She'd thought for sure he would stop by to ask to go to lunch or dinner. She picked up her book and sighed.

Bella couldn't stop the sudden leap of her heart and sucked-in breath, as Alec walked into the room the next day to check on Noah. She came within an inch of saying, 'I missed you yesterday' before clamping her lips together.

"Morning, Bella…Noah. "I don't know if you heard, but we had some freezing rain last night. I'd let your family and friends know not to risk coming to visit today. The roads are icy, and the temperature won't rise above freezing until tomorrow."

"Okay, I'll call them."

Noah's face fell. "Will I still be able to go home tomorrow?"

"Ninety-nine percent guarantee. Temps are rising into the high thirties tomorrow."

He breathed out a sigh of relief.

As Alec rose up after examining Noah, Bella issued an invitation—her words coming out in a rush. "Would you like to have lunch with Noah and me?"

Alec's eyes flashed with an emotion Bella could not identify before his mouth curved up. "Sounds good. I'll let you know when I'm free."

***

The morning dragged as Bella waited to hear from Alec. He poked his head in the door at eleven-thirty. "Ready to go?"

"Yes." She turned to Noah. "We'll be right back, honey."

He gave a quick nod and returned to the game he was playing on his iPad.

Back in Noah's room, Alec swallowed the last bite of his cheeseburger. He turned to Bella. "Has the medical transport been arranged?"

"Yes, Daniel took care of it yesterday." She hoped her tone hid her distress of having to say goodbye and never seeing Alec again. "We're leaving around three tomorrow."

"Roads should be clear by then."

Bella forced a bite of her sandwich. She wasn't hungry but had to show a positive attitude for Noah's sake.

Noah smiled as he chewed. "I can't wait."

Bella swallowed. Her gut churned as she cleared her throat. "I guess you're stuck in the hospital for another night. Would you like to share dinner with us?"

Alec averted his eyes from her gaze. "I'm having dinner in the cafeteria with some colleagues tonight. But thanks for the offer." He rose from the chair with his tray.

This time Bella struggled to hide the swift pain that squeezed her heart. "Ah…okay…see you tomorrow."

With a smile and a backward wave, he left the room.

"Mom, what's wrong?"

"What?" Bella eyes swiveled to the bed.

"You look sad."

Bella pulled in a breath and plastered a smile onto her lips. "Nope, not sad at all...looking forward to getting home."

"But..."

"Come on finish your meal so we can play "Star Wars" for the zillionth time."

Noah laughed as he took a bite of his chicken finger.

Bella inhaled the chilly air deeply and sighed. She shifted her position slightly, and ice salt crunched beneath her shoes. Standing to the left of the hospital's automatic doors, she tilted her head to look at the multitude of bright lights that seemed to wink at her and gazed at the night sky. It was nine o'clock, and Noah was fast asleep. She had left his room to clear her head. She pulled the zipper of her ski jacket up tighter under her chin as a shiver crept through her. Bella lowered her head. The streets were empty—nothing stirred in the frozen landscape around her.

She crossed her arms over her chest and hugged herself. *What is wrong with me? I shouldn't be having these feelings about a man who is still mourning his wife.* She leaned her head back and stared at the stars again. *Please Lord, help me to expunge these inappropriate feelings from my heart.* She waited. Silence. Bella lowered her head...her eyes welling with tears. She pulled in a deep breath, trying to stem this sudden flood of emotion, but the tears slipped over her eyelids and streamed down her face. The doors swooshed open behind Bella. She lifted fingers to her face and dash away the wetness.

"Bella? Is that you?"

Bella froze. Footsteps came abreast of her. She shifted her head away. "I came out to get some air."

"Are you all right?

The tremor in her voice was giving her away. "Fine. I should get back to Noah." She turned away, but found her way blocked by the handsome doctor.

The light from the lobby shone on her face. "You've been crying."

Bella heard the distress in Alec's voice. Her cheeks inflamed with embarrassment as she lowered her gaze to the pavement. "It's nothing."

A cold hand grasped her chin with a gentle touch and lifted it until her violet eyes locked onto his deeply troubled blue eyes. He lowered his head and placed his lips gently against hers. Bella's heart leapt, as Alec deepened the kiss and his arms enfolded her. She kissed him back with all the pent-up emotions of the last few days. Her heart beat rapidly against her ribs.

Alec's hold on her abruptly loosened, causing Bella to stagger and almost fall into Alec's chest. She straightened quickly. Though his face was in shadow she clearly saw that he was stunned by his own action.

"Bella, I'm sorry. I shouldn't have..."

"No...no it's alright...I..."

Alec shook his head, his face a mask of guilt and sorrow. "I'm leaving soon...for Africa, and I...I...Bethany."

Anguish flooded Bella's soul, the words forced out in a whisper, "I know you loved your wife with...with all your heart..." She paused dashing away more tears. She looked up at Alec's handsome face. "It's too soon...I understand that you..."

Alec reached out and grasped both her hands stopping her words. "Bella..." His eyes widened. "Your hands are like ice! You need to get inside before you get frostbite."

He turned with one hand in his grasp. Once inside the lobby, Alec dropped her hand. "Bella..."

Curious heads turned in their direction.

Bella heaved a sigh leaden with sorrow. "No, Alec... please, it's okay." A sudden tumult of emotion swirled painfully in her stomach. She had to get away from Alec before she lost her composure again. "I'll see you tomorrow morning." She turned and hurried to the elevators. As the car rose, she bent over and grabbed her stomach with hands that shook. She drew in a long breath and straightened as the ding announced her floor. She entered Noah's room and walked to the bathroom.

She stared into the mirror. *Deja vu* slammed into her—red rimmed eyes, beet-red nose, and black streaks trailing from her eye lids to her chin. She shook her head fiercely. No! I will not go *there* ever again. Bella's knuckles whitened as she grabbed onto the sink and pulled in cleansing breaths. She bowed her head and prayed silently. Fifteen minutes passed. Her heart slowly calmed, and her stomach settled. She lifted her wash cloth off the towel rack and cleaned her face with a hand that no longer shook. She exited the bathroom undressed and pulled on her pajamas.

Bella pulled in another long breath and forced thoughts about Alec to the back of her mind. She stepped to the side of Noah's bed. Her fingers lightly caressed his hand. A smiled trembled on her lips. Noah had to be her priority. No more illusions of "happily ever after"–it was nothing but a fairy tale.

The elevator slowed to a stop. Bella drew slender fingers through her loose curls. During morning rounds, Alec had asked if Bella would have lunch with him in the cafeteria. She wanted to say no...*no, needed to say no*...but when he looked at her with those guilt-ridden eyes, she hadn't had the wherewithal to refuse. She was every bit as guilty for wanting him to kiss her.

Bella had left Noah in a multitude of good hands. As soon as the roads had been announced safe to drive on, her father, mother, Alicia, Charlie, and Daniel had arrived for a last visit before she and Noah left in the medical van. They had wanted to leave with Bella, but she insisted that they stay at the resort. Her parents, friends and their families, still had two days left to ski and enjoy themselves. After a short debate they had reluctantly agreed to stay at the resort instead of driving back to Williamsburg.

She stepped out of the elevator, squared her shoulders, and breathed in deeply. Bella walked briskly to the cafeteria. Alec was seated at a corner table staring out the window. She paused for a moment memorizing every detail about this man she cared for so deeply–the man that would soon be lost to her forever. There would be no texting or emailing…she needed a clean break. She had survived saying goodbye on the cruise ship, and she could do it again.

Alec turned as if sensing her presence and rose swiftly to his feet. She walked up to the table and Alec pulled out a chair for her. She sat down and he returned to his chair.

"Bella, I…"

Bella reached out and laid a hand on the fingers that Alec had folded together on the table. "Please, may I speak first?"

Alec tensed, but nodded.

"There is absolutely no reason for you to feel guilt or shame about kissing me. If anyone should feel shame, it's me for having inappropriate feelings for a man who is still in mourning for his wife."

Alec opened his mouth to speak. Bella squeezed his hand, and he pressed his lips back together. "I'm here to make a deal. If you let the shame and guilt go—so will I." She gazed into his eyes waiting.

Slowly, Alec's shoulders relaxed, and he gave her a rueful smile. "Deal."

"Now, see, that wasn't so hard, was it."

Alec chuckled. "How do you do it? No matter what negative thoughts or feelings I'm having, you always manage to lighten my mood and make me laugh."

Bella shrugged her right shoulder. "It's a gift."

Alec laughed harder, Bella joining in. As their mirth quieted Alec folded his two hands around Bella's hand. Tingling shot straight up her arm. She silently congratulated herself when Alec showed no reaction. His voice was subdued as he spoke. "I'm attracted to you...I'm going to miss you ...more than you think I will. I want you to be in love again...but I'm not..."

He cleared his throat. "I need to be completely honest with you. I dream of my wife and girls every night...the dreams...feel...real. And for a reason I don't understand, in the mornings, when I wake up...instead of feeling sad, I'm happy...ready to go out and conquer the world." He sighed. "I still feel them here." He placed a hand over his heart. "And here." He lifted the hand off his heart and pointed his finger at his forehead.

Alec squeezed Bella's hand as he looked into her eyes. "Last night I didn't dream of my family, and when I woke up....the pain...it was like losing them all over again."

Bella gently pulled her hand out from between Alec's and smiled though her heart was breaking all over again for his loss. "I understand. Really, I do. You and I were broken into a thousand pieces with our losses and the time it takes to heal...to mend those pieces back together...is different for everyone."

Alec's eyes shone with moisture. "You are without a doubt the most amazing, understanding, and kind woman I have ever met. And I will pray that God gives you the happiness you deserve."

Bella's eyes danced. "Alec, you used the words "God" and "pray" in the same sentence. Give me a couple of weeks and I'll turn your doctor's trip to Africa into a mission trip."

Alec stared at her in mock horror. "God forbid...and I mean that in the most reverent way."

Laughing, Bella rose to her feet. "Come on, let's get our meal. I've got a lot to do before we leave."

"I just have one question."

"Yes."

Alec's grin reached ear to ear. "Do you think one of the servers could mix me up a Roy Rogers?"

Bella's grin was just as wide. "Who knows? The Bible does say, 'with God all things are possible.'"

The medical transport pulled up beside the curb in front of the hospital's main entrance. Alec pushed the wheelchair, carrying Noah, through the doors to the van. The percentage of surgeons who wheeled their patients to their vehicles for the trip home had to be miniscule... but then most surgeons didn't have the relationship that Alec had with Noah. Noah didn't think of Alec as just his doctor...he considered him a friend...and vice versa. Bella's eyes grew moist as she watched Alec help Noah into the van.

"Is something wrong?"

Bella turned to Charley blinking back tears. "No... um...just sad for Noah. You know...missing out on ski-ing."

"Oh, sure...and I'm Mother Teresa." Alicia's voice oozed with good-natured sarcasm. "You're thinking about a certain surgeon that shall not be named."

Bella whipped her head towards the van and back again. "Shush, Alicia, he might hear you...and you're wrong. Alec and I are friends."

Alicia cocked an eyebrow. "Oh, really? That's not what Noah told me, your parents, and Charley."

Bella's eyes widened with horror. "What!"

John laughed. "Honey, she's joking. Noah didn't say anything."

Bella narrowed her eyes at Alicia.

"Okay, sorry…jeez." Alicia hugged her. "Skiing isn't the same without you."

Bella hugged her back. "You're forgiven. I'll see you when you get back to Williamsburg." She loosened her hold on Alicia and hugged Charley and then her parents. "Let's all meet at my house for dinner the day you get back."

"I'm in." Charley smiled at Bella.

Ginny's eyebrows peaked. "Bella, no, you have Noah to take care of. You won't have time to cook for thirteen people."

"Who said anything about cooking?"

John barked out a laugh as Alec walked over to their little group. "Noah's settled in for the trip home. Is his father coming to see him off?"

Bella gave a slight shake of her head. "He left two hours ago. Michelle is feeling a little under the weather."

"Well, I guess this is goodbye then." Alec's smile looked a trifle forced.

Bella's heartbeats were thrumming in her ears. "Thank you, for all you've done for Noah. I…um…pray that your trip to Africa is everything you hope it will be."

"Me, too." His fingers reached down, grasped Bella's hand and brought it up to his lips. He pressed a light kiss on her knuckles. She sucked in a soft breath as he released her hand. "I'll be forever grateful for everything you've done for me." He glanced around at their small group. "Be safe driving home."

As he turned and walked back inside, Bella wrestled her heartrending emotions into a choke hold and smiled at her friends and family. "Love you guys...I'll see you in a couple days." She quickly turned and strode to the passenger side of the medical van.

In the dark bedroom, Bella stared at a white ceiling she couldn't see. She sighed with pleasure. *Sleeping in my own bed under my own comforter.* She was ready for her first decent night's sleep in a week. Her lips lifted in the corners as she thought of Noah. She wished she had half his energy and agility. He whipped around the house on his crutches as if he'd been born with them. He was already begging for a sleepover with his friends. *Five rowdy boys staying up until at least midnight.* Bella was exhausted just thinking about it.

Unbidden, Alec's handsome features collated in her brain. Memories of their five days together flooded her mind as an invisible hand clenched her heart. Bella shook her head on the pillow. *No, I have to let him go.* Bella forced the memories back into the dark shadows of her mind and turned on to her side. As she drifted into oblivion, a single tear slid down her cheek.

Bella took a sip of her mimosa. The corners of her lips slowly curved up as she gazed at the white charter and fishing boats bobbing gently on the inlet waters. *It's so lovely and serene.* It had been two years to the day since she and her friends had gathered at Rudee's restaurant in Virginia Beach. Alicia and Charley had protested loudly when Bella insisted on Rudee's for their April birthday celebration. 'No, not happening,' Alicia had said, 'I'm putting my foot down.' Bella laughed at the memory.

"What's so funny?" Alicia pulled her eyes away from Charley.

"You."

Alicia's forehead furrowed. "Me? I didn't say anything. Charley was talking."

"I was remembering the look on your face when I said I wanted to go to Rudee's for our birthday brunch."

"I'm still trying to figure out how I lost that argument." She smiled ruefully. "But I'm glad I did. I love this restaurant. You were right. No point allowing a bad memory to spoil future good memories."

"Hear, hear." Charley raised her flute. "To the future… and more good memories."

The three women clinked their glasses together.

Alicia sipped then set her flute down. "Tell Charley about Noah?"

Bella's eyes shone. "Noah kicked the winning goal at his soccer game yesterday."

Charley laughed with glee. "How wonderful! I guess his leg has completely healed."

Bella nodded.

"Speaking of Noah's leg…have you heard from Alec?"

Bella sighed with exasperation. "Charley, you know we didn't exchange emails or phone numbers." The corners of her mouth curved upwards. "But, I do have one tidbit of info that I found out this week. Alec left for Africa in January."

"How did you learn that?"

"I got a call from the hospital about one of Noah's bills, and I asked."

Charley sighed. "Well, I guess that's that."

"What's 'that?'

Alicia leaned over the table with a conspiratorial whisper, "You were supposed to marry Alec and live happily ever after."

Bella started. "Charley, wherever would you get such a crazy idea?"

"It was obvious. I saw it in both of your eyes the day you left the hospital.

Bella cleared her throat. "So, changing the subject…" She lifted her flute in the air. "To my best friends and the sacrifices they made for me when all I wanted to do was sleep my life away." She sipped her drink.

Charley's eyes brimmed. "Oh, Bella, you know we would do anything for you."

"And did…over and over for more than a year."

Alicia reached a hand across the table and squeezed Bella's fingers. "Because we love you."

Bella's eyes welled. "And I love you both so much."

Alicia raised her flute. "Here's to finding a handsome prince who loves Jesus for our BFF…Bella.

"Amen, sister." Charley said.

Alec's face suddenly forced its way out of the shadows of Bella's mind where it had stayed hidden for the last four months. She immediately pushed the memory back into the recesses of her mind. "I'm perfectly happy with my single status–thank you very much."

The waiter walked over with the bill. Charley snatched it insisting on paying. "You both can buy me a latte during our afternoon shopping spree."

"Well, that will break the bank at two dollars and fifty cents each." Alicia remarked.

Charley stuffed a fifty and a ten-dollar bill in the check holder and closed the flap. "Come on, let's go, daylight's wasting away, and the cutesiest pair of heels are calling my name.

Laughter filled the air as the three best friends rose from their chairs.

✦ ✦ ✦

The streetlight gave off a comforting glow as Bella stepped from her car and into the darkness. She was looking forward to a quiet evening. For whatever reason, Noah's gaggle of friends preferred her home to their own when gathering together, which seemed to be every day of the week except Saturdays and Sundays.

Noah was away at his father's house for the entire weekend. Bella's lips curved up in a smile. He absolutely adored his baby brother. And she had to admit, that sweet baby had helped her put away her lingering resentment and find a way to accept and be at peace with Daniel and his new family.

She shut the driver's door, and heels tapping, strode to her front porch. The motion light came on as she paused to find the key to the front door among the other keys on her ring.

"Mind if I join you?"

De ja vu slammed into Bella, and she froze in place. Her head swiveled to the right. A man stood in front of the gently swaying porch swing. For a split second, Bella thought she had conjured Alec from thin air just from thinking about him. She sucked in a breath as she gazed at the emotions splayed across his face—hope, desire, and a possible fear of rejection. Her heart started thudding in her chest, and her body trembled.

"This time I'd like to take a leap of faith. I love you, Arabella." Alec opened his arms wide.

Bella didn't need to think about it even for a second. She walked straight into his arms. After a lingering kiss she brushed her lips against his ear and whispered, "I love you with all of my heart."

Two years later . . .

Christmas carols softly filled the air of the large den, as Bella gazed fondly at her husband from the oversized recliner. Alec sat on the couch bouncing their one-year-old daughter, Carabella, on his knee. She was giggling with glee. Bella's eyes filled. She knew Cara would never replace his other daughters but was grateful their first baby had been a girl. Alec's love for this daughter was a special sight to behold. She placed a hand on her swollen belly, sighing with contentment. This child would be a boy.

Alec glanced over his smile disappearing, as his gaze locked on to her tear-filled eyes. Bella smiled and mouthed the word, *happy*. He mouthed back, *me too*. She looked around the room, her smile softening as she gazed at her loved ones. Today was her parents annual "Sunday before Christmas" get together for their three 'girls' and their families. Kelen and Noah were roughhousing with her parents' 6-month old golden retriever, Brandy. Cameron was texting on his iPhone.

Charley's three girls, taking advantage of their parents' lack of attention, were sneaking chocolate candy and cookies from festive trays scattered around the room. Bella laughed.

"What's so funny, honey?" Ginny placed a hand on her shoulder.

"Charley's girls."

Ginny laughed. "At least one will have a bellyache tonight." She glanced over at Alec, who was laughing and joking with John as he held onto his squirming daughter. "So different from Daniel," she murmured.

Bella caught the words. "Why was I so blind, Mom?"

Ginny squeezed her shoulder. "To use an old fashion word, you were 'besotted.' You refused to acknowledge his faults."

"Is it wrong of me to be glad that Daniel cheated on me?"

"No...his actions led you to the true love of your life."

Bella looked up into her mother's face. "I don't think I ever told you the story of why Alec came back."

"Sure you did. One of the doctors in Africa with him was a Christian. He started a Bible study, and Alec joined the group. His faith grew, and after a few months he knew he loved you and came back."

"That's all true, but that wasn't the entire story."

Ginny came around to the front of the recliner and pulled over an ottoman to sit on. "Okay, I'm listening."

"The last day we were in the hospital, Alec told me that he dreamed of his wife and girls every night and because of those dreams he woke up energized and ready to conquer the world." Bella sighed. "It broke my heart because I had fallen in love with him."

"I knew you had, honey."

Bella shifted back in the chair. "He told me that a month or so after he started the Bible study, he stopped dreaming about his family. He said it was painful in the beginning, but he began to realize the dreams were a crutch–that he could now rely on God to get him through his days."

Tears welled. "A few weeks later he started to dream about me…and he realized that he had made a mistake… that he loved me." Tears slipped over her lids. "Sorry, Mom, I'm hormonal."

Ginny rose up and gave her a hug and then pulled back. "God has truly blessed you and Alec with each other."

"Yes, he has…he really has."

A door slammed close by, and Charley and Alicia strode into the room. John looked over. "How was your walk?"

"Freezing." Alicia and Charley chorused.

"Hot cocoa coming up." Ginny hurried to the kitchen.

"You've been crying again, Bella," Alicia said.

"How…"

"Black streaks down your face." Charley giggled. "You really should get the water proof mascara."

Bella laughed as she struggled to rise from the chair.

Alec rushed over to help her up, slipping an arm around her expanded waist. "Are you okay, honey?"

Bella looked around the room, her heart full. "How could I not be?" Her eyes widened.

Alarm filled Alicia's face "What?"

"I think my water just broke."

Charley yelled at the room at large. "We're having a baby!"

Shouts of joy erupted from twelve throats at the same time. Chaos ensued as the adults collided with each other or tripped over children looking for shoes and a coat for Bella.

As John walked over with Cara, Bella looked up into Alec's eyes and whispered, "I love you."

Alec wiped a black-streaked tear off her cheek. "And I love you…always."

www.ingramcontent.com/pod-product-compliance
Lightning Source LLC
Chambersburg PA
CBHW030653120726
47905CB00001B/184